Holding Pattern

Holding Pattern

Jenny Xie

RIVERHEAD BOOKS · NEW YORK · 2023

RIVERHEAD BOOKS
An imprint of Penguin Random House LLC
penguinrandomhouse.com

Several chapters previously appeared in slightly
different form in the following:
chapter 1 as "The Fitting" in *Hyphen Magazine* (August 23, 2016);
chapter 5 as "Villa Palms" in *Narrative* (February 2016);
chapter 10 as "Rehearsal" in *Gulf Coast Online* (Summer/Fall 2016);
and chapter 14 as "Lucky Frank" in *Joyland* (April 2017).

LIBRARY OF CONGRESS CATALOGING-IN-PUBLICATION DATA
Names: Xie, Jenny, author.
Title: Holding pattern : a novel / Jenny Xie.
Description: New York : Riverhead Books, [2023]
Identifiers: LCCN 2022043854 (print) | LCCN 2022043855 (ebook) |
ISBN 9780593539705 (hardcover) | ISBN 9780593539729 (ebook)
Classification: LCC PS3624.I4 H65 2023 (print) |
LCC PS3624.I4 (ebook) |DDC 811.3—dc23
LC record available at https://lccn.loc.gov/2022043854
LC ebook record available at https://lccn.loc.gov/2022043855

Printed in the United States of America
1st Printing

Book design by Alexis Farabaugh

This is a work of fiction. Names, characters, places,
and incidents either are the product of the author's imagination or are
used fictitiously, and any resemblance to actual persons, living or dead,
businesses, companies, events, or locales is entirely coincidental.

For my parents

Holding Pattern

1.

Heartbreak was its own kind of incandescence that morning, scrubbing the world raw with its floodlight. I felt acutely out of place among Marin's pristine streets and quaint signage, its veneer of health and wealth an insult I couldn't answer. As we entered the bridal shop, my mother wrapped a hand around my biceps and squeaked her excitement, and this grated on me, too: Not so many years ago, she might have clung to me like this, her breath a lank cloud of vomit and liquor.

Inside the shop, a series of alcoves illuminated a froth of white dresses. The other clients were expensively dressed, model-esque women with the exception of a boy in a basketball jersey who was slumped on a clear acrylic bench, frowning at the handheld Nintendo between his knees. I cast a line of hope in his direction, seeking an acknowledgment of our mutual misery, but he kept his eyes trained on the game.

"Good morning, ladies!" A bridal consultant tottered toward us, legs bound by a black pencil skirt. "Welcome to Francesca's," she said in chirping tones.

My mother fitted her sunglasses onto the crown of her head, removing her hand from my arm. My grief swelled again to the boundary of skin. "Hi, I'm Marissa—we have ten o'clock meeting." Her halting English, which I'd grown accustomed to, newly rankled in the marmoreal perfection of the shop. "This my daughter, Kathleen. Today she find the dress for wedding."

The consultant, who introduced herself as Greta, pumped my hand. "So exciting! Congratulations on the engagement, Kathleen."

"Actually, she's the one getting married. I'm her maid of honor," I said.

Greta's smile froze. "Oh, that's wonderful. Why don't you girls come back with me?"

As we followed her, my mother whispered in Mandarin, "Let's have fun. Don't worry about how much it is."

This excursion, and the Big Sur wedding that was three months away, was being financed by her fiancé. Brian Lin owned a software company called Wayfindr that, as far as I could understand it, leveraged personal data and real-time location to herd people into buying lattes or visiting the zoo. When they had started dating a little more than two years ago, my mother had said "I'm going to love him" in the same tone she might have used for "I'll finally be able to redo the kitchen."

Money had always been elusive for us. We were diligent with our frugality, elevating it to a kind of morality—especially after my parents' divorce. Birthday parties I attended caused agonizing negotiations over the spending limit, and inevitable shame when the kid unwrapped a mountain of presents more titillating than mine. Trips to the movies were tolerated only if we strung together three back-to-back screenings. I learned the strange pleasure of self-denial, of trying on a pair of jeans I'd lusted after for weeks only to slough them off and leave the would-be version of myself hanging in the dressing room. In that way, everything in my adolescence was calculated against assimilation, every precious dollar diverted from the frivolity of fitting in bringing us closer to the middle class. At the grocery store, my mother paused in each aisle as she sifted through the stack of coupons she'd dutifully harvested from the mail. Often, by a trick of sales and double coupons, the store owed *her* cash at the register. It had seemed like a triumph, however measly, over the system.

Now we entered a cavern of dresses arranged by color, the fabrics a rustling hedge of satin and silk. I had never liked frills, to my mother's frustration. Warmth crept up my cheeks. I felt as though I were choosing lingerie in front of an audience.

"My bridemaid wearing pink, purple," my mother told Greta. She tapped her phone, enlarged the Pinterest image—Brian must have shown her how to use the app—and held the screen aloft. "I think long dress. My daughter like a size six."

"Ten," I amended.

"So pretty," said Greta, nodding at the screen. "Any preference in neckline?"

"Not strapless," I said, my words colliding with my mother's, "No straps."

Greta laughed, exposing a long incisor. "Opinionated women!

Okay, let me just grab a couple of dresses that I think you'll *adore*, and I'll meet you in the dressing room."

The private room had a trifold mirror at one end and a padded bench at the other. My mother set down her bag and began walking heel-toe, heel-toe toward her reflection, her body contoured by performance wear. I'd only been back in California for a week and I was still adjusting to the new Marissa Cheng. This woman was happier than the one I'd grown up with, more robust. This woman was empowered and had means—or at least she would be marrying her means atop a seaside bluff come August. With her new fiancé, she sailed under the Golden Gate Bridge, hiked, climbed sandstone boulders, ran loops in the Oakland hills. All things unimaginable for the Marissa I knew, who had spent her spare hours cleaning the house and watching television, a bottle of wine beside her. But now, as she described her recent outings with Brian, my gaze grew slack, and her face separated into two overlapping orbs. Then I studied the unfamiliar features. It wasn't that the nose had grown or the lips had migrated, it was that I was seeing her from the perspective of a stranger, as if for the first time.

There were, of course, real physical changes: at fifty-three, my mother had always been petite, but now she was trim, her hair smartly angled toward her jaw. Her recent weight loss had revealed the delicate planes of her face, like petals flaking away from a shrouded bud. She had traded her mom capris and department-store blouses for athletic gear. In her spandex pants and fleece half-zips, she looked sporty and self-possessed, the type of woman who might race up a switchback with a mantra pulsing in her chest: *If it doesn't challenge you, it doesn't change you.* I missed the old Marissa. At least she would have provided a dreary comfort.

As we waited, she swept a strand of hair from her face, then flinched and swore.

"What's wrong?" I asked.

"It's my bracelet," she said in Mandarin, holding out her wrist so that I could see the matte-black band. Someone could mistake it for a minimalist watch; it had a square screen that glowed green when she tapped it, revealing a countdown. "It gives me a shock if my hand gets too close to my mouth during fasting hours. I still have an hour and fourteen minutes until lunch. I can also deliver manual shocks if I'm about to make a bad decision—have a cupcake, for example." She paused. "Or have a drink."

I looked at her, aghast. "I'm sorry—it *shocks* you? Why would you do that to yourself?"

"To be more disciplined," she said matter-of-factly. "I sized down for my wedding dress, you know. It has to fit." She encircled one wrist with the other hand, touching the middle finger and thumb to- gether, and then moved to measure my forearm, too.

"Mom, that's awful." I shook her off. "You don't need to lose any more weight, and definitely not through torture."

She ignored me, fiddling with the device. She'd been chroni- cling her diminishing body, but she'd never mentioned this. I won- dered what other torments she'd adopted in the manic renovation of her life.

Ever since my father's infidelity barreled through our home twenty years ago, my mother had been managing grief, uncertain finances, and an eternal homesickness for Shanghai. For most of my grade school and undergraduate years, she'd medicated with drink, the habit eroding her until she was as faceless as a river rock. Then she'd met Brian—the same year I'd met Oren, my ex—who had jolted her back into being. Something I hadn't been able to do for her, though I'd been there all along. I watched her body turning in the mirror now, her reflection somehow more familiar than the flesh.

Greta burst through the curtain, pink gowns draped over her arm like deflated bodies. She hooked them on the wall and said breathlessly, "Okay, ladies, here comes the fun part. I grabbed a couple in different sizes so you can get a feel for what you're most comfortable in, and keep in mind that we can always get them custom fitted."

"Beautiful," my mother said in English, sighing. She plucked one dress out by its plastic covering and cocked her head at me. "You want try on?"

It had a sweetheart neckline, which I'd opposed to avoid the burden of cleavage, but I obliged. Both women watched as I stripped. Discarding my raglan T-shirt and denim shorts, exposing a soft belly and the hump of flesh under my bra band, I found that I had transcended physical lumpiness—I had somehow become spiritually lumpy. I stepped into a ring of chiffon while my mother fussed at my front, jerking the dress over my breasts, patting me down as if it would make me smaller. Her armpits smelled like spoiled milk and lemons. I regarded the black bracelet warily, bracing for a shock.

"High class," she said, fingering the thin beaded band at the waistline. She stepped away, freeing my view of the mirror and the trio of reflections. I remembered the fragments she'd told me about her rationed childhood in Shanghai, when she woke hours before dawn to line up for her family's precious share of rice, pork, eggs, and other scarcities during the end of the Cultural Revolution—including the cloth with which she would learn to sew her own dresses. How she'd clutched the coupon book in her pocket to keep it safe, shivering in the half-light. Things had been even more dire in the country-side, where our relatives shared a single pair of trousers, wearing them in rotation whenever one of them left the house. It never seemed like the right time to ask for more details; against these stories of suffering and famine, my mother's reticence, my shyness, and the mundane needs of the moment always won out. Now, my mother clapped her hands with delight as Greta closed my dress, cinching the breath out of me.

"I don't know about this," I said.

"Try put hair down."

I tugged it out of its ponytail, but it retained an unflattering crease where the elastic had been. "What is this, a six?"

"Yes, it is," said Greta.

"Well, that's the wrong size."

My mother toggled into Mandarin. "We'll do something about that before August," she said, then switched back to English. "So pretty. Look like princess."

I gritted my teeth. "Why don't we try another?"

The last time I'd dressed up had been a mere month ago, though it felt like another lifetime—it'd been another wedding, an intimate party in the backyard of a dive bar, which I'd attended with Oren, suspecting nothing. I had been ecstatic, caught up in the delicious pooling amber of other people's love, imagining looking up at him at the altar.

Oren had had to dump me twice. The first time, he made such a kind and gentle incision that I hadn't recognized it as a severance at all. When he left our apartment to spend a week away, I took it as a chance for the two of us to regenerate, to reconnect as more intentional, lucid versions of ourselves. It was only when he returned and unfurled the air mattress that I understood—understood with my whole body the way, as a child, I had recognized death in the mute outline of my pet rabbit from across the room. I'd had to endure the same speech from him, delivered just as tenderly, though a bit more emphatically. "It wouldn't be fair to pretend," he'd said, and the realization that he'd practiced that line drained the world of its color. "We'd be denying ourselves the kind of love we both deserve." But I'd thought what I deserved was Oren.

After the breakup I'd keened in my adviser's office until she granted me a leave of absence. I had been struggling in my classes anyway. Oren was five years into the cognitive psychology PhD program at Johns Hopkins, and was relocating to Gainesville for an internship at his top-choice university. Me, on the other hand: I was back at home with a useless master's degree, preparing for my mother's matrimony instead of mine.

As Greta leaned into me, disentangling my bra from the hanger strap of another dress, I saw where the dark foundation ended on her jawline. She looked at me, and our eyes snagged.

This dress had a lace yoke that cut into my armpits. My mother hummed a note of distaste.

"I don't think this is the one, either," said Greta, wrinkling her nose. "I'll head back and grab some final selections, and you'll have a chance to think through your options."

"Thank you very much, Greta," said my mother. As soon as Greta left the room, Marissa shifted her civic smile—the one she used with waiters and bank tellers and lost tourists—on me. Then it faded into a slack line of disappointment. "You're making her uncomfortable," she said in Mandarin.

"What do you mean?"

"You're standing there like a *si ren*, stone-faced at this, stone-faced at that. These are designer pieces, Kathleen."

I hadn't told her about Oren. Telling my mother would make it real, a fact outside of myself that would go on the family record. Instead, I leaned into my irritation. "I'd feel a lot better if you didn't make me squeeze into things that clearly don't fit."

"They *will* fit," she insisted. "You don't plan on staying this big, do you?"

I saw it then: her old face, her eyes filled with arctic dark. We were picking up an old conversation. Part of me felt relieved that the woman I wanted to hold accountable, that I wanted to accuse, was still there.

"Of course not," I said. "I was thinking of getting a cattle prod—you know, the new diet trend."

"Say what you want about it, but it wouldn't hurt to put a little more effort into self-improvement. Your cousin Ingrid just lost ten pounds."

"How is that possible? She weighed ten pounds to begin with."

"And she just got into Harvard Business School."

"Related, I'm sure."

"Of course it's related. It's called discipline. Hard work. Determination."

"You're being so superficial, Mom. You can't judge someone's work ethic by how thin they are."

She tutted. "Don't twist my words."

"I get it, okay? Ingrid is brilliant and perfect! I'm sorry I'm not Ingrid!" My mother was good at this—forcing me into desperate, exaggerated stances that I thought I'd outgrown.

"I'm not asking you to be perfect, and I know you're not Ingrid." She looked down at her hands and then spoke into the mirror, where our faces were less searing. "You're always too defensive to listen. I wouldn't worry about you if you were a man. Money, looks—you need them to survive as a woman."

"I'll be fine."

"*Kan ba*," said my mother. *We'll see.*

A bolt of rage shot through me. "You didn't have money *or* looks before you met Brian," I snapped, "so don't act like you knew what you were doing."

"At least I knew what I was missing. When I think about how hard I worked to raise you—"

"Yes, you, mother of the year! You must not remember the nights that I cleaned up your piss and put you to bed. I've come as far as I have because your life was depressing, not because of any magical parenting." My words went agitatedly in and out of Mandarin, picking up shards of English.

"I was sick," she said, sounding stricken. Her features deflated. I tried to hold on to my anger as the seconds ticked by, but it only curdled into hot shame. Finally, she said quietly, "When you have kids, be sure to have more than one, or she'll grow up too selfish to think of anyone but herself. That was my mistake."

Her attacks could be so masterful, aimed from a shocking distance, each word a precise shaft. Sometimes they made me stagger in anger; other times, like now, they delivered me to a smothering darkness. I looked at her face, its beauty clarified by fury, and understood how much she loved me. I heaved the words at her feet. "Mama," I said, "Oren broke up with me. And I told the school that I don't know if I'm going back."

"*Shenme?* What are you saying?"

"Oren doesn't love me. At least not enough."

A hesitation, and then she surprised me by encircling me with her arms. I tried to relax into their unfamiliar hardness, feeling the new architecture of her body, but the gesture made us both too self-conscious to be any real comfort. "Don't worry. You'll rest at home. Spend this summer on yourself, and you'll feel better enough to go back to school."

"That's what you're focusing on?"

"Xiao Mao," she said, using my pet name. She rubbed my shoulders and looked around the dressing room, as though remembering that we weren't like this: We weren't articulate with affection. "Now is the time to focus on school, your career. Someone even better will come along, *ni xiangxin*."

A wild loneliness settled in my body. But what did I expect? She'd never shown much interest in my relationships, perhaps preoccupied by her own dramas, perhaps afraid of further burden. She knew that I'd meant to marry Oren, which had always felt like enough information. I was also reluctant to share my life. Growing up, I thought being aloof would make me less vulnerable to the times she would come home from work and slump toward the bedroom without saying a word, or the times she would drink and screech. It hadn't occurred to me until recently that maybe her reciprocal coolness had been a way of feigning strength.

"If it was meant to be, it would have been," she continued. "Maybe there's something to learn from this."

"This is not helping."

"You're always the one being broken up with," she said in a tone of pity and accusation. "Maybe that's saying something, too. And you know I never thought he was very good-looking. He has giant eyes, like a bug."

I'd heard enough. "I'm going to the bathroom," I said.

I punched my arms through the sleeves of my shirt. It was my fault for expecting anything but judgment and blame. Sweeping aside the dressing room curtain, I felt oddly menacing. Bull in a china shop, I thought, picturing a hoof impacting the encrusted throat of a gown, a spray of Swarovski crystals studding the air.

The restroom was down the hall, across from a door marked EMPLOYEES ONLY. I paused at a water fountain. Leaning into the dribble, I heard Greta's voice say in muffled tones, "That's not even the end of it. This morning he tells me he can't do dinner. So I'm supposed to entertain his sister alone. Like, what? I'm sorry, there isn't enough wine in the world to make that worth my time." The door swung open before she'd finished her sentence and the final words rang out in the corridor. The workroom tittered; the door closed again.

Greta and I stood facing each other. She touched the side of her blond bun, then laughed airily and said, "Sorry. Watercooler talk."

"It's okay," I said, glad for the distraction. "We all have that one relative."

"Gotta love family." She swept an arm toward the end of the hallway, inviting me to walk. She said, "You and your mom are so cute. It's sweet that you're supporting her as her maid of honor."

It was hard to imagine the dressing room scene as sweet, but I was relieved that we appeared so to an audience. "Sorry we're being so indecisive with the dress."

"Not at all! We're going to find you The One." Greta said it with a flourish of capital letters. "In fact, while I have you here, let me get your opinion." Her skirt made shushing noises as she led me to a corner of the main floor, where she paused before a rack of dresses.

She slid a hand across the shades of cream as if gliding across piano keys. "These are technically bridal gowns, but they come in other colors, too. I had this one in mind as a maybe—what do you think?"

As she pulled it out of its plastic sheath, I felt a surprising prickle of interest. The dress had two elongated petals over the hips and braided straps that harnessed the collarbone. She raised it in the air and rocked the hanger back and forth, undulating the skirt. "It really moves," she said.

"I don't hate it," I said.

"Okay, okay, getting warmer. How about this?" Greta held another dress against her body and slow danced with one hand on its hip. The asymmetrical seams and draping reminded me of a candle melting—an effect I liked, immediately and mysteriously.

"I'll try that on." Then, with some relish: "My mom's going to hate it."

Greta waved her hand. "You can't go wrong with this label. Veronika Kraus. She's an up-and-coming designer from Austria. Her stuff has an edge," she said, and laughed in a way that made me wonder how much the dress cost. "I'll meet you back in the room in five."

My mother was seated on the bench, scrolling through her phone, when I returned. "Well, I didn't get the job."

"What job? You're applying for jobs?" Marissa had been working at the Macy's perfume counter for the past six years. It wasn't ideal, but she had finally settled into a routine after so many years pinballing between gigs.

"College administration." Marissa clicked her tongue. "I made

it through the final rounds, but 'It was an extremely difficult decision,'" she parroted in English. "At the last meeting they made it
sound like they were looking for someone young and perky."

"You're perky." A silence lasted just long enough to make me regret my omission.

"*Suan le*," she said finally, her eyes faraway and roving. "My English gets in the way. But I'm not going to let this get me down. I am
not a talentless woman! That's one of my mantras."

"*That's* your mantra?" Despite the apparent changes, Marissa hadn't
outrun her old insecurities. "Mom, you shouldn't think that." The hard
words she often spoke to me were echoes of the bitter things she told
herself, I knew, and the cruelty her own parents could dole out.

Greta returned with more dresses slung over her arm. "Okay, ladies, ready for round two?" She gave me a conspiratorial look and
said, "I found one I think you'll fall head over heels for."

Constructed from panels of gleaming silk, the dress had a barely
restrained energy: gathered fabric created a cowl-neck and a slanted
waistline fed into a skirt of irregular pleating. The fabric felt cool and
good on my skin, like a bed I could drowse in. I put it on and immediately felt taller. It had a resonance, like the final vibration of a
struck bell.

"I love it," I said. Despite myself, I wished Oren could see me in
it. I found my mother fiddling with her phone in the mirror. "What
do you think?"

She looked up and seemed to see the dress for the first time. "Oh,"
she said, her features warping. "No, too busy."

Greta jumped in. "It's so couture! She just shines in it."

"Look like children made this, use bedsheet."

"Do a little twirl," Greta urged.

I did, then stood facing my mother, plucking at the material. She raised one hand to her cheek but didn't say anything.

"You still like the first one."

"I don't know how to say. First dress very joyful, so young."

Greta leaped to my defense, pointing out the dress's attributes, guiding my body with her fingertips as she turned me and lifted my arms. But the magic was evaporating from the seams as she spoke, its plumage revealed as rags. I watched my mother tune out, her mind clearly circling the disappointment of the job. A small, ghoulish part of me cheered the setback in her sparkling new life, but the rest of me was worried. I worried that offices might reserve careers for people like Greta instead of people who had emerged from astonishing darkness, that this version of my mother would never shed those vestigial mistakes, would find new ways to punish herself.

"Never mind," I said, unable to bear the pressure of Greta's fingers on my shoulder. "Let's just go with the first one."

Relief flooded my mother's voice. "You sure?"

"Whatever."

"Thank goodness. That thing would have gotten you laughed out of the wedding," she informed me in Mandarin.

"Get this off me?"

Greta gripped the skirt of the dress and shimmied it over my head. "I'm so glad we could find a dress that both of you love. Francesca's prides itself on being the boutique for everyone," she declared. The statement was so canned, so automated, that it clamped the appointment shut.

"I know what looks best on you," said my mother, shouldering her purse. "Come on, you can tell me more about Oren at lunch. There's a new poke place I've been meaning to try." She glanced at her bracelet. "I have an hour to eat."

I didn't know whether to be impressed or alarmed at how coolly she had recovered, but I did register with grim respect how coolly she had won.

2.

LB was smoking outside when I got to the bar. Vintage marquee lights spelled out THE ROOSTER overhead, warming the slopes of her cheeks and burnishing her leather jacket. Her brown shag had been gathered in tiny pigtails, and rhinestones accented the corners of her eyes. She held her arms open as I approached, pulling me into a hug. "Kath, you're here, you're really here!"

"It's been so long." I surveyed the entrance, which was plastered with stickers and festooned with the usual graffiti, the people huddled in tight circles. "I'm stoked to see you play, finally."

"I know—and here of all places." LB's new band, Towers, a sludgy dream-pop outfit, was headlining tonight at The Rooster, our old stomping ground. When we were in high school, LB knew one of the bartenders, and their ongoing flirtation meant a steady supply of flavored vodka and rum and Cokes. Spinning on the cracked leather barstools, spinning in the taxis home, we convinced ourselves we were above the parties our peers were throwing—never mind that we hadn't been invited. The bar hadn't changed much, and neither had the neighborhood of worn, ivy-lashed homes and liquor stores with winking lights. In the thick of wild fennel obscuring the chain-link fence behind the property, crushed cans and empty chip bags hung like baubles.

"These are cute." I flicked a pigtail.

LB had a low, dopey laugh, same as I remembered it. "My camp kids are an endless source of hair inspiration." She was teaching yoga and drums at a camp in Berkeley for children with names like Rainer and Truth. In the fall, her band, Towers, was going on tour. She'd quit her job as a development coordinator at a women's health non-profit to figure out her next move. Unlike me, she seemed to know what she loved, who she wanted to be.

"How's being home?" she asked, her mouth flattening with concern. "Have you told your mom yet?"

I sucked in a breath. "Yeah. I meant to wait, but we got into this argument when we were trying on dresses, and I just blurted it out. She's really fixated on me finishing my degree, which I thought would be the case."

LB's face crinkled in sympathy. She had also been a caretaker for her mother, who would spend whole days in the backyard shed she'd converted into a studio, creating sculptures out of pantyhose, papier-mâché, chicken wire: engorged, intestinal things. Theresa Hinman was loving but distracted, and LB picked up the slack—cobbling together lunches for herself and her younger brother to take to school, writing down messages on the notepad by the phone.

"I hope she doesn't pressure you to do anything you don't want to do," LB said. "I mean, at this point, do you have a gut feeling about going back?"

"Right now, no part of me wants to go back."

She chuckled at how immediately I'd responded, smoke purling from her nostrils.

"God, just . . . It's this constant publish-or-perish mindset, and everyone is so hypercompetitive that I feel like I'm losing sight of why I'm actually there. I thought I wanted to . . . I don't know"—I gestured helplessly at my own naivete—"contribute to a well of human knowledge about touch and cognition, but everything we find out just points to the need for more research." I scrunched a shoulder to let someone pass. "It didn't help to have Oren around, either. He was so *in it* and motivated that it made me feel like I'm never going to make it if the field is full of people like him."

"Well, you shouldn't compare yourself to Oren. Or anybody." LB jammed the butt of her cigarette into an ashtray. "But it sounds like you're pretty clearheaded about the program, and that's important to pay attention to."

"Maybe. I don't know. It also seems inconceivable to walk away." I'd already sunk so much time into it, and there was always the hope that something in me would be reignited. I cringed to think how my cohort, who could masticate a single morsel of gossip for weeks, would feast for years on my departure. "Sorry to vent. Can we get a drink?"

I put a hand on LB's shoulder as we jockeyed our way inside and up to the bar. Red light bathed the interior, blurring the faces of the people we edged past. Kitschy paintings of kittens and clowns and old posters featuring buxom, bud-lipped women covered the walls. A row of flashing pinball machines framed the entrance to the next room, where another band was finishing their raucous set.

"Something else, LB?" It was Eugene, bald and wearing his customary bow tie, behind the bar. He brightened when he saw me. "Kathleen! What a surprise! You home for the summer?"

I smiled. "You know it. Got back a couple of days ago."

"Well, this is cause for celebration. Let me make you something special. I've been fucking around with this bacon-infused bourbon."

"Can you make that two something specials?" LB glanced at her phone. "Cool, Andrew's on his way."

Several years had passed since she'd started dating Andrew, my high school boyfriend, and we'd long since recalibrated our friendship. Today, however, I felt the old envy and insecurity prowling the edges of my thoughts. It seemed that everyone around me had found their person.

Andrew and I had broken up before college, agreeing that a clean goodbye was preferable to forcing the relationship to limp along. I left for the East Coast, and he enrolled at UC Berkeley, where LB transferred to after two years of community college. There, they'd begun to date, breaking the news to me over the winter holidays when we were stoned and halfway through a pizza. I thought they were a good match—he, responsible and good-natured; she, idealistic and gentlehearted, if a bit impulsive—but there would always be the node where the three of us intersected.

"How are you doing? Have you talked to Oren at all?" asked LB.

"No," I said, "but we still watch each other's Instagram Stories." That morning, he'd posted a video of a squirrel eating a croissant— unremarkable content, but I'd watched it four times, trying to place the park where he'd recorded it, straining to make out what someone was saying in the background. A woman's voice. "I know I should stop, but it feels nice to have this tiny peephole into his life. And by nice I mean it's absolute torture."

"That's the thing, isn't it? People used to be able to pretend their exes didn't exist. Now they haunt you on the internet."

"If I were smart I would just block him."

She rubbed my shoulder. "And you will, whenever you're ready. This shit's hard."

Last year, for one of my courses, I'd read about a study involving lab rats and reward levers. In one scenario, a rat would press on a lever and that would always yield a treat; in another, nothing would happen. In the last scenario, a rat would press on the lever and a treat would be produced, but inconsistently. The rats in this last group pressed the lever most often. That's what it was like scavenging through social media for traces of Oren: a light blinked on when-ever I found a new post. I was used to knowing his days in excruciat-ing detail, so any morsel was a reward. "What's that grain—?" he had shouted near the end, from the other room, and I had interrupted him, already knowing the answer to his question because I'd had the same salad: "Farro!" Yet when these glimpses came to me, sugar-coated nuggets dispensed by the algorithm, they did nothing but emphasize the unknown: what the tweet referenced, what was just out of frame. Anyway, I was undeterred. I would abuse the lever. Pain and pleasure stimulated the same parts of the brain, secreting endorphins and dopamine.

We carried our drinks into the next room, where a sparse audience stood in silhouette against the stage and the performers were on their knees, one yodeling into a microphone and the other nodding over his equipment. LB bobbed to the music. She was always an easy presence, so grounded in her own body. I had a mental scrapbook of her over the years, jittery and giddy coming in from the cold, sucking beads of blood from her scrapes, legs grasshoppered wide to pee in the dirt. Her bandmates, three women, drifted toward us, and I fumbled with their hands in the dark. At the end of the set, LB draped her arm across my shoulders and tipped back the rest of the cocktail. "I'm going to go get set up," she said.

As soon as she left my side, the anxiety that had been trailing me all day stepped into her place. I ordered a beer from Eugene, trading sentences every time he passed me at the bar. Then, with a tilting sensation, I spotted Andrew by his backward cap and held up my pint in his direction.

"Welcome back," he said through our hug. "How are you?"

"What has LB told you?"

"Everything." He laughed and adjusted his thin, gold-rimmed glasses. He'd started growing a mustache, which was new. As I answered his questions—yes, it was bittersweet to leave Baltimore; no, I didn't think Oren and I would be friends—I gripped the edge of the bar with one hand as though it would buck me off and reveal just how tenuous a hold I had on things.

"But what's new with you?" I said.

"Not much, to be honest. Just working as many shifts as I can, saving up, you know. I'm studying for the LSAT. Making Mama proud, as they say." Andrew lifted his cap, raked his greasy brown locks. He resembled his mother, a Korean woman, while his brother took after their German father.

"You're at the new place, right? On Shattuck?"

"Yeah, the bougie Thai place. The money's pretty good. I want to go somewhere this summer. Luke and I—you've met him, right? My roommate?"

"Once or twice. I've heard stories."

"I'm sure you have." He smirked. "Anyway, we're talking about taking a trip somewhere in July. There's this pet convention happening in Vegas that he's trying to convince me to go to."

I laughed. "Wow, I didn't expect that sentence out of you."

"So Luke's latest thing is making his rat Milo famous on Instagram so that he can coast on brand partnerships. It's *not* an utter failure so far," he added incredulously, fishing out his phone to show me the feed. Instagram user @meetmilotherat had more than eight thousand followers. There were photos of Milo asleep in Luke's palm, the gray half of his body nestled into the white, or looking into the camera with his pink ears curled like pea shoots.

"He's pretty stinking cute," I said, "but he's still a rat."

"Don't let Luke hear you say that. So at this pet convention, all these influencer animals show up. Cats, dogs, ferrets, pigs. Hedgehogs. Lorises."

"Cats. Cats get famous."

"That's what I told him. But Luke's like, 'Oh, cats are played out. Cats are dicks.' I think he just doesn't want to be responsible for something that lives as long as a cat. How this got started, he has this yoga-wellness-woo-woo friend who gets eight hundred dollars a pop for posting selfies of herself, like, drinking organic juice."

"Eight hundred *dollars?*"

"I mean, granted, she has an insane body. The biggest ass you've ever seen."

I rolled my eyes. "Well, I hope Milo has a dump-truck ass."

A line of synth bloomed from the stage, and we made our way over. I was grateful for the chance to compose myself; the drinks were beginning to weigh on my limbs, unwinch my field of vision. LB was on the drums, a microphone bent to catch her yips as the beat quickened. The tattooed bassist swayed and sang with her eyes closed, voice pirouetting over the music. Andrew and I wove to the front of the crowd.

"They sound so good!" I leaned in to say.

"I know, they've been killing it."

LB had played the drums all through high school and college, but this project was different from the others, the sounds expansive and unpredictable. Clouds of reverb and eerie synth thickened the air; the guitar slunk along on drowsy riffs and then punched through with sudden muscle. My best friend was radiant, her expression beatific, the drumsticks fluttering in her hands.

Cradled by the noise, my thoughts rounded by the drinks, I danced woozily in place. Andrew nodded along. Standing close in a crowd carried me back to the time when we'd dated. We were configured in the same way, but now he wouldn't draw me toward him for a kiss or claim a shoulder with an arm, though I could imagine the familiar heat and pressure. I knew I was in the tender time following a breakup during which everything had an unbearable resonance. Watching starlings spiral and warp in the air, tracing their slow arabesques against the sinking light, could bring me to tears. Deleting old voice mails, I'd stumbled across a message from Oren, its mundanity slamming into my chest like a battering ram.

We'd been looking at engagement rings—an exercise I'd always thought I'd despise, a submission to the wedding industrial complex. But everything was different with Oren. He was emotionally fluent, kind, generous, humming with ambition and enthusiasm: *a lightning bolt and a mountain*, I'd described to a friend after the first few dates. He was classically handsome, with dark hair and a dramatic profile, like a ridgeline. I'd fall asleep listening to his percussive typing as he thrilled about the correlation between gestures made on an iPad and knowledge retention in children learning math. He was blindly supportive, which veered toward stifling. "You don't really want to do that," he'd reassured me when I'd brought up switching to marriage and family therapy. "You're so brilliant. You need to keep going.

You're needed in this field." I couldn't muster telling him that every-thing I was doing seemed thin and bloodless because I feared that his affection hinged on his admiration for me. In that suspicion at least, I was right. I'd watched him pack for his internship interviews and driven him to the airport and waved until the sliding doors had closed behind him, long after he'd already turned around.

THE BASSIST, PHOEBE, invited some people to her place after the show. Friends coagulated, bumping along the human current. Traffic lights raised their orange palms, beamed their walking men, and the sidewalk purred underfoot like a treadmill belt. I staggered up the steps to a Victorian somewhere in West Oakland. It was packed with mismatched sofas and armchairs, books haphazardly stuffed onto shelves, plant fronds luxuriating in the dim light.

I had a six-pack of Tecate that I didn't remember buying. I plowed through the living room to the kitchen, which was garishly lit in comparison, revealing faces ruddy with excitement, mouths shouting good news. Phoebe stood on tiptoe to pull glasses from the cabinets and her shirt rolled up to reveal the velvet hollow of her hip bone.

"You want a whiskey?" she asked.

I took a moment to focus on her face. "Yes, please."

A clatter of ice, a swell of amber in the glass, and then I trundled back to the living room. I folded myself between the marigold arm of a crushed-velvet couch and a man with chin-length curls.

I saw, across the room, Andrew standing in a circle with LB and some people I didn't know. She was chatting and rubbing his back, lifting a palm to make a gesture, then placing it back between his shoulder blades. It was the kind of easy, unconscious touch that I hadn't known I would crave until it was gone. Before Oren, I hadn't been so accustomed to the heat and salt of skin. When would I stop dividing time this way: before Oren, after Oren?

"Can you scoot over?" I asked the man beside me.

He flicked his head at the people seated next to him. "I would, but there's not really any room."

It wasn't a joke, but I laughed, as if proving to myself that I was having a good time.

"How do you know Phoebe?" He was barely looking at me, his eyes skidding sideways from behind a shroud of hair.

"She's in the band with my best friend." I pointed her out. "LB Hinman." My arm landed heavy on my thigh.

"Yeah? I'm her neighbor."

"Lucky you."

"Yeah, she's all right."

"Did you see them play? I didn't see you at The Rooster."

"Nah, I've seen them a bunch of times already. They've only got a couple of decent songs."

I screwed up my eyes. "Has anyone told you you're kind of an asshole?"

"Oh, sure. I'm the first to admit I'm an asshole. Saves everyone a bit of time." His voice was a deep, nasal drone. "Wish being honest didn't automatically make you an asshole, though. I'm allowed to dislike my neighbor's music. And whatever the fuck *this* is." He flicked a hand at the speakers, which emitted a shower of glossy, electronic notes.

"Must be exhausting."

"What?"

"Hating on everything."

He bounced one knee. "No one said anything about hate. What's more exhausting is being precious about everything we produce. Most stuff is shit, a lot of it is mediocre, and that's okay. It's all part of the soundtrack to the next mass extinction event, anyway."

I laughed again at his joylessness. "You're really good at parties."

"I'm just being realistic. We could all benefit from a little humility. Part of that is knowing and accepting how it'll all shake out."

"Or," I tried, "you can make something. Change something. Celebrate something. Not everything needs to be judged on some arbitrary, cosmic scale."

"I *am* celebrating something. I'm celebrating my neighbor's above-average music and the attractive women who seem to enjoy it."

"Okay." I planted my empty glass on the coffee table. "I gotta make my rounds."

I shimmied off the couch and slammed down the hallway. Bodies, throbbing to the music in a doorway, parted to let me inside. It was someone's bedroom, a white comforter like a pane of milk across the mattress. Stretching out my fingers, I pressed down on the covers until the cool fabric closed around my hand, absorbing my forearm. It was like taking a drink of water. I slid forward until half my body was on the bed, temples pounding. The room canted from side to side.

"Feeling comfy?"

I rolled toward the voice. It was Phoebe.

"I'm sorry. I can get up." I wiggled in place. "Your bed is really nice. A lot nicer than mine."

"You don't have to move. I'm just using the bathroom." She pointed to a slim door obscured by a laundry hamper.

"Okay. I'll wait here."

I heard her peeing through the wall. The sound tapered to a trickle, then there was a pause before the gurgling flush and the hiss of the faucet. When she emerged, wiping her hands on her jeans, I said, "So what's the deal with your neighbor?"

"Oh, did you meet Tyler? I don't know, he's sort of awkward, but I invite him to these things. Maybe because I feel bad for him. Why? Was he bothering you?"

"Yeah." My mind swerved. "Did you know I used to date Andrew?"

Phoebe cocked her head to the side. "No, I didn't." She was humoring me, a patient smile hovering between us.

"Yeah. It's cool, though. We're highly evolved friends." My eyes dragged across her face. With her head tilted back, eyes half-lidded, only slivers of her wet corneas were visible. "Never mind. You're just trying to enjoy your party. You're a good host, and you have a nice bed. Thank you for letting me lie on it."

"No problem. Make yourself at home," she said, turning to go.

I couldn't bear the tundra of the bedroom, so I indulged the sudden crush. "Wait, wait. Before you go. Can I have a kiss?" I needed to believe that good things were possible. That beginnings were still possible.

She released a puff of laughter, then bent to press her lips against mine. They had the buoyancy of two peeled sections of a clementine. When I opened my eyes, there was no one there. I hadn't kissed anyone but Oren in years.

I clattered into the bathroom, squinted at the mirror. I thought I could see my mother's face sliding under mine, could feel the same wildness and relief she must have felt when she'd drunk as much as I had, and bent to suck water from the sink. When I looked up, I was myself again, or a puppet that looked like myself, jolted by strings manipulated by a dark hand. It was liberating to relinquish control.

Later, snaking deeper down the hallway, I found the backyard, where people were dancing, their faces silver in the moonlight, then orange over a shuddering flame. My hair swung back and forth, the tendrils catching in my mouth, my scalp growing swampy with sweat.

"There you are!" said LB, falling into rhythm beside me. "I've been looking for you everywhere."

"I'm right here," I told her, putting my arms around her neck. Her body smelled familiar, sweet and tinged with funk, mushroomy. We rocked from side to side until I lost her, until I was rocking with no one. I wanted to go home.

The house was emptying out. Someone called my name, but I didn't stop until I collided with someone on the stoop. "You," I said, uncertain if I was whispering or shouting. "The asshole." I registered him as a wavering tower, hair like a brown fern, a deep mouth suddenly connecting with mine. It was incredible how reptilian my response was, how little it mattered who the mouth belonged to.

Tyler gripped my hand and walked me to the bottom of the stairs. "Conveniently," he said, "I'm right here." As he jostled with the door to his downstairs unit, I surmised that what was about to happen was inevitable; it had practically already happened, so I might as well get it over with. We staggered into the dark apartment and stripped each other in his kitchen, sending plastic glasses clapping across the tile. Oren's body was so familiar to me that this new one seemed unreal, one I could only understand through negative space: not Oren's neck, not Oren's chest, not Oren's waist. His face was a shifting veil of shadow except for the silvery glint of teeth. Clamping my mouth closed as his hips slammed into me, I bit my cheek and drew a slick of blood, sharp and sweet.

3.

Qilai le," said my mother, her fist curled around the pull of the blinds, her body slowly taking shape in the morning's frail light. With hazy panic, I wondered if she had tracked me down in West Oakland and barreled through a stranger's door to find my naked body smeared in his sheets, but I began to recognize the room as my own. "We're heading out in twenty minutes."

"Can't you knock?"

"You have to get dressed."

"Why?"

"We're going running at the lake." Free of makeup and bared of hair by a headband, her face was pale and frank. Her body, sheathed in black spandex, had a dolphin's sheen and tautness. It was clear that she expected me to run the loop around Lake Merritt with her, which would total some ten miles. Deciphering the clatter in the kitchen, I gathered that her fiancé, Brian, was here, too.

"I'm not going," I said. "I don't run."

"Yes, you do. The wedding's in two months, and you have a dress to fit into."

I clutched the comforter closer around my face. "I'll hit the gym later."

"You should spend more time with Brian."

"I'll spend plenty of time with Brian. After I sleep."

My mother paused and changed tack. "When did you get home last night?"

I searched for an answer. A bleary memory of panning for clothes on Tyler's kitchen floor. Digging the slime out of my belly button with a wad of toilet paper. Shame, revulsion, and exasperation pressed my body deeper into the bed. "I don't know. Two?" I guessed conservatively.

"If you don't get enough sleep, you'll get wrinkles."

I writhed. "So let me sleep."

"Nineteen minutes," she said, and left the room. I knew I wouldn't be able to drift off again. I would do penance for ruining her image of militaristic precision while Brian was here. She would come back.

I rolled onto the floor and crawled until I could clamber onto my feet, like the three stages of evolution in a diagram of an evolving primate.

When I slumped into the kitchen, Brian was feeding stalks of kale into a blender.

"Kathleen! Good morning!" An American-Born Chinese—an ABC—he always spoke English with me. He regarded me over the top of the blender. "You coming with us? You must be pretty beat."

"Just a little groggy," I said, trying to sound game.

"Well, this will perk you up." He brandished a fistful of apple slices and threw them into the mix. Brian, at forty-eight, was five years Marissa's junior, and appeared still younger with his deep tan and resonant voice. Today he wore an athletic T-shirt that accentuated the ridges of his chest and arms. His receding hairline and faint wrinkles around the eyes were the only indications of his age. I had met his teenage son, Chester, last Christmas, and had been unsettled to find him similarly walnut brown and wrapped in muscle. Aside from scattered meetings over the school holidays, we were strangers to each other, and I distrusted his cheerful haleness, as though he'd been an As Seen on TV product. His presence somehow made the apartment look smaller and drearier than it already was.

Brian started the blender, and it engulfed the kitchen with its demonic gargling. Under this assault, I retreated back to my bedroom. I'd taken down the childhood posters—the Backstreet Boys, the tiger cubs—and corralled the stuffed animals into the closet, but it wasn't hard to excavate the child who'd lived here, written the names of her crushes in tiny letters on the baseboard. She'd chosen a lime-green paint for the walls, and I was paying for it now. The rest of the home had also stagnated in time, evidence of a life cobbled together from curbside finds and yard sales, the cheap fixtures and lopsided cabinets still clinging on from the '90s. Marissa had not sloughed off this part of her life, perhaps biding her time until she could trade up.

I crouched in front of my suitcase—I wasn't sure how I'd retrieve the rest of my things, undisturbed in the apartment close to campus that Oren and I had shared—and yanked a pair of leggings out of the tangle. I willed myself not to remember the calm blade of morning light that woke us in our bed back there. I would not re-member the creak in the floorboards under his bare feet and the sound of the grinder pulverizing coffee beans. I would not think of that place as our home. As I pulled the leggings on, I noticed a stip-pling of bruises across my ass cheeks in the full-length mirror. "Why did you do that?" I whispered.

The smoothie waiting for me on the kitchen counter was green and capped with foam. Its bitter, vernal coolness did nothing to clear my clouded thoughts, but I knew it was good for me to swallow.

THOUGH WE STARTED at a brisk jog, my mother was determined to stay a few paces ahead as though to demonstrate progress, per-sonal growth. She pumped her arms, elbowing her way past houses with cracked, paved-over yards, sun-bleached tricycles listing in the driveways, the scrum of trash and dog shit lining chain-link fences. In August, she would move in with Brian and leave the neighbor-hood for good. They weren't living together to avoid stretching her commute, she said, though I thought it had more to do with some deeply programmed belief that the relationship wouldn't be truly solidified until marriage. In China, it would be inconceivable that a younger, richer man would want to marry someone of her age— or any woman past thirty, she often reminded me with a hint of warning—and she still harbored a shred of mistrust. I couldn't help but feel sentimental about our migrating elsewhere, though the Lau-rel District of my childhood, sleepy and residential, was already disappearing, making way for farm-to-table brunch spots and craft beer dens populated by hip parents and their well-dressed babies.

At this hour, the streets were sparse, the green hills and gold turrets of the Mormon temple blurred with fog. It was impossible not to think of running alongside Oren on the rare occasions when I'd joined him on his morning jogs, our strides syncing and then breaking away as we traversed the park. That was the dastardly part of a relationship, the way it shaped and buffed the world into a faceted gem that reflected the both of you, together, and then suddenly you, alone. The toxic fug of the night before still circulated my body, pinching my side.

Brian slowed to run abreast of me. "Your mom tells me you just earned your master's. That's fantastic."

He didn't know about my leave of absence, I realized. "Yeah, it feels good to have it under my belt," I said, keeping my response terse. Brian, however, was not so easily deterred.

"Your research had something to do with touch, right? Haptics and cognition?"

"Yeah, exactly," I huffed. Brian wore a polite, expectant look, and I resigned myself to giving him an explanation. "Basically, I gave these kids tangram puzzles to solve. But the pieces they were working with had different textures. One group got traditional wood polygons. Another group got this unpleasant, gritty sandpaper. And one got soft velvet pieces. We'd time them to see how quickly they could re-create the patterns we showed them."

"Wow, that sounds fascinating." I didn't know him well enough to detect flattery, but he said it with convincing enthusiasm. "And? What did you find?"

"So, in terms of shortest solution times, the kids who got the velvet pieces did best. Then the control group, then the sandpaper group. The difference was most obvious when the kids spent a lot of time handling and playing with the tangram pieces. So my thesis mapped this correlation between pleasurable touch, which stimulates the orbitofrontal cortex, and better cognitive performance."

"Orbitofrontal cortex?"

I nodded, anticipating the question. "The front part of the brain that perceives reward, which then trickles down to impact how you feel and behave."

"Incredible," said Brian, and again it seemed to be genuine, which somehow made me feel worse. "You're doing incredible work. So you're happy with the program?"

"It's a good program," I said, which was only a half lie. In the beginning, it had been electrifying. I'd thrust myself into academia, slavering to be published and then to present at conferences despite the lukewarm support of my adviser. I'd enjoyed teaching and the implication that I had a role somewhere, in someone's life. I couldn't pinpoint when it had all started to feel insurmountable: the idea of tying my life to the work and the institution.

"What about you?" I deflected. "I heard Wayfindr just released all these new features. I don't really know how it works, to be honest."

"No worries—it's hard to keep up since we're constantly iterating. Well, I'll give you the elevator pitch: Wayfindr leverages real-time data and machine learning to help people discover hidden gems on their way from point A to point B, which supports local businesses and ultimately strengthens the community." We cantered past a storefront with brown butcher paper taped to the windows; the number of the psychic who used to occupy the building was still painted on the glass. "For example, take Wonder Wool, right? Boutique yarn store in the Mission. In one month of using Wayfindr, they increased the number of walk-ins by forty-two percent, the number of sales by thirty-five percent, and revenue by twenty percent. Unheard of, really, without an app like ours to redraw the map."

It sounded like a flippant way of describing gentrification, and I wondered if he'd listened to my spiel with the same skepticism. Neither of us could avoid using the flawed, alienating language we'd inherited through academic or corporate life. "Isn't Starbucks your biggest client?" I said, feeling mean-spirited.

"That depends on what you mean by 'biggest.' If you're talking sheer number of locations, sure. But there are so many use cases from both the business and consumer side. In a sense, our biggest client is our core user. In research, we've heard from newcomers who use the app to navigate their new hood, old-timers who want to get out of their routines or save money on their usual purchases, and everyone in between." He hopped over a jut of concrete where a tree root had rumpled the sidewalk. "Anyway, you should pop in for lunch sometime. All our food is locally grown and organic, and the chef used to work at Chez Panisse."

He began to recite last week's menu, but my attention was on following the two bicyclists who shot past us, trailing a shouted conversation and passing a thermos back and forth. Watching them curve around potholes back toward each other, I felt nausea unfurl in my throat like a flesh-colored flower. Saliva flooded my mouth, forcing me to swallow again and again.

"I'm sorry—" I interrupted, veering across the street toward a coffee shop. "I think I have to stop."

I wove through the line at the counter and burst into the bathroom, which was thankfully vacant. I had just hunched over the toilet when I retched, my back rounding horribly. A spurt of green liquid clouded the water.

"You okay in there?" said Brian through the door.

"It's fine." My voice echoed in the porcelain bowl. A second wave made me lurch forward, and I was thankful for it: the long, violent contraction of the body asserting itself, the choking acidity that streamed from my throat. I was a conduit, a hose of poison. I let the convulsions grip me, the snot clog my nostrils. Soon I couldn't see through the tears wrung out of my face.

When I was empty, I flushed it away. There was a newspaper clipping framed on the wall next to the mirror, where my blotched face hung—it was an interview with the café owner, an Ethiopian woman who had named the business after her dead son. I skimmed it out of a sense of duty, as though it would protect her against apps like Brian's. Then I walked straight out, avoiding eye contact with the patrons who combed me with their curious gazes. My mother was still jogging in place like a video-game character at an invisible boundary.

"I need to go home," I said.

"That's probably for the best," said Brian, his face a mask of concern. "You must be dehydrated."

I nodded. My mother seemed satisfied. As she pressed on, she flicked her calves behind her, light glinting off the Nike swoops on her shoes.

THAT NIGHT, Marissa pointed her chopsticks at me, the ends doused in black bean garlic sauce. "You need to start planning my party."

Brian was staying over again, which meant we were eating at the table. It was a tight fit in the kitchen nook, elbow brushing elbow. A frustratingly competent cook, he'd made dinner, and now the demolished fish lay in tatters of flaking meat. The tablecloth was meant for picnicking, with its waxed surface and red-checked pattern, and our paper napkins had been saved from take-out orders: familiar details I wouldn't have noted except for Brian's intrusion.

"What party?"

She probed the fish, came away with a greased morsel. "You know, the 'bachelorette party.'" She pronounced the phrase in careful English.

I laughed. "*You* want to have a bachelorette party?" I passed a look of incredulity to Brian, who did not return it. He was beaming at his fiancée, ruffling the fish with his chopsticks.

"Why not?" She sat up straighter. "*Laowai* do it all the time. I want to go to Vegas."

I plucked a filament of bone out of my mouth. "Just because white people go to Vegas for their bachelorette parties doesn't mean you have to." I hadn't forgiven her for my miserable morning. "Don't you think you're past that point? And what would you even do there? Not drink, of course."

"Oh, there's plenty to do," Brian chimed in. "You can hit the casinos, see a show."

I resented him for his graciousness, but I knew it was true. Vegas had been something of a family tradition with Baba, who had taken us not long after we'd arrived from Shanghai. He'd been in America for two years then, and he introduced us to the most American place he knew, a mirage of the West with its unctuous neon lights and the pervasive whisper of cash. I'd been so young. In my mind it was like an amusement park, the ersatz halls of Caesar's Palace—which sounded so grand in Mandarin, *kaisa gong*—and its ceilings painted like a storybook sky. The fountains reeked of chlorine and were glutted with coins. I had photos of myself as a toddler sporting a bowl cut and a fanny pack, making a peace sign next to the camels of the Sahara Desert, so frequently repainted that their bodies sagged with color. We didn't have any other family, so we went there for Christmas, too, posing next to hotel lobby trees and their attendant piles of empty boxes wrapped in festive paper. Even back then I sensed something counterfeit about our holidays. Once, I'd seen an off-duty Santa smoking a cigarette by a chain-link fence, dozens of cards advertising call girls tucked in the steel lattice like lewd wallpaper.

After the divorce, after my mother found out about my father's *xiao laopo*, his little wife, we never went back. Maybe a girls' trip would be her way of reclaiming the city, asserting her triumph over the past. The thought depressed me, which made me feel meaner.

"I didn't have a real wedding the first time," my mother continued. It was bizarre, her entreaty, as though she were a child desperate to attend a sleepover or have a toy. "I want to do it the right way."

Mama and Baba had met in a doctor's office in Shanghai. She was taking her father, my *waigong*, to get his kidney stones treated; he was bringing his little sister in for an ear infection. Lanky and gregarious with incendiary ideas about democracy, my father stood in blazing contrast to the suitors my mother had endured at her parents' bidding, but his was a poor and provincial background—his folks were rural *waidi ren* who'd found their footing in Shanghai as a schoolteacher and a factory worker during the Cultural Revolution—while my mother's family had risen in status, thanks to Waigong's military education and post in submarine research.

So they conducted a furtive love. They wrote letters on thin, translucent sheets of rice paper. They met at noodle stands between their college campuses and lurched down dappled streets with my mother standing on the back pegs of his bike, skirt rippling around her shape. The honeyed musk of *bai lan hua* still made Mama nostalgic for the creamy buds he would buy to pin to her blouse, the street peddlers peeling back the cloth on their wicker baskets so that she could choose the most luscious floret. Waipuo and Waigong eventually sniffed out the romance, and my grandfather staged a half-hearted hunger strike, but by then it was too late: I was already a curl of flesh in my mother's womb, had been carried through the swarm of a student protest.

Baba had long ago married his *xiao laopo*, and now he and Leslie lived in Pasadena. They had no children, though not for lack of trying. We spoke here and there on the phone, careful not to disturb the polite scrim we'd erected between us. "This is good news," he'd said about Marissa's engagement, "happy news," and I took his words at face value because it was too exhausting to do otherwise. Growing up, though, I'd always burrowed close to him, the more affectionate parent whose heavy breath felt like a benediction as he read me stories about the Monkey King and his magnificent adventures.

When Baba left, my mother retreated into a private chamber of grief. In college, when I'd read about Mary Carlson's research in a Romanian orphanage—how a lack of touch made the children rock listlessly, rendered them silent and strange—I wondered whether the swift loss of tenderness could have stunted my growth somehow. Nowadays doctors call this a failure to thrive. At my age, however, that would have been a hyperbolic diagnosis. It was far more likely that the inexplicable flares of anger I felt toward my mother were just adolescent angst. But I'd never stopped studying touch, perhaps trying to understand my sense of deprivation, although I'd wandered into a suffocating, theoretical thicket instead of getting closer to the truth.

"Nothing wrong with wanting the bells and whistles," said Brian. I watched him suck his teeth and wondered what it was about him that had resuscitated my mother after all my years of looking after her. What refulgent love for him, and where was that light for me?

"I guess it would be fun," I relented. Maybe there was something to learn from Brian. Maybe instead of dwelling on my resentment I could get back to what I had wanted all along, which was to make Marissa happy. Which was, in other words, to feel like an adequate daughter.

MY MOTHER ANSWERED the beeping dryer as I cleared the table, and Brian cut up a watermelon for dessert. The knife slid easily through the rind, yielding two crisp and glistening halves.

"Thanks for cooking," I said, holding a plate under running water.

"Oh, anytime," he said. He sliced slowly, methodically. "It's always nice to be able to cook for other people. Gets boring when it's just you. Do you cook much?"

"Does microwaving takeout count?"

He chuckled. "Chester's not a big cook, either. He makes a decent sandwich, though." He picked up a chunk of watermelon and shaved the rind clean with his teeth. "I think it's cool you're doing this for your mom."

"Yeah. I mean, if it's what she really wants. I was just caught off guard."

"Don't think she doesn't know it's a weird ask." They had talked it over beforehand, I realized, which shouldn't have come as a surprise, but it irked me to remember that Brian was upstream of Marissa's thoughts now and could tamper with them before they drifted to me. "But she trusts you. She can be a harsh critic, but she speaks highly of you."

"*That* I don't believe."

"Really. It's a cliché of parenthood, but she's hard on you because she loves you. And being an only child, you're getting that times ten. And your mom—yeah, sometimes she can put things bluntly. She has high expectations. As she should. I mean, look at everything you've accomplished."

I worried a bowl with the sponge, intent on scrubbing away the irritation building in my chest at Brian's paternal tone. "I'm guessing she hasn't told you that I'm thinking of leaving the program?"

He concentrated on cubing the watermelon. "No, she hasn't. But, hey, if that's how you're feeling—"

"I'll never hear the end of it."

"It might take her a minute to come around, but in the end, it's your decision." He used the flat edge of the knife to transfer the fruit into a bowl. "It's been really motivating meeting Marissa. She never feels defeated. Never wants to settle. She wants the best for herself and for you. I think coming to the States at a certain age, escaping a certain regime, you fall into a survivor mindset, and you never really leave. My parents were like that. Tough. Disciplined to a fault. They could seem insensitive and demanding, but they made sure I got going on my own path. I wish Chester had grown up around them more. I wish he'd seen the days of us eating Spam and watered-down rice for dinner."

"Hey, Spam and rice porridge got me through the first two years of school."

Brian scrunched up his face. "Are you kidding? I'm waiting for Tartine to 'discover' it and put it on their brunch menu for fifteen dollars."

I laughed—the first time I'd laughed that day.

My mother emerged from the hallway. One arm hugged a laundry basket to her hip; the other was threaded through a stack of plastic hangers. "How long does it take to cut up some fruit?" she said.

"Cracking the whip as always," Brian said conspiratorially, and I saw that he was truly enthralled with Marissa, had spun her misery into heroism.

The TV program we settled on followed ex–Playboy Bunnies who worked at competing lumber mills in Alaska. My mother and I knelt on the carpet by the hamper, folding each article into a neat rectangle, assembling a kind of truce.

On the screen, an old photograph of Bunny Libby, her slender body encased in a satin costume, preceded her present-day confessional. The years had caused her features to bloat and spread. She was struggling to keep up with the chipper, she told the camera, and the dust was getting into her lungs.

"You see what happens when you don't take care of yourself?" said my mother.

Our sorted piles of underwear were growing on the carpet. My mother smoothed a pair of my boy shorts, tucked in the sides, and laid it on top of the others. I glanced at Brian on the couch to see his reaction to her criticism, but he was either absorbed by the TV or willfully creating a perimeter around us.

I'd dismissed their relationship as economic—instigated by loneliness and buoyed by the prerequisite amount of love, but Brian's unflagging earnestness made me reconsider. He offered a shortcut to the kind of life she'd always envisioned, yes, but he also drew strength from her relentlessness, her past. Marissa bridging two countries and the various epochs of her own life formed a through line that reinforced and inspired his own narrative. For her, it must have been intoxicating, reanimating, to prop someone else up after so many years of scrambling for support.

My mother shifted on her ankles and drew another pair from the hamper, a mesh panty with slack elastic I'd purchased for Oren to appreciate. She gathered up the corners, then gave it a pat as she set it down. It was a motion she'd performed hundreds of times, maybe thousands. It struck me, watching her, that despite all of my complaints, I could never repay her care, not even for the number of times she had folded my underwear on her knees.

PROPPED UP IN BED with a book I wasn't reading in favor of scrolling through Twitter, I could hear Marissa and Brian's mumblings coming through the walls in dark, indecipherable shapes.

After a while, her footsteps traveled down the hall and my door swung open.

"Kathleen?" She was in a T-shirt and underwear. Her face was glossy with night cream. "Here, I need you to look this over when you get a chance." She sat on the edge of the bed, placing a paper on the nightstand. I saw her name boldfaced across the top and realized it was her résumé.

"You don't want Brian to help you with it?"

"He will, but I want you to look at it, too."

I picked it up and read: *Eager team player and strong leader.*

"Why are you looking for a job all of a sudden?"

"*Wo lao le.* I can't work on my feet all day anymore." As if to demonstrate, she crossed an ankle over her knee and picked at a wart on the ball of her foot. Scratching the protuberance, she said, "I've already given too many years to Macy's. I've always thought I should be doing meaningful work. I'm very smart, you know. I always graduated first in my class."

After university, she'd been funneled into a job with a state-owned electrical company thanks to her *guanxi* with a school counselor, though she lacked the actual expertise to be a project overseer. Her manager had a lashing tongue—calling her *gou shi*, or dog shit, when she misread the plans—but he never fired her; as one of only three women in the ranks, she was good for morale. My mother had always felt that she'd wasted her education, though some would say she'd been lucky to land anything at all in those lean times. She never escaped the sense of imminent failure, either, in any of her subsequent gigs. She would be berating herself for a mishap at work and then crumple in panic, panting for air with her head between her knees on the kitchen floor. I wondered if terror still overcame her or if she still felt tempted to disappear in wine.

"Do you regret coming here? To America?" I asked. We were both surprised at the question, its intimacy.

"Knowing what I know now, I wouldn't have come. I would be speaking my own language, living in my own city." She smoothed the blanket around my waist, her confession a kind of permission to touch. "But there were so few opportunities then. Turning down a chance to come was unthinkable. And I found a different version of happiness here, didn't I?" She patted the résumé and walked back down the hall.

4.

After indulging my misery for two weeks, LB made me download a dating app. We were in her loft at Dolly's, a West Oakland co-op converted from a former packing warehouse for Dolly's Sweets, a now-defunct cookie company—the members called themselves Dolls in tribute. LB's place was on the fourth and topmost floor, its high ceilings traversed by pipes from which she'd hung ferns and streaming pothos. An expansive grid of windows faced the street, the panes cranked open over a mattress raised on shipping pallets. Aside from the bathroom, the space was completely open.

We were each nursing our fifth Aperol Spritz, lying in opposite directions on the couch, our ankles knitted together. With LB, touch came naturally; we'd spent so much of our childhood jostling each other, scrambling to turn the pages of trashy teen magazines and rub our wrists against the perfume samples, or pinching each other's pores to eject globules of sebum. The ease I had with her didn't translate to other people. Oren had had to coax me into creating our own language, a calligraphic system of strokes and caresses. The first time he'd kissed the back of my neck—I'd been bowed over a textbook—I'd yipped with nervous laughter.

LB sprung up from her side to snatch the phone out of my hand and started scrolling through photos to add to my profile.

"How does every single picture of you have Oren in it?" she said, slouched low against a pillow so that her chin flattened against her chest.

"All the good pictures of me are on his phone."

"You don't take selfies? Oh, hey, it's me! Aw, I remember that day." She flipped the screen around to show me the picture. It'd been taken a year ago at the county fair. We were squatting next to a pygmy goat at the petting zoo, its bristly face cocked at the camera; LB's baseball cap was crooked, and she was making the metal horns sign with her hand. "I've got one hand on a go-oat," she sang in the strained, spiraling voice of Alanis Morissette, "and the other one's giving a metal sign."

She raised her glass from where she'd placed it on the concrete floor and slurped from her luminous drink.

"Whoops, that's a nude. What angelic tits you have, Kath, seriously. But shouldn't you keep these in a separate folder?" She tsked. "Oh my God, you only take selfies with dogs. Whose dogs *are* these, even?"

Later, when she'd finally cobbled something together, we huddled next to each other and thumbed through hundreds of faces. Men in plaid flannels held their prize fish up to the camera; men flexed in front of mirrors at the gym. They loved to travel, and held dear the notion of pineapple on pizza, and would only trust you if their dog liked you. They were GGG and ethically nonmonogamous, and punctuated their wholesome portraits with a snapshot of themselves in Burning Man regalia, rosy and powdered with desert dust at sunrise.

"He's cute, sorta," said LB, pausing.

I hummed an indecisive tone. "Oh, no, he's a moderate."

She swiped his photo away, condemning him to the digital abyss. "Not gonna lie, this is rough. Guess we can't all inherit our best friend's exes."

I had always been grateful to LB for preserving our friendship through her candor and optimism, her disarmingly vulnerable way of saying things like "Kath, I wouldn't go down this road if I didn't feel like there was a real chance at happiness at the end of it" when she'd first started dating Andrew. "I really need your blessing." She was the sort of person who sought blessings, who looked out for signs of goodwill from the universe—a ring of mushrooms parting the grass, an exquisite rock plucked from the riverbed—and made you a believer, too.

An ad popped up next. *Need a hug? Cozy up to cuddle therapy*, it read, accompanied by a photo of a couple snuggling by a campfire, a blanket draped over their shoulders. We snickered at its cheesiness.

"I'm sorry, come again?" I said. My glass collided with my teeth and I repositioned it, tipping the drink into my mouth and gesturing for LB to click through.

The website that loaded was for Midas Touch, a self-proclaimed cuddle clinic with locations in San Francisco, Oakland, Brooklyn, and (coming soon) Austin. Hygienic photos of people spooning in bed or curled up on the couch ran alongside a friendly, sans serif font. Whoever had art-directed the photo shoot had been scrupulous about representation, as though they'd had a check mark beside every race, gender, age, and size.

"This is *so* creepy," said LB. "Is this a cult?"

"It's either a cult or a millennial sock brand."

I clicked on the About Us page.

Take a hands-on approach to happiness. Studies have shown that a kind touch lowers stress, boosts your immune system, and releases oxytocin—you know, the hormone that gives you the warm and fuzzies. It's time to get back to basics: unplug and unwind with a wellness consultation with one of our trained cuddle providers.

"What on God's green earth," LB breathed. "The founder's a babe, though."

The creator of Midas Touch was Abigail Brown, a woman with a spiraling mass of red hair, whose thin lips were tilted in a knowing half smile. "'The seed for the cuddle clinic was planted during her one-year solo trip around the world, when she made so many meaningful connections—but still craved the simple, soothing comfort of touch,'" read LB bombastically. "'Over the past two years, Abigail has consulted with experts in touch therapy to develop the Midas Method, a code of ethics and cuddling manual.'" She widened her eyes at the screen. "This is wild. Is this based on any science at all?"

"To be fair," I said, "there *is* this thing in social psychology called the Midas touch. Like, if a waitress touches you at a restaurant somehow, puts her hand on your shoulder or something, you tip more. And students participate more in class if they're touched by the teacher—no, not in a molesty way—and basketball players score more points if they high-five or hug each other."

"Ew!" she shrieked. "Of course you would know that. Look," she said, tapping on the Start Cuddling button, "they need brains like yours. 'Become a certified cuddle provider and earn up to $100 an hour.' I'm signing you up."

"No!" I grabbed for the phone, but LB twisted away. "I'm going to get so many spam emails."

"Hey, I'm doing you a favor," LB said. "This is a job. One that pays four times as much as I'm making."

I tried to imagine what it would feel like, holding a stranger, but instead my brain substituted Oren, the stubble I grazed when I sought his lips in the dark. A slow sadness, like cold mud, saturated my body, and my eyes welled. I was always within reach of pain; it could assault me at any time.

"Sent!" LB dropped the phone and noticed my tears. "Oh, no." She confiscated my glass and looped her arms around my neck, pulling me close. "See? I'm healing you with the incredible power of touch."

I laughed through a shudder. "Thanks." I blinked against the dark of her shoulder for a while and then pulled back, wiping my nose with the inside of my collar.

"Have you, like, tried being angry?" she asked.

"Yeah, I'm angry," I said indignantly. I regularly cycled through my list of grievances: that Oren had kept his unhappiness from me, that he'd unilaterally decided the relationship was past saving. That he hadn't been present to support me through school because he was too busy excelling, that he hadn't admitted that he found my lack of motivation unattractive. It was a dark pleasure, seething about these things, flattening him into something easier to discard.

"Have you been so angry you've broken something?"

A pause. "What are you trying to get me to do right now?"

"Come on!" she exclaimed, flinging her hands up, looking around her space. The light cascading from the warehouse windows sharpened the knolls of the mussed sheets on her bed, revealing the whirligigging dander in the air. She launched herself toward a long dresser, its surface a tableau of books, candlesticks, and pert-eared plants, and brought back a mug. It was white with a teddy bear pattern running around it.

"I'm not going to break your mug," I protested.

"Just try it," she said, shaking it at me. "It might be satisfying. I hate this mug. This mug is cursed. I accidentally stole it from the kitchen at work and now this woman named Cheryl is asking everyone for it, and it's too awkward to put it back now. It must be destroyed."

"How? Where?" I grasped the handle.

"On the floor! We'll sweep it up! I mean, you'll sweep it up!"

I walked a few paces into the center of the room and conjured my apartment in Baltimore, how empty it had seemed after Oren had gone, how unconquerably vast, and I hurled the mug against the floor, where it petaled into several pieces. The sound came hot and bright.

"How did it feel?" asked LB.

I let out a breath I hadn't realized I'd been holding. "Good." I started gathering the shards with my shoe. "That felt good."

THE NEXT DAY I had an email from Midas Touch: *Little spoon or big spoon? Let's get to know each other.* It opened with a testimonial from a cuddle provider named Drishti, age thirty-six, in San Francisco: *Seeing my cuddle clients is the absolute highlight of my week. Midas Touch takes care of the scheduling and payment processing, so all I have to do is show up and snuggle. I always leave feeling like I've made a difference.*

I told myself I was reading it ironically, but something compelled me forward. I didn't believe in the sanitary veneer Midas Touch presented, but that only made it more alluring. Here was research of the flesh, so far from the hermetic experiments of school. So many relationships and flings had made me suspect that I was less fluent in touch than other people: I marveled at how easily other bodies warmed to mine, yielding like butter whenever my hand grazed the back of a neck, the slope of a thigh. I tensed when they kissed me in public as though it would help to fortify the borders of my body. Oren had had to encourage me toward him, saying when I pressed my lips to his bare shoulder once, "I like that. You never do that." But it was less complicated with strangers. I was only afraid to reach for someone I was scared of losing.

The next steps to becoming a certified cuddle provider, the email explained, were to complete a background check, take an online training course in the Midas Method, and pass an in-person Cuddle Aptitude Test. After that, I would be added to the directory for clients to book within my available days and time frames.

At worst, I reasoned, my nerves swimming with a strange electricity, it would be a good story to tell; I could already imagine LB's eyes inflating with shock and glee. I clicked on the button—Get Started—marveling at how even the most innocuous copywriting could feel like a benefaction to someone like me.

MIDAS TOUCH WAS in downtown Oakland, occupying the sixth and seventh floors of a building that had once been coworking offices. Long ago, in high school, I'd peed in the front courtyard out of desperation after leaving a show on Telegraph Avenue, squatting behind a concrete planter while my friends stood as lookouts. Now, the elevator doors opened to a landing of dark tile and mirrors. Glass doors bearing the company's logo, a golden palm radiating lines of energy, slid open as I approached, beckoning me to the front desk.

"Hi," I said to the woman at the computer. "I'm here for my Cuddle Aptitude Test?" She was intimidatingly put together, like a gift, presentable, with her dun blond bangs in a crisp line across her forehead and small gold hoops pinned to her ears.

"Great, just one sec," she said, swiveling to the monitor. As she searched for me in the system, I ogled the open office behind her. Everything was unsettlingly neat: There were rows of standing desks lined with marigold felt dividers and white orb pendants hanging above the employees, headphones clamped over their ears. Fiddle-leaf figs and voluminous palms grew lustily out of burlap-sack planters.

"Kathleen Cheng?" asked the woman.

"Yes, that's me."

"Perfect. I have you all checked in. If you'll have a seat in the waiting room, someone will call your name in a couple of minutes."

"Thanks." I walked in the direction she pointed. The walls were gallery white, hung with blown-up photographic prints of nuzzling bodies, composed to abstract the joist of a collarbone or the swell of a stomach.

I was both impressed and distressed with how seamless it all felt, as though I'd stepped through the app into a physical manifestation of the brand. Everything about the start-up was studiously youthful, friendly, conscientious, cool. During the online training, after every video segment a quiz would slide onto the screen. *Your male-bodied client becomes physically aroused during the session*, it read. *How do you handle the situation?* I'd tapped on *Take a break from cuddling and assess how you're both feeling*, and a flare of confetti had showered the screen.

The waiting room was wrapped in a hushed taupe felt, and a curvaceous built-in wooden bench wrapped around three sides, accented with circular cushions. There were knotty wooden blocks dispersed as side tables, adorned with dried flowers and eucalyptus. Ambient music bled softly into the room. I sat down on a cushion and studied the large canvas on the opposite wall, its blotches of sienna and fern green.

Soon, someone walked in and I straightened, but it didn't seem like he was there for me. We glanced at each other—he, a forty-something white man in a checkered button-down; I, a visibly tense woman in a black T—and decided not to disturb our private spheres. He took a seat on the bench and pulled out his phone. A client, I realized. I imagined gathering him into my arms, feeling the shifting of his spine and smelling the faint tang of coffee on his breath, and my nerves flared again, both in agitation and with an odd longing. I felt protective of this human creature.

I sat examining this feeling until a woman around my age entered the room. She was tall and plump, with shining cheeks and a gap-toothed smile. "Kathleen? Thanks for waiting. If you're ready, I'll take you to our therapy rooms." She glanced at the man waiting. "Wayne, let me know if you need anything."

"I'm great, thank you," said Wayne, holding up the phone as though it was proof.

She introduced herself as Nadia—"senior cuddler and community liaison"—as she led me out of the waiting room and up a carpeted stairwell. "Do you have any experience as a professional cuddler?" she asked.

"No, not professionally."

"Most of our cuddle providers don't have formal experience,

but that's not a problem," she said, her high-pitched voice ringing with a slight echo. "I've been at it for four years now, so let me know if you have any questions. At first I was doing it on my own, but then I found Midas—or, more accurately, they found me. I helped beta-test the whole thing, smoothed out the kinks. And here we are: the bathrooms—there're changing stalls if you need to get into something comfier—and the therapy rooms." We'd emerged on the next floor, where a long hallway connected meeting rooms encased in frosted glass. I could see dim silhouettes in the occupied spaces; a touch screen at the door closest to us counted down the minutes left in the session. She took in my silence. "Not what you were expecting?"

I couldn't put it into words—the eeriness of commodifying intimacy, the company's willfully cheerful answer to the urgent and pervasive loneliness of existence. Studies on the physiological benefits of touch were sparse, and questions around ethics stayed the hands of caretakers, doctors, and therapists. Midas Touch seemed poised to satisfy a primal need, but what about the ethics of privatizing touch at all? In the end, profit would be the only metric that mattered. Despite their breathless DEI statement and inclusive brand identity, Midas Touch was tailored to a privileged, urban, tech-savvy few. "It's very regulated," I finally said lamely.

"Oh, absolutely. Everything's been streamlined to feel as safe and comfortable as possible." Nadia unlocked a door with a string of numbers and held it open to let me pass.

Here, a low platform bed took up most of the space, draped with a fringed coverlet, and a slim leather couch hugged one wall. A wooden coffee table held a brass tray of melted candles and a singed nub of palo santo in a marble bowl.

"Go ahead, have a seat," said Nadia. She took her place on the couch, then leaned over to wedge a finger into the back of her sneakers. "We just ask that shoes stay off the furniture."

Unsettled by the sudden familiarity in the room, I stepped out of my flats and sat beside her, maintaining a cushion's width of distance.

"So the first thing I want to point out," said Nadia, "is that there's a camera in every room that monitors the session. This is just to ensure that everyone is complying with the Midas Method, which, as you know, includes cuddling, conversation, and companionship, but is completely nonsexual." She gestured to the white camera mounted in a corner. "If you feel uncomfortable in any way, it's your right to terminate the session, and that'll flag the user in our system for a follow-up with the safety team. Nine times out of ten, that will result in them being permanently banned. Not that it happens very often— less than one percent of the time, to be exact." She flashed a reassuring smile. "Do you have any questions before we begin?"

The misgivings I had were jumbled in an impossible knot. I shook my head.

"Okay, feel free to let me know if anything pops up. Otherwise, how about we start with you showing me The Armchair?"

The Midas Method included a guide to cuddling positions that ranged from basic poses, like spooning, to more elaborate choreography. *Start with something simple*, the training had advised, *and let the rest come naturally. Feel free to incorporate stimulating movement, like back rubs and head scratches, with the consent of the client, checking in periodically to make sure you're both comfortable and relaxed.* I'd studied the illustration for The Armchair, recognizing it as the way Oren would often hold me: he lying on his side with his knees bent at a right angle, I resting on my back with my legs hooked over his, as though in a seat. I guided Nadia to the bed and into the pose, suppressing a laugh at the strangeness of our bodies connecting so unceremoniously, as though we were models performing for a camera. My arms encircled her shoulders as she settled into my lap, and I could feel the warmth and give where her breasts began, and I smelled coconut shampoo.

"Are you comfy?" I asked, hoping that she couldn't feel my sputtering heart.

"M-hm. This is nice. Are you?"

"Yup." I cleared my throat to stifle a cough. I waited for further instruction, but it did not come. Thirty seconds passed, then a minute. I marinated in my own self-consciousness until it deepened and metastasized into a kind of horror. To disperse the feeling, I tried to think about the science of what was happening: the unmyelinated C-tactile fibers in the skin responding to tenderness, the insular cortex of the brain processing sweetness. While I labored, Nadia was breathing deeply, letting the air graze the back of her throat so that she emitted a light snore, and I wondered if she were falling asleep.

I closed my eyes. I focused on the rise and fall of her body pressing into mine. Gradually, my thoughts lost their rigidity, began to drift. I became less aware of time and more aware of the heat coalescing between us, my consciousness sinking until it was a small, eyeless seed within a broadening galaxy of flesh, bone, blood, nerve, steady and alive. It felt like a meditation, a color dawning inside my head. Apparitions of sound and image ballooned and dissolved, forming a diaphanous tunnel that transported me back: the tick of a car signal, windshield wipers clearing a swirl of snow. Oren's hands climbing over the wheel as we cruised left. The tires dragging through slush on the road. I was telling him about Brian, how flushed my mother sounded on the phone. Maybe they were taking things too fast.

He glanced at the directions, the blue line charting our path. "I think I turned too soon."

"That's okay, we're close, I think." I cleared a patch of fog on the window and watched it regain its milky opacity. "Did you hear me? I'm worried she's going to get hurt."

"Have there been any red flags?"

"Other than an alien abducting my mother and replacing her with a freaky clone? No. Can you imagine Marissa *running*?"

"What's so bad about her wanting to be more active?"

"It's not bad, it's just . . ." I arced against the seat, stretching my back. "It's alarming. It's like everything she went through—that *we* went through—didn't count or matter. All she needed was to meet some dude?"

He patted my thigh. "I'm sure it's jarring, but if she's happy, what's the point in overthinking it?"

Comfort, encouragement—Oren offered them readily, but he had a hard time acknowledging when things were off. He did this when I talked about Marissa, about school, about us, as though the troubles of my life could seep into and taint his. It was because he saw my life fundamentally as a reflection of his own, a shadow that couldn't survive without its counterpart. It was lonely to trudge through my doubts, though at the time I'd dismissed them as my own insecurity and anxiety.

The truth was, my body had sensed the relationship straining before the breakup. Oren and I had stopped touching each other. The sex was still there, but not the palm caressing my lower back as he passed me in the kitchen, not the sardine squeeze of our bodies stretched across the couch. We fell asleep with just our ankles intertwined, and I would wake up huddled on one side with the covers while he lay exposed in the dark. These were inches that felt like miles, the negative space between us like runes we'd refused to decipher.

Nadia sighed and shifted, and I miraculously moved with her, and we nestled facing each other with my chin buried in her hair. I felt as though I'd landed a dazzling gymnastic maneuver, but it had come naturally. My body had known what to do.

5.

For his first two years in California, my father was without family, but he was not alone. For one, he shared a duplex with six other tenants, all of them subject to the vigilant proprietorship of Mrs. Yee. He was earning his master's degree in computer science, presumably among colleagues, and waiting tables at a Szechuan restaurant called Golden Lotus. He sent letters back home to Shanghai, and every couple of months, when he could afford to hear my mother's voice, he'd place a long-distance call. "I miss you," he said, "unbearably, unbearably much." But he must not have been so lonesome because he had found a lover, a woman named Leslie Fang, though we wouldn't know that for a while.

When my mother and I finally joined him, we lived in the duplex, too, but when I was six we moved to a brown stucco apartment in Anaheim. Compared to the single bedroom we had all been sharing, Villa Palms was the pinnacle of luxury. An eponymous stand of palms sprang from the central courtyard, and the pool was clear and blue as a windowpane. The promise of Disneyland, though I had never been there, presided over my imagination, like heaven or Santa

Claus; I loved to watch other families leave on their expeditions, donning Mickey Mouse ears and trailing the slick scent of sunscreen. At night, fireworks thudded against the sky, the raining sparks as reliable as the next day's sun.

I was proud that we lived there, proud that we had the dignity of a living room and kitchen that was ours alone, away from the *shushu* and *ayi* who would tease me and pinch my cheeks. Mrs. Yee could no longer squawk at me for standing on the couch or straying from the plastic mats she had laid over the carpet. About a year in, that idyll dissolved.

It was a Friday—I remember because I'd brought home a manila envelope from school fattened with the week's in-class assignments: the life cycle of a butterfly, painstakingly colored in with scented markers, math worksheets stamped *Outta this world!*

My mother sat at the small table by the window, poring over the classified section of the newspaper, planning our route of attack. Every Saturday, in the bleary hours of the early morning, we wound our way through the suburbs on a tour of the best garage sales. She would circle the most promising ads—the ones that mentioned home goods and children's clothes, the ones in nice neighborhoods—and plot out each stop on her ragged map of the city, its creases furred with use. The holy grail was a Japanese sale, advertised with star icons on the top line, where the garage door whirred open at exactly 7:00 a.m. to a waiting crowd, and the items were impeccably sorted, marked with color-coded stickers to be tallied up at the cashier's box. Our apartment was full of secondhand items that Marissa had ruthlessly haggled down.

Her face was shrouded in the black whorls of her perm.

"What is this word," she asked in Mandarin, sounding it out, "'humidifier'?"

I hooked my elbows over the table and pored over the column of text, hoping that it would come to me. Through the slanted blinds I could see the neon plashing of swimsuits hitting the pool. "I don't know," I confessed, scrunching the skirt of my dress. "You have to sign this envelope."

"Here, you do it." She handed me the pen and reached for her electronic English-Chinese dictionary.

"That's not allowed!"

"Don't fuss." The dictionary emitted small beeps as she typed the word into the display. Bringing my nose to the envelope, I mimicked her signature, which was itself ersatz, improvised when she moved to the States. My hand cramped around each labyrinthine *S*. I worried that I would get into trouble, my name emblazoned on the board in yellow chalk. My teacher already disliked me, I feared, because I didn't follow directions, though the truth was that I often couldn't understand them.

"It doesn't look right."

My mother glanced at my work and clicked her tongue. "Oh, well."

I rolled the pen back and forth on the table with my palm.

"Are you hungry?" she asked. "If you're hungry, get yourself a slice of cheese."

"I'm not hungry," I said, though I loved unwrapping the rubbery surface of a Kraft American single and peeling off slivers of yellow matter. Hoping to redeem myself, I began to pull papers from the envelope. I set them on the table in silence, then ventured, "I drew a butterfly."

"Mmm," my mother grunted. "Very good." She slid the map over the newspaper and hunted for an address, tracing the street with her finger. I wanted to bury my face in the downy filaments of her white sweater, but I knew she was in an impatient mood. Her eyebrows strained to meet over the bridge of her nose. It seemed that around me she was always tired and anxious, but when my father got home from work, she relaxed and elongated, a sunning reptile.

"Look," I tried again, tapping the drawing. "One wing is red and orange, and the other is blue and green."

She tsked in annoyance, fingertip holding her place on the map. "I'll look at it later, *hao ma*? Be a good girl. Go outside and play."

I LAY ON a concrete bench by the pool and watched the breeze animate the long fingers of a palm frond overhead, roiling with a sense of injustice. My teacher had doled out rare praise about my butterfly worksheet; why couldn't my mother do the same? The canopy heaved against the sky, and I fantasized about running away, how frantic she would be. I imagined filling my backpack with clothes and Kraft singles and hitchhiking to Disneyland, where I would find a new family, maybe even a white one. I pictured sitting down to dinner wreathed in the tulle of a princess dress, the table laden with chicken nuggets, heaps of fries.

"Whatcha doing?" Brianna, who was my age and lived in apartment 2G, dispersed the vision. Her face blinked above mine, brown hair hidden under a flower-pattern helmet.

I sat up. "Nothing." I focused on the pristine white roller skates on her feet and gasped. "When did you get those?"

"Today," she said smugly, and lifted one foot to show off the clear wheels, speckled with glitter. "My grandma got them for me. Wanna see me skate?" She propelled herself down the walk that encircled the pool. Her movements were stiff and juddering, but I watched in awe as her body grew smaller, disappearing and reappearing between the steel bars of the fence as she reached the far side of the water. Her little arms swam unsteadily through the air, and her hair flapped behind her. Brianna's extended family lived nearby, and her aunts, uncles, and grandparents were forever anointing her with gifts; sometimes I got her hand-me-downs, so I didn't totally begrudge her the good fortune. This, however, was a windfall I couldn't bear. Just last Saturday, on our yard sale excursion, I had begged my mother to buy an old pair of skates, but the owner had been adamant about the price. With every shake of her head, the hope drained out of my body. I held the sacred shoes, running my fingertips over the weathered skin.

"It's too dangerous," my mother had finally said, to justify giving up. "You'll break your bones. Maybe when you're older." The truth, of course, was that we couldn't afford it. There was never enough money, never enough time, never enough energy.

Brianna finished her lap and came to a stumbling halt, grinning widely enough to show the gap in her teeth. My jealousy made her face seem grotesque, a rictus of indulgence and excess. "It's so fun! Do you know how to roller-skate?"

"Sure," I lied, seeing my chance. "Can I try them?"

She hesitated. "I just put them on."

"Come on, you'll have them the whole rest of your life. I'll let you go first the next time we play mermaids." Mermaids, in which we took turns describing our tresses and shimmering tails, was a favorite game of ours, and whoever went first got to claim long, tumbling red hair.

"Okay, but just for a minute," said Brianna, and she sat down to unlace them. I plopped down beside her and eagerly transferred each offered skate to my feet. They were too big, but I yanked the laces with as much force as I could muster, feeling a surge of excitement as they fused with my body, became a part of who I now was: sporty, speedy, carefree. Using Brianna's shoulder as leverage, I stood up and took a few clattering steps.

"You're not very good," she said dubiously.

"I'm just getting used to these," I said. "They're different from the ones I had."

Leaning into each movement, I found, would coerce the wheels forward. I pumped my arms for extra speed, winging them from side to side as I clung to my balance. The pathway underfoot rumbled with cracks and pebbles, and the jittering in my knees made me feel like a rocket ship reverberating before takeoff: as I struggled forward, I imagined flames and a billowing cloud in my wake, the roar of my progress drowning out Brianna's voice as she called me back in shriller and shriller tones. Then my mother, drawn outside by the girl's shouting, added her voice to the din: "Slow down, slow down!" But I was beyond slowing, didn't know how to slow, my legs working maniacally beneath me to keep me aloft, the greased ground careening underneath, until finally with an elated hoot I missed a turn and crashed against the concrete and the rock bed of a palm, skinning my hands.

Brianna dashed to my side and burst into tears. "You messed up my skates!" she squealed. "My brand-new skates!"

Dazedly, I looked down at my knees, scored with bright, welling blood, and then at the once immaculate skates, which now wore long black scuffs on the leather. I was sorry to see them marred, but part of me was thrilled that I had been the one to do it.

My mother appeared and lifted me by my armpits into a sitting position. Her fingers raced to unknot the skates. "*Wo bu shi gaosu ni ma?*" she scolded as she tugged them off. "Too dangerous! Break your bone!" she said in English, and then hoisted me to standing, grimacing at my legs, which were now smeared in dirt, blood, torn skin. She gripped me by my shoulders and steered me toward Brianna, whose face had gone blotchy with crying. "Say sorry," she instructed. "Sorry for to damage your new skate."

As I watched Brianna's nostrils flare and sniffle, the shock of the fall finally registering on my skin as spreading trails of fire, it occurred to me that if I'd had what she had—if my mother had bought those old skates—none of this would've happened. My mother's grammar jangled in my ears, further evidence that though we'd moved out of Mrs. Yee's home and into our own apartment, the things we wanted were still inaccessible. She gave me a shake as though to jostle the apology from my lips, and I tore myself out of her hands. "Sorry *for damaging* your new *skates*." I said it into her startled face, exaggerating my corrections. Her arms were still raised, describing my shoulders in the air. It felt good, so I said it again: "*Damaging* your new *skates*."

My mother set her features, which made her both terrible and beautiful. "Baba will deal with you when he gets home," she said, which deflated my anger into a flat blade of fear.

MY MOTHER'S PUNISHMENTS were swift and unexpected: a slap across the cheek, an incisive word, a vise closing around the wrist. When she delayed discipline for my father to exact, however, the wait itself was a kind of torture, each sluggish hour choked with threat and rebuke until, finally, I felt the crash of the belt. I dreaded the stony mask that dropped over his face as he ordered me to lie across his lap with my ass cheeks exposed and goose-pimpled.

Having washed and bandaged my scraped legs, my mother was preparing dinner with menacing efficiency. Hot oil sizzled in the kitchen. I stole in, foot sheepishly caressing foot, as she threw a colander of bok choy into the wok. The hiss of it drowned out the Chinese talk show playing on the radio, and steam plumed around her face. Oil bounced over the stove like translucent fleas. She used a pair

Jenny Xie

of chopsticks to spread the greens around, then lifted the lid on a pot of soup. I tried to make eye contact, but she worked around me, shunting me aside with her hip as she reached for a jar of chili garlic sauce.

"I can do the vegetables," I offered, hoping to earn forgiveness.

"Then do them," she said, and afforded me one expectant stare.

I took my position over the wilting bok choy and nudged them from side to side until they turned a slick, vivid green. Every so often a flick of oil would sear my wrist, and I accepted the pain as punishment for what I'd done. The surest way to avoid a spanking, of course, was to apologize, but doing so would unearth my embarrassment of her and the way we lived.

My mother encased me in a web of quick, practiced movements as she plated the vegetables, turned over the chicken wings. She held a ladle of the soup to my lips. "Taste," she said. It felt like an olive branch.

I blew on the broth, ruffling the surface. I took a sip and deliberated. "More salt?"

She sampled it, nodded, and handed me the canister. "*Yi diandian.*"

I liked being near her, playing house with her. It usually took a task to lasso our bodies so close. Beyond the bargain hunting, I loved driving around with Marissa on Saturday mornings before the streets crawled with life, the feeling that only we and the birds were awake. Being in the kitchen was not so different. The pots trembled, and the radio swam in and out of audibility. It was just the two of us: my

mother at the wheel and me by her side, with time still before the rush
of the world.

"WHAT A FEAST," said my father when he walked through the door
and saw the spread. He was a thin man with slumped shoulders and
dorky, square-framed glasses, but today he cut a terrifying figure. I
wasn't sure if helping in the kitchen had granted my freedom. He
kissed my mother on the cheek, then bent down over me. I shied
away from his lips as though they, too, could bear violence. "What's
wrong? In a bad mood?" He tugged on my earlobe and wandered
into the kitchen. The faucet ran.

When he came back, we took our seats at the table. He tapped his
chopsticks against his bowl and said, "Eat. Eat." I ladled soup into a
bowl, catching slivers of bamboo, chunks of turnip and oxtail. It was
still scorching, but I slurped a mouthful, hoping that my parents' idle
talk would stall any conversations about me.

To my relief, my mother asked about work. Having left his serv-
ing gig, Baba was now a software engineer. He started on an anecdote I was too distracted to follow. He sucked and smacked as he
talked, periodically dabbing his greasy lips and laughing his high,
barking laugh. My mother listened with relish, swaying in her seat. I
scarfed my food, hoping to find refuge in my room. Maybe I would
turn the lights off and end the day; tomorrow would be a fresh start.
I tore into a chicken wing. I gnawed on a leaf of bok choy.

Because I was eating so hastily, because it sent me into a coughing fit, we didn't hear the knocking at first. As my father thumped my back, however, and my eyes cleared from watering, we heard the insistent tapping at the door.

My mother shot me a dark look and said, "Tell your friend you can't come play."

I wondered if it could really be Brianna. My mind spun with what she could want to say so urgently—maybe that she'd forgiven me for ruining her skates or that she was sorry for hollering about it? I slid out of the chair to answer the door.

The person who stood on the other side, however, was not Brianna. It was a woman—young, like my teacher. She might have been pretty, but I would always remember her as a nightmare figure with a distended mouth and dark, swimming eyes. Her fingers picked at the wooden buttons running down the front of her dress, which was sky blue with white clouds, a detail unshakable from memory because I stared at it in lieu of her tormented face.

She pointed a rigid finger into the room and screeched in a dialect I remembered from Shanghai. It was what my parents spoke when I wasn't part of the conversation. "You tell her! You tell her about us!" She pressed against me as if to walk through me, and I let her pass.

My mother rose with a rapidity and decisiveness that later I would turn over and over in my mind. It was as though she'd been waiting for this moment to come. "Get the hell out or I'll call the police. I'm serious."

But the woman addressed only my father, who remained at the table looking pale and shrunken. "You promised you'd tell her." Her voice broke, and her head lolled to one side. "You're trying to kill me. You want me to die. What kind of man are you?"

"I told you to get out!" My mother strode over and seized the woman by the forearms.

The woman wailed. With her arms held by her head, it looked like she was imitating a cactus. "Is it so wrong to tell the truth? I'm just telling the truth," she said. I had never seen adults behave this way. It was like a horrific game.

"Get Xiao Mao into her room," said my mother.

My father staggered to his feet and ushered me out of the living room, where the two women were fumbling with each other, slippery as eels.

In my room, I fell onto the edge of the bed. Baba looked like he wanted to sit down, too, and tell me one of his made-up stories, but instead he rubbed his mouth as through trying to wipe it off and said, "Stay in here, okay? The adults need to talk."

Before the door closed, I asked, "Baba, do you know her?"

His face was a rectangle between the frame and the door. His lips were flat, a low range on the horizon. "I do know her," he said. "I must have owed her something in a past life."

For hours I tried to hear what was going on, but their urgent voices were impossible to unknot, and eventually I fell asleep with my clothes on.

. . .

WHEN I WOKE UP, no one was home. The food was as we had left it, a layer of fat congealing over the soup and the chicken bones still ragged with meat. I had a vague and optimistic idea that it had all been a horrid misunderstanding. I poured myself a bowl of cereal and sat on the couch to watch the morning cartoons. Then, when still no one had returned, I visited the kitchen to swallow a spoonful of sugar. There was the sense that nothing I did now counted; I existed some-where between the past and the present moment, hidden from the conscious universe.

Then my mother clambered through the door as if hoisting herself out of a manhole. She joined me on the couch and we watched *Pinky and the Brain*. "Precipitation," she said. The mice were planning to hijack a tornado and take over the world. "I just learned that word."

Eventually she slid onto her back and rested her head in my lap, eyes inflamed and searching the ceiling. I'd never felt her weight press into me with such abandon. I didn't dare move in case I dis-turbed this new creature, my mother's perfect head, soft perm, and heavy skull. I stroked her twitching eyebrows and wiped away the wetness at her temples until I lost the feeling in my legs, as though I didn't have legs at all and had fused with her instead.

FOR THE NEXT several weeks, my mother wept, baptizing her face and hands with grief. She threw open suitcases and paced around them, telling me to gather my things because we were going back to Shanghai. "But what about Baba?" I insisted. In the end, her despair circled in on itself, hardening into a dense growth that hung like an anchor. She found work at a Chinese take-out place, and after work she drank. It still wasn't enough: Before too long, we would have to leave Anaheim, make our way up north to move in with a family friend named Tiffany.

Most of our things were in boxes the night I came inside for dinner and heard the radio playing not my mother's usual talk show but a Chinese oldie. *My love is real*, the voice lilting over a waltzing beat. *The moon represents my heart.* While the range hood droned, I peered into the kitchen and found my mother dancing. Dancing! With her back turned, she rocked from one foot to the other, and her arms floated from side to side. I clutched the doorway, hoping she wouldn't turn around.

It was only as I watched her sway that I realized my father had left for good. I felt joy and sorrow like two successive hammer falls. I couldn't articulate it then, but I was stunned by my mother's resilience and vulnerability, her womanhood, and saw how that would one day be mine. I had never dreamed that life could be so breathlessly vast. I stood as still as I could to let the knowledge sink in, afraid that even the tiniest movement would send me tumbling back to childhood and pull my mother out of her reverie, stay her rejoicing feet.

6.

After Luke posted a video of @meetmilotherat lounging on a miniature swan floatie meant to hold a beer, backed by a sauntering '70s track, his Instagram followers swelled to just under twelve thousand—a blip in influencer terms, but a triumph in the rodent category. Apparently, the clip had bounced to Twitter and Reddit before hitting the local morning news. Luke, who now considered himself Milo's brand ambassador, had celebrated the occasion by taking a tab of acid.

"People want to see a varmint with influence," he said, pacing back and forth and periodically tossing his mat of dusty blond hair. Luke was thickset with a long, mournful face, reminiscent of a bloodhound. "This isn't just about Milo. This is paving the way for rats to be taken seriously. This is about upending the food chain."

"I thought this was about monetizing how quirky he is," I said. I'd come over to Luke and Andrew's apartment to bring LB a spare bike lock; she'd left hers behind at summer camp. The three of us now sprawled on the carpet, audience to Luke's proselytizing. Milo sat on Andrew's shoulder, sniffing at his earlobe. He was a dumbo rat, which meant he had bigger, rounder ears than other specimens, his body white with a silvery hood.

Andrew had been in this apartment since his sophomore year of college, and I'd seen the growing pains: the stacked milk crates giving way to floating shelves, couches dragged in from the street ceding to minimalist sectionals. Where there had once been dusty blinds were now hanging ceramic planters and healthy, coiling vines, their leaves burnished with light.

"You're right," said Luke. "Let's talk shop. What kinds of sponsorships should we be landing?"

"'We'?" said LB. "Will the proverbial we be getting a cut of this?"

"Everyone here gets free merch," said Luke, waving his hands as though to appease us.

"Did you see that Nightshade and Nymph plugged that vegan cheese brand?" said Andrew. "It's another account Luke's been obsessed with," he explained to me and LB, "run by this witchy thot. I believe the caption said something about, like, alt cheese. 'For those who dare to be different.'" He traced scare quotes in the air.

I searched Instagram until I found the account—@nightshade_andnymph. The grid was largely populated by selfies, taken by a woman with ink-black hair that changed from frame to frame, now coyly spilling over her cleavage, now messily bundled on top of her head, now spiraling out of the square. She was pretty—pale, long-nosed, dark eyes in a perpetual droop, her lobes stretched around black plugs. Interspersed throughout her feed were photos of a black rat and a gray rat—presumably Nightshade and Nymph—and their litter of pups. "Whoa, she has more than sixty thousand followers," I said. "Including Andrew."

He shrugged. "Market research."

Luke squatted to look over my shoulder and groaned. "How am I supposed to compete with thirst traps?"

"Why does it have to be a competition?" LB held out her arm, making a bridge for Milo, who scuttled into the scrawls of her hair. She wore a camouflage T with the sleeves and neck cut away to reveal skin warmed to a deep olive hue. "I mean, yeah, you're in the same space, but you can still differentiate your brands. She's cool and sexy—you're silly and goofy. That's going to attract totally different people."

"Yeah, it's not a zero-sum game," said Andrew. "Her gaining a follower is not you losing a follower."

"She could even help you!" said LB. "Someone who finds her account might find yours."

"You're not going to be happy if you make this about who's doing better than you," I chimed in, wishing I could take my own advice. "There's always going to be someone more established to compare yourself to."

"What do you think, Milo?" LB asked in a baby voice, reaching to stop the rat from scampering down her back. His pink tail tapered around her neck. "Here, go to Aunt Kathy."

Before I could protest, she cupped the rodent and passed him to me, downy and writhing with energy. His delicate, padded feet traveled along the back of my hand, up my forearm, dropped into my lap.

"He likes you," said Andrew. "He knows you're used to handling rats."

"Only in lab," I said. "Hardly the same thing." Lab rats were bred to facilitate different branches of research—obesity, leukemia, respiratory disease. We treated them as humanely as we could, but the grim efficiency with which I'd had to work with them cured me of any sentimentality. The focus was on advancement: So much was to be learned from these creatures. As Milo's nose flitted in the air, whiskers flared to map my size and shape, I remembered how the whisker system illuminated neural processing, working like hands to deliver tactile information to the brain. As my thumb grazed the silken petal of his ear, I thought of how rat pups deprived of touch suffered developmentally—how researchers could stroke them with a wet paintbrush, mimicking a mother's quick, grooming tongue, to remedy this. Milo ascended the front of my shirt, hanging on with his claws, and to my surprise, I laughed at his curiosity.

Luke took a seat on the carpet. "I'm sorry, guys. That's great advice. I just can't talk about it anymore because I'm frying."

"I can't believe @meetmilotherat is actually working," I said. "No offense." Luke had had a few harebrained ideas before, including an app that would crowdsource lottery tickets to increase the chances of winning. He had borrowed money from his dad to hire a developer, but two weeks in, he'd blown the budget on catered info sessions for the public.

Andrew pressed his lips together and raised his eyebrows in a way that said *Me, too*, and I laughed, partly at the pleasure of being signaled in secret. He took off his glasses and polished them with his shirt. I'd missed how utterly legible his face became without the frames. It had to do with him being defenseless, unable to see more than a couple of feet. I was being nostalgic for us, I realized, and was certainly alone in doing so. I watched LB put her chin on Andrew's shoulder, in the same divot where mine had rested.

My phone buzzed, and I felt a leap of vertiginous hope that it was Oren. We'd had a few brief exchanges regarding logistics—a new Netflix password, an email from our landlord in Baltimore—and though these were largely transactional, they still rang in my head. I'd finally muted all of his social media accounts, a loss that felt somehow more obliterating than watching him leave the apartment for the final time and walking back upstairs to face the plundered bookshelf, my paperbacks listing in the spaces where his had been. Social media was the last remaining tether.

A few days ago, his familiar icon had popped up in my Twitter notifications: He'd liked my reply to someone. In a moment of weakness, I clicked through to his profile to see that eighteen minutes prior, he'd subtweeted a professor we'd often complained about, a message that seemed to be solely for me. I'd agonized about whether to like it, my thumb hovering over the heart icon, until it'd vanished from his timeline, the opportunity sucked back into the abyss. That was how we made contact now: asynchronous finger taps on screens we caressed to life dozens of times a day, sending digital ciphers as inscrutable as tea leaves.

I scanned the text. It was my mother, asking for a favor.

"Hey, I have to pick up some wedding stuff while I have the car. Anyone want to come with?" I asked.

"I've got band practice, unfortch," said LB. "I'll head out, too."

"Andrew?" I wasn't in the mood to be alone.

"Sure, I'll come. I haven't seen your mom in ages."

"I want to come," said Luke.

I shot him a dubious look. "Okay, but please act as normal as possible."

AS NORMAL AS POSSIBLE, for Luke, meant bringing Milo along for the ride in his carrier, but thankfully, the woman from whom we collected the glass terrariums for the wedding didn't notice. They were gingerly stacked in the back seat now, tinkling orbs striated with soil, sea glass, and succulents, remnants from another wedding that my mother had found on Craigslist to use as table centerpieces. I imagined it wouldn't have been outside her budget to buy her own, but salvaging these must have satisfied an old need to survive through bargaining and thrift. Brian must like that about her, I thought—that canniness.

I eased toward a red light, the bass from someone else's stereo dribbling into our car and making the terrariums quake. "I drove by your house the other day," I told Andrew.

"Creep."

"No, on the way to the store, I mean."

"Sure, sure." He smoothed his mustache. "You should've stopped by. My mom asks about you, you know."

"Really? Still?" I remembered the hum of activity in Andrew's house, how his mother was always producing treats. She'd knock on the bedroom door to bring us plates of sliced oranges or hunks of cakes she'd dusted with matcha. "Make him study," she'd entreat me. "You're a good student." And when his father came home from work—six foot three, balding, bearded—it was another ruckus as he kicked off his shoes and thundered about the house, checking on his boys. I used to envy Andrew for having a parent who'd grown up in the States. He and his father could talk about anything: classic rock, skateboard lore, mobster movie trivia.

"Oh, yeah, she's dying to catch up."

I gave him a sidelong smile, knowing that he would read in the silence my regret at not being able to say the same thing. Andrew and Marissa had had a few strained encounters, but for the most part we'd avoided my home to avoid facing the gulf of difference between our families.

"Your mom's been sober now for how long?" he asked as traffic began to spill forward.

"More than two years," I said. "As long as she's known Brian, basically. But she's gone through other periods of not drinking." I felt compelled to add that, as though to say that I had been there all along, that I'd made a difference, too.

· · ·

WHEN WE ARRIVED, the door was already open. Marissa was on the phone with someone, waving Andrew and me toward the kitchen table as we trundled in with the boxes. She read the numbers on her credit card and then muffled the microphone. "Thank you. Right there is good," she said in an exaggerated whisper, eyes grazing over Andrew, blank of recognition. "Yes," she said into the phone. "Three, zero, six."

On our second trip from the car, she was hunched over the terrariums to admire the arrangements. The black bracelet strapped to her wrist gleamed like an engorged leech, and an oversize Wayfindr hoodie hung on her frame.

"It's good to see you, Marissa," said Andrew, setting down his load. "Congratulations on all the big changes! Kathleen's told me all about it." He stepped toward her for a hug that she received with one arm, the other still holding a globe aloft. Her disoriented smile told me that she hadn't placed him. I swallowed a cold stream of embarrassment, recalling the few times she'd received us in high school with a lubricated grin that Andrew had pretended not to notice.

"I was just over at Andrew's house," I said by way of explanation, hoping the name would ring a bell. "He offered to help."

"How nice," said Marissa, maintaining a sheen of hospitality. "Yes, I not see you for so long. You are live in Oakland?" She was fishing for clues.

"Yeah, yeah," said Andrew, hitching up his sleeves. "Still here. I work at that restaurant now, White Elephant? On Shattuck?"

"Oh, I have to try it," she said in a tone of polite dismissal.

"Come in anytime—we'll hook it up." Andrew looked to me, then cleared his throat and said, "You must love having Kathleen home to help with wedding planning."

"Yes, she need responsibility, I think, something for plan when she confused about life." Marissa hugged a cardboard box to her chest and hefted its weight. "Wedding give us lots to do—" She faltered as a blur zoomed across her feet. I registered it as Milo just as she sucked in a shock of air and dropped the box, glass peeling open and sending a spray of dirt across the floor.

"Bad Milo! Bad Milo!" It was Luke, suddenly thrashing through the apartment, swiping at the rat to halt his pinballing progress. "I'm sorry, he's not usually like this," he said, chasing Milo as his tail wriggled down the hall toward the bedrooms.

"This your rat?" my mother asked incredulously.

"I'll get a broom." I hurried after Luke, who was hopping from foot to foot as the rat traced a ragged trail down the corridor. "What are you doing?" I hissed at him. "I told you to stay in the car."

"He was getting antsy," he said. "He's so freaked, he never bolts like this."

"Just get him back in the carrier," I said.

Marissa wrenched the broom out of my hands as soon as I got back to the kitchen. "You go, you go," she said to Andrew. "It okay, you go."

"It's our fault——" Andrew said, stepping back as she swept through the rubble.

"I'll help her," I told him. "You make sure Luke's okay."

Andrew retreated, muttering an apology, and I bent to rescue shreds of moss and dirt-clumped plants from my mother's short, furious strokes of the broom. Once we were alone, she muttered in Mandarin, "*Zhen meiyong.* I asked you to do one simple thing. Who are these people?"

"You don't remember Andrew from high school?" I dumped the plants into the sink. "The person I dated for years?"

"Yes, yes, I remember now," she said, shoulders working. "Sometimes the past should just stay in the past. Are you hanging on to Oren like this? How can you move on if you don't know how to grow up? And that boy—is this who your friends are? Running around with rats, and stuck working at restaurants?" As she stooped to collect the debris into a dustpan, my remorse hardened into resentment like the convoluted lines of a loose knot being yanked into clarity. In light of that morning's conversation, it was clear Marissa belonged to the camp of comparison and competition, and she expected me to slough off anyone who wasn't participating in the contest for rank and clout. She was a social climber, I fumed, who thought that now that she'd straightened out her life, she could cast judgment on mine.

"Andrew's not *stuck*," I said. "And I'm not going to just move on. He's someone I've always been able to count on, which is more than I can say for you."

Marissa said nothing, emptying the dustpan in one brusque movement.

"I'm going to go check on them," I said.

Andrew and Luke had cornered Milo in the bathroom, but in a flash, he scampered through their legs and down the hall once more. I dropped to my haunches and caught the rat in my hands. I rose, cupping him close enough that his furry face filled my field of vision. I felt his flittering heartbeat in my palm, the bulb of heat, and marveled that I'd kept his brethren at such a clinical remove all those hundreds of hours I'd spent in the lab. Now there was no screen of data, no calculations to be made. I looked Milo in the eye. A rat had precious few years to live—even this moment would account for a notable fraction of his time before the final flash and bleed of color. It was a life too brief to bother with statistics, like all of ours in the end.

7.

> **The Spoon** really needs no introduction, but we better start with the basics. In this position, you both lie on your side, front facing back. From here, the world is your oyster: try intertwining your legs, curling up like a ball, or switching places (see: The Jet Pack).

Passing the Cuddle Aptitude Test added me to the directory. The app prompted me to upload a headshot, add a bio, and set my availability. I filled out a skeletal profile—*Let's hug it out*—but it didn't take long for the appointment requests to come in. Most of them were accompanied by a brief message. Alireza, forty-nine, wrote that he was going through a divorce and had started a new remote job, which meant he wasn't getting a lot of physical contact. Jamal, who was a year younger than me, said he was looking forward to cuddling ☺. Curtis, fifty-five, shared that his regular cuddler had moved away. I studied their pictures and reviews and felt the strange resolve to know them, to inflate the smiling photos into physical beings. It was like reeling in an infinite fishing line: I felt pinned to the narrative, both in control and held captive, convinced that some relief or understanding would be thrashing on the hook as long as I kept with it.

My first session was with Alireza, shy and soft-spoken, as inexperienced with professional cuddling as I was. I'd counted it as a positive until we were together. Holding him was nothing like holding Nadia, who had poured herself against my body like wax hewing to a mold. I tried to channel her assured and professional demeanor but couldn't still my fluttering nerves, couldn't shake the sensation that I was watching someone else conduct my life—until, that is, we rose from the couch and we climbed inelegantly into bed, and I dropped back into my body like an anvil. He was tense, his ropy muscles radiating a surprising heat as I nestled against his chest. I stroked his shoulder, and he gave a short whiff of laughter.

"Does that tickle?" I asked. "Would you like me to stop?"

"No, no, I like it. I think I'm just nervous. I'm sorry."

"Don't be sorry. It's my first cuddle, too," I found myself admitting. I felt a creeping guilt; this wasn't what he'd paid for. I didn't know where to put my hands, which were suddenly clammy and as unwieldy as cymbals. His breath, an oily broth, washed over me as he blinked at the wall.

"You mentioned that you're going through some life transitions in your message," I said, to break the uncomfortable silence. "Is there anything you'd like to talk about?"

A barely perceptible frown dragged on his features, and I regretted bringing it up. I should have stuck to small talk. But Alireza, it turned out, was eager to speak. He started hesitantly, his sentences thawing and flowing as he went on, his body relaxing in tandem. He had cheated on his wife, he told me, and most of their family and friends had rallied behind her, but none of them had had to endure the loneliness of their marriage. "She worked all the time, traveled all the time," he said. "I started putting dinners on her calendar just to see her. But if I complained, she accused me of being lazy and not understanding the value of her work. We had totally different versions of happiness. It's a familiar story, I guess."

My caresses gradually slowed, grew longer and more luxurious. "What kind of happiness did you want?" I asked.

His body flexed, pulling me close. "This. I wanted time. I wanted touch."

It was stunning to come up against the truth so fast, like staring up at the gray veins of a sheer granite cliff. I was grateful to him for being a real person; it made me feel like a real person, too.

Jamal was on the other end of the spectrum. He was hale and effusive and took the lead in guiding us to the bed, where I lay on my side, using his stomach as a pillow—one of his favorite positions. His fingers wove through my hair, worried out the knots. The conversation was light until, nearly at the end of the session, Jamal told me that the last time he'd seen his father at the hospital before he died, Jamal hadn't hugged him goodbye.

"I wanted to do it," he said, "but I couldn't. I can't explain it. It took everything in me just to reach out and grab his hand. But cuddling you, here—it comes so naturally to me. Isn't that funny?"

I thought, mistakenly, that providing some context would help. I talked about skin hunger, a famine exacerbated by technology and Americans' near criminalization of touch. "But we're programmed to want skin-on-skin contact," I said. "It lowers your heart rate, blood pressure, and cortisol, the stress hormone. It boosts your immune system." I told him that when they massaged premature babies for fifteen minutes three times a day, they gained weight 50 percent faster than the ones left in their incubators.

"What does that have to do with anything?" he asked.

I floundered. "I'm just saying, you shouldn't feel too bad. It's natural to want and need touch, but everything around us enforces this idea that touch can only be violent or sexual, and that can make us more withdrawn. *This*"—I patted his stomach—"might come easily because it's controlled, in a way, so it's sanctioned." Even as the explanation unspooled, I sensed his annoyance. He didn't want to hear about neuroscientific data chafing against societal trends. He wanted to talk about his father, dulled and pale and untouched except for the stab of the IV. Afterward, he rated me three out of five stars: *Dominated the conversation.*

Curtis, who had been coming to Midas Touch for more than a year, taught me to massage his earlobes the way his regular cuddler had before she moved away. With his head in my lap, I leaned over him and circled my thumbs over the buttery tissue.

I enjoyed our silent communion, though I realized a little later that within the hush lurked a permissiveness. I was resting on my back, eyes half-closed in contentment, as Curtis's broad, plump hand roamed over my collarbone, my arms, the tops of my thighs. When his palm slid under my shirt to massage my stomach, he asked, "Is this okay?"

I nodded, though alarm shot through my consciousness like a light spearing the dark. It was easy to rumple a T-shirt, I reasoned, unsure why I was convincing myself of this; surely clients brushed navels all the time. Curtis's hand, however, traced lazy, widening circles that were hard to track, sometimes fondling the edge of my bra, at other times careening downward just past the elastic of my cotton shorts. I waited for him to rein himself in, and then I waited for myself to speak up, but something had plugged my throat. I worried, ludicrously, about offending him, accusing him of something he wasn't doing—but then his hand swam up to explore the flesh in my bra cup and thumbed the nipple. "I prefer not to be touched there," I said in a phlegm-lined voice, and realized how useless the security camera in the room really was. I kept waiting for someone to interrupt and end the session, but no one was coming to help—not even me.

"Sorry," he said. "Sometimes I get carried away."

On the app, I filed a report, selecting Inappropriate Behavior as the reason for my complaint. Someone from customer service followed up for more details, and as I typed them, the incident seemed at once humiliating and already inconsequential. I still ended up giving him four stars.

* * *

MY FOURTH SESSION was with a man named Phil Hayes, who sent no message with his appointment request. When I met him in the waiting room, he startled, then pocketed his phone and stood up to greet me with the mien of a chastised schoolboy, which was funny given that he was around my father's age, face wreathed by a gray-streaked shag that connected to a trim beard. He wore a short-sleeve black button-down and black trousers, a watch with a russet leather band.

"Sorry if I seem a little out of sorts," he said. "It's my first time here."

Clients could see the number of ratings on each cuddler's profile, but for some reason, I suppressed the urge to reassure him that I was relatively new here, too. It was easier, more authoritative, to use the corporate *we* and welcome him to Midas Touch. "Our room is just upstairs."

When I tapped in the code and the door unlocked with a whir, Phil paused, as if managing the impulse to bolt. I saw my past self then: It was astonishing how just a few trips to the cuddle clinic had inoculated me against its blithe posture of wellness, crafted to make you feel ashamed of your hesitation about paying or charging for touch, insufficiently evolved.

I slipped off my shoes, and he obediently followed suit. I pictured our mute gray forms in the security footage, vulnerable in our socks. "Would you like to lie down?"

"Sure," he said, a pleat of worry between his eyebrows, but he maintained a faint smile.

Phil was pliable, his head settling into the crook of my arm as I lay on my back, his leg and arm draped over me. "Am I crushing you?" he asked.

"Not at all." This was my favorite part of each session, the first tentative shifting of weight and the slow choreography of limbs, the way our bodies gradually resolved. It was comforting, the way total strangers knew how to come together and give in to their exhausted animal yearnings.

"How's your day been?" I asked. It was a question the Midas Method suggested, something innocuous and open-ended that helped gauge what the client was feeling. *Some clients and sessions will lend themselves to conversation. Others will fall into a comfortable, meditative silence.*

"Busy," said Phil. "We were on-site today, pouring foundation." Though he had a measured, timid way of speaking, Phil was forthcoming about himself. He ran a design-build firm in Alameda and was currently constructing a home in the Oakland hills for a tech executive and a jewelry designer who'd met at Burning Man ten years ago. Now they had two kids, a German shepherd, and an inexhaustible budget. The site was dense with trees, he said, with views of the bay, so the rear of the house would comprise glass walls that would glide open to connect the living room with a cantilevered deck. This led to a separate guesthouse, which doubled as the wife's office and jewelry workshop, and a cedar hot tub and sauna.

I listened to his deep, thrumming voice, compiling the house in my imagination. I pictured a dog loping across the deck, haze and water visible through the trees. We'd seen homes like this, my mother and I, whenever we'd ventured into the hills that vaulted up from our earthly apartment. Phil described an inconceivable way of life, the house shaped by the arc of the sun and the rational lives of its residents, the materials chosen to weather and age so that the design seemed inevitable, as though he'd excavated the structure from some buried dimension.

"Have you always wanted to design homes?" I asked.

He paused, rolled to face the ceiling. Blood rushed back into my arm without the compression of his weight, and I sat up against the pillows. "I have, I think, in one way or another," he said. The fine lines traversing his face mapped his buoyant expressions, the articulate eyebrows. "My dad was a contractor and woodworker. He taught me a lot about craftsmanship and self-sufficiency and respect for natural materials. He would take us out to the woods—me and my brothers—and we'd build lean-tos and such with whatever we could find. I grew up with the idea that shelter was essential and had to be built with respect for the land."

"That's beautiful."

Phil scooted up against the pillows until we sat in bed side by side. He placed a hand over mine, our fingers interlacing. "What about you? Have you always wanted to be a cuddle provider?"

I laughed, dropping my veneer of professionalism. "To be honest, I didn't know it was an option until about a month ago."

"No kidding." He thumbed his nose with his free hand. "Well, in my amateur opinion, you're a natural. I feel better already."

I flexed my hand under his, tightening the grip. "That's nice to hear."

"Really. I hope you don't mind me saying—it took a lot of convincing to get me here. I was a major skeptic about the whole thing." He cleared his throat. "My wife, Diane, passed away two years ago. I've been in therapy to deal with the grief, but a friend told me about Midas Touch, and it's starting to make sense. Loneliness is such a part of the body. Might take another body to address it."

Our eyes met, his a glacier blue. "Get comfortable," I said, indicating that he should slide down to put his head on my lap. "I'm glad you came. Do you want to talk about her? Diane?"

His head lay heavy against me. I raked my fingers through the striated hair. "I could go on and on about her," he said. "You're going to regret asking."

OVER THE COURSE of the next several sessions, I learned that Diane was a creature of habit and discipline. She jumped on her spin bike every morning and kept up a ten-step skin-care routine of mysterious foaming salves and elixirs. Before she left for work—she was the director of marketing at a fashion start-up—she outlined to-do lists on the fridge whiteboard: *Wish your brother a happy birthday*, she'd remind Phil. *Water the plants and feed the goldfish*, she'd write for the twins, Aster and Ada.

"Those are pretty names," I said, rubbing his back.

"Diane chose them," said Phil. "They're both in college now. It was hard for them to leave home so soon after she died, but then again, maybe it was good to get a fresh start."

Diane was also prone to worrying. She tracked everyone's whereabouts on her phone and often turned the car around to check that she'd indeed shut the garage door or turned off the burner. Never would she risk parking the vehicle in a questionable zone or let the meter run out for even a minute; she took rules as unquestionable law. Her scrupulousness arose from being the eldest of three sisters, said Phil, speaking about his late wife as though she were another home he'd fetched from oblivion, an inevitable woman shaped by light, landscape, air. Their mother had suffered stroke after stroke, each one gouging away her faculties of speech and movement until it took the woman fifteen excruciating minutes to put on a sock.

"Diane had to grow up quick for the sake of her family," said Phil.

"What did she look like?" I asked.

"Well, she was born in Beijing," he said. A flare of trepidation went arcing through me. This was a familiar interaction: people I'd just met telling me that they had an Asian sister-in-law or my dates divulging that they'd had a string of Asian girlfriends. It was exhausting to confront, again and again, my interchangeability with the purportedly monolithic population of Asian women, but sometimes I gave them the benefit of the doubt. I let Phil continue.

He drew her with the care of a craftsman. Diane had a strong, square jawline and large, wide-set eyes. She wore a constellation of freckles and her hair in braids around her head, or in rolling waves down her back. Even in the end, when she was weak and emaciated, he found her cuttingly handsome.

The memory of her was so precious to him that it felt like a privilege to be entrusted with it. I wondered whether our sessions, once routine, would lose their sheen, but it seemed like the opposite was happening: The more often we met, the more keenly I sensed his need, which hung swollen and fragrant like an overripe fruit. It gave me an intoxicating sense of purpose and power. My mere presence, my care, was a great benevolence to this man. *If only I could've had the same effect on Marissa*, I thought one day in the elevator.

Sometimes it felt as though Phil was depositing a memory for me to preserve, intentional with the details. "Diane and her sisters grew up in a shingled house in Massachusetts with a backyard that bled into the woods," he said. "They used to sneak through the trees and pretend they were witches."

One day, they gathered twigs, blooms, and leaves to mash in the pit they'd dug in the loam, shrieking when the sap-slick tangle made their hands boil with blisters. Diane squealed with them, but she was secretly enthralled, convinced that they'd struck a deep well of dark power. When they returned home with their dirt-bruised bodies and red hands, their mother roared, stripped them of their clothes, and sent them to the shower. Diane suffered a vicious lecture. As the eldest, she shouldn't have been leading her sisters through the woods. She had given them rashes—and what if it was permanent? What if the skin didn't heal, and she and her sisters had to grope through life with their disfigured hands, never to be married? Shameful girl, hissed the mother. Behaving like a boy. Diane listened, but she wasn't hearing: She was concentrating on her newfound powers, reaching inside her magic as though plunging her hands into black oil. That night, her mother had her first stroke: a mild one, decades before she would be seized by another. Diane had been convinced that she'd caused it, and worried that in a way she really had. She'd never told anyone this before Phil, and Phil had never told anyone before me.

I wondered how Diane would feel if she knew her husband was coming to me for comfort and divulging her secrets. She would be exasperated, I supposed, that he'd found a Chinese cuddler out of everyone available, but relieved that he was no longer in agony. And anyway, Phil and I weren't romantic, weren't even friends—just two people at either end of a transaction.

8.

If you're craving some face-to-face time, try
Mirror Image. Both cuddlers lie on their side
facing each other, legs crossed at the calves or
ankles. Thread your arm under your pillow
for some extra support, or bring it in for a
full-on hug.

After leaving Villa Palms just before my eighth birthday, my mother and I found refuge in the home of Tiffany Guo, the daughter of an uncle's best friend who owed something to our family through a chain of debts and favors. We were only meant to stay in the spare bedroom of her Oakland home for a couple of months as we got our footing, but it stretched to a year, and we became a makeshift household: Tiffany, the husband she would eventually leave, and her son, Gary, with whom I played first-person shooter games that sublimated my anger into pixelated bursts of blood. In retrospect, despite how unmoored I felt, the Guo house was a lifeline.

We had an audience that compelled us to keep performing life, that stilled my mother's communion with booze.

My mother trusted Tiffany's opinion in matters of style and beauty, so Tiffany was here to oversee today's hair and makeup trial. I thought her taste was more a symptom of money than of sense, however. A divorced lawyer who now dated rich men in six- to eight-month rotations, Tiffany routinely jabbered about her Botox injections, laser facials, and shopping sprees, sometimes bequeathing us last season's clothing, though on us they looked like costumes. Tall, rotund, and large-chested with a chemically flattened sheet of black hair, she had a gravitas that pulled off ensembles of leather, mink, and monogram patterns.

"Eat a burger and get a boob job," she prescribed now, with a wry smile, as Marissa rotated in a white Prada sundress. The crisp poplin ballooned around my mother's body, making her look like a child clown. "It looks chic a bit oversize, anyway," said Tiffany, slurping her tea.

"The fabric does feel really nice," said my mother. They were speaking Shanghainese—Tiffany and her ex-husband had also grown up in the city—the dialect's lilting vowels ribboning through the air like the notes of a familiar song. I could understand it, but struggled to speak it, garbling the intonations. "Are you sure you don't want to keep it?"

Tiffany grimaced, repulsed by the idea. "No, no, too many people have seen me in it. Keep it, alter it, or give it away if you want."

"Who would I give it to?" said my mother, but she retreated to the bedroom to change. The dress would hang in her closet like a talisman, calling forth plentitude from the universe. Tiffany had implanted the idea that finery was a woman's prerogative, that her life should be garlanded with richness and delicacy. Sometimes I regarded it as a crass, superficial obsession; in my more sympathetic moods, I recognized it as an emancipation from the lean decades.

"Your mom, she is so shy accepting gifts," said Tiffany, switching to English. She had a formal way of speaking, her accent giving the words a subtle curl, but she had moved to the States for college and was readily fluent. "The bachelorette party—have you booked the hotel already?"

I nodded; a lie. I wasn't sure why I was putting it off, but my mother's outburst when I dropped off the terrariums had made me burrow further into inaction. If she didn't think I was capable of an errand, never mind organizing a bachelorette party, then a sour impulse wanted to prove her right. It had been exhausting enough to write an email in the unrelentingly cheerful tone of a maid of honor.

Hey, ladies! So excited to celebrate Marissa with you in Las Vegas next month. The temps will be soaring into the triple digits, so don't forget to pack those swimsuits :). Let's make this weekend extra special for the bride-to-be!

It stank of disingenuousness. I wasn't excited. As cruel and selfish as it sounded, my mother's happiness gave shape and heft to my bereftness. I begrudged her the entire carnival. What was I going to do—buy penis-shaped straws? Pink sashes that read SHE SAID YAAAAAS?

"I've got it under control," I assured Tiffany.

She drained her tea and looked me over. "You're getting darker. Are you remembering to wear a hat outside? Sunscreen every day. Tans are for *laowai*."

Tiffany was always candid with me. We'd witnessed the hard facts of each other's lives, which made us family. She knew how pre-occupied my mother had been, how things had deteriorated after we'd secured our own apartment. Some nights, it was Tiffany who drove my mother home from one of her short-lived gigs preparing take-out orders, mending clothes, waitressing; Marissa knew she could always call Tiffany when she'd snuck too many swigs of vodka. I would spend weekends at the Guo house when my mother was working, doing homework at the kitchen table. Tiffany made the same dishes that my mother did, although spicier and sweeter, everything cloying and overcooked. Her husband cloistered himself in the office or watched World War II documentaries on TV or herded Tiffany into the bedroom to bellow about a disrespectful comment she'd made, and I would hear her wounded voice winding through his growls like wind rising from a bestial fray. Sometimes, when the shouting led to objects thudding against the walls, I found Gary pale-faced in his room and asked if he wanted to play video games.

THE MAKEUP ARTIST, who introduced herself as Rae, stood on the landing gripping a rolling makeup case and black director's chairs.

"Cute place," said Rae as she lugged her equipment inside. She set up the chairs in the living room and then riffled through the black case, which she had unlatched and expanded as if lifting the wings of a dead beetle. "Thanks for letting me take over. I promise you, it'll be worth it." She had a hoarse voice and a ready smile. "Remind me, Marissa. What's the vibe of your wedding, and what look are you going for? Do we want to go dark and dramatic"—both palms glided over her eyes in a slow game of peekaboo—"or do we want something a little more fun and fresh?"

My mother shifted in the chair. "The wedding in August, outside. I think better do more fresh, like make younger."

Rae nodded. "I read you loud and clear, Marissa. That'll be easy with your skin. You're already glowing! That's how you know it's the right decision, when the bride glows." She grinned at me, her bushy eyebrows catapulting toward the brim of her cap. "Are you excited for the wedding? You get to see your mom walk down the aisle— how dope is that?"

"Pretty dope," I said, chastised by her enthusiasm. A better daughter would be more effusive about her mother's wedding, I thought. Then I realized it was a line my mother would have leveraged against me.

"Give her glitter eyeliner," advised Tiffany from the couch. She sat facing us as though we were a television program. "It's the latest look. I see all the bloggers putting it on."

"Don't worry, we'll definitely add some shimmer," said Rae. She finished prepping my mother and then stepped to me, pumping a clear slime into her palm before slathering it on my face. Her small hands exerted a firm, gentle pressure, and I felt responsibly handled, a dog at a practiced groomer's. I closed my eyes, grateful to have an excuse not to speak, and sat anticipating the next expensive-smelling serum. When I felt a light mist on my face, I peeked through my eyelashes to see Rae brandishing what looked like a silver pen.

"What's that?" I mumbled, trying not to move my lips as the makeup set.

"It's an airbrush," said Rae, now pointing the apparatus at my mother's face. "The great thing about it is, you don't get the creasing or cakeyness of liquid or powder foundation. It's literally like Photoshopping your face."

"Feel very light," agreed my mother.

"One cannot have pores on one's wedding day," I said drolly.

Lacking mirrors, my mother and I looked at each other to see the effect. Her face had been eroded to a smooth, tan surface, the perfect absence of wrinkle and blemish placing it somewhere in the uncanny valley. I was reminded, too, of our echoing features: the high, round cheeks, the sparse straight brow, the pinched mouth. Looking at photographs of Marissa at my age always revealed our likeness, a kind of time travel that transported me into the frame, curled my own hands around the stem of an umbrella and inflated my hair into a tumbleweed perm. Once, I'd pointed this out to her, our similarity, and she'd peered at the photo and said, "No, I was prettier. My nose is taller and my face is slimmer, see?"

"All your pimples gone," said my mother.

"I'm not going to airbrush my face every day," I said in case she suggested it next.

"And how did you and your fiancé meet, Marissa?" Rae asked.

"Oh, you know, I meet him in class—how to say?"

"It was a business seminar," I said. Tiffany, who'd heard about the seminar from a marketing executive boyfriend, had encouraged her to go. I'd edited the meet-cute story for the wedding website, feeling as though I was writing the plot of a Hallmark movie. *Marissa, who was considering going back to school for a business degree, decided to give it a shot. The speaker that day was Brian—a smart, charismatic entrepreneur who inspired Marissa in more ways than one.*

"I go to thank him after and we talk for one hour," she said. "They close the room while we still talking."

"That's so romantic!" said Rae. "So you're in business, too?"

"No, no. I sell perfume for many years, but I try to learning something else. Before I not have time to think about career. Just be a mom and make sure Kathleen have opportunity. Everything I do is for Kathleen."

Rae was filling in my eyebrow with quick, artful strokes, each staccato brush of the pencil stoking my surprise at Marissa portraying herself this way, the self-sacrificing mother. I watched Rae's look of concentration as her hand tipped back my forehead and felt as though she were an agent sent to conceal and contour our story. In this version, I was the burden and Brian the shining knight who had rescued Marissa from distress.

"*That* I know all about," Rae said. "I have a six-year-old son, which is a job on top of my normal job, right? This kid walks right by his dad to ask me for a sandwich 'cause he likes the way I make 'em." She huffed through her front teeth. "So when did you know this guy was the one for you?"

"Right away. I call Tiffany the next day and tell her, I think I meet my husband."

"I couldn't believe it," Tiffany chimed in. "But I don't believe in marriage. I'm happy being fat, divorced, and rich."

"A lot of people I know could learn something from your attitude," said Rae, laughing.

"My first marriage just practicing," said my mother. "But you cannot control when you meet right person. For me, it's fifty years waiting."

It was startling to hear her be so sincere with a stranger; she hadn't said as much to me. She didn't speak to me about love—only the politics of marriage and choosing well. I turned to look at her, but her eyes closed as Rae moved in with the pencil. "I hope my daughter be patient, too."

The makeup artist cooed. "You're absolutely right. Never settle."

BY THE END of the appointment, my mother and I were unrecognizable. Stiff with powders, sprays, and gels, we smiled into the camera and turned our heads with queenly slowness so as not to disturb our sculpted hair. Tiffany adored the handiwork, and as Rae packed up her bag, she urged my mother to try on her wedding dress.

"For the full effect," she said as my mother headed to change.

I blinked into the empty room from under a thicket of false eyelashes.

"She looks so beautiful, doesn't she?" Tiffany sighed.

"I've never heard her say that. About meeting Brian." I inched a finger into the base of my coiffed hair and scratched the scalp. "Why was she giving that woman that whole fairy tale? Everything is for me, blah blah blah, I hope my daughter finds the right person, blah blah."

"Well, it's true."

I scoffed. "Maybe that's what she tells herself." Then, under Tiffany's reproachful gaze, I located the barb. "She doesn't say these things to me. Maybe she'll tell you, or Brian, or the makeup artist, but not me. It's like everything I did to try to help her didn't matter."

Tiffany sat back against the couch cushions, hands wedged between her thighs. "Of course it matters." She leaned in, black hair slipping from behind her ear. "Trust me, she knows how lucky she is to have you. Maybe it seems like Brian changed her life with a snap of his fingers, but all that time she survived was for you. Do you know how many times I found you two asleep at the house? Homework on your lap, pencil still in her hand? She tried to make sure she didn't fail you. She didn't tell you in these words, maybe, but you can imagine she is too ashamed for words."

It was an elusive memory, but I could catch drifts of it if I concentrated: the sheen of graphite on paper and the microwave humming with leftovers. My mother's head bobbing forward on a stream of sleep and then snapping to attention. What else had I forgotten?

As I struggled to answer Tiffany, my mother announced herself by singing the wedding march. "Dah, dah, dah-dah," she crowed, taking long, regal steps until she came into full view. Her presence altered the air like the changing of the seasons. I had seen the mermaid silhouette and lace sleeves hanging in her closet, but animated by her body, the dress had a breathtaking brightness and velocity.

"Brian's going to pass out when he sees you," said Tiffany, clapping.

As my mother walked the perimeter of the room, each ivory bead that clung to the gown flaring with light, I understood that no matter how alike we might have looked, or how much time we'd spent together, we were distant as stars. She was like anyone you loved, in that way—the more intimately you knew her, the more closely you beheld the wild, unbreachable distance that would keep you from perfect understanding.

9.

As the Beatles famously sang, sometimes you just want to hold their hand—and that's exactly what you're doing with **The Clasp**. Because it's so approachable, this position is the perfect appetizer for what's to come.

The first time Phil messaged me, I was at Brian's celebratory barbecue in the Outer Sunset, where he owned a squat yellow house with an arched entry shrouded in bougainvillea. In the backyard, a portable speaker thumped reggaeton—not what I was expecting in his music tastes—and smoke from the grill wound into the overcast sky. Wayfindr had raised forty million dollars in Series C funding, and the occasion had congregated gaggles of twentysomething employees and investors in calculatedly casual puffer vests and checked button-downs. A couple of guests lobbed beanbags in a game of cornhole on the lawn, at the back of which were a row of planter beds voluminous with chard and tomatoes, a wheelbarrow with a deflated bag of soil. A neighbor's tabby cat hunched on a sun-bleached fence, its slitted eyes turned against the breeze.

Brian was a veteran in the start-up world, having skipped from venture to venture, selling some and consulting for others. He'd given TED talks and guest starred on business and technology podcasts. He roamed the backyard now, collecting hearty, thumping congratulations, and Marissa trailed a step behind him; even from a distance I could see the nervous flexing of her lips as she was introduced. She looked the part, dressed in a zip-up fleece and a plain baseball cap, but she'd been on edge during the car ride over as though a poor social show would call off the wedding. She'd chewed the inside of one cheek, blamed me for making us late. To explain my erratic hours at Midas Touch, I'd told her that I'd gotten a summer research position at UC Berkeley, arranged through my adviser. I knew that the truth would precipitate too many questions, whip up a gyre of anxiety that it was inappropriate work. She'd already been skeptical of my field; in her mind, she'd come to America to place me on a preordained road of law, medicine, or science.

Tiffany was here, too, along with my mother's current coworkers, waifish Meredith Wong and demure Joyce Yu, who made up the rest of the bachelorette party I was heinously behind on planning. I stood beside them holding a paper plate, feeling obliged to keep them company though we'd already exhausted our topics: Vegas, school, my marital status. Though she'd invited them, my mother seemed to be keeping her distance to better insinuate herself with this new crowd.

I felt embarrassed, on her behalf, to have her thirst for prestige so plainly exposed.

"Maybe you'll meet someone here," Joyce said to me in an angelic voice.

Nothing seemed less likely, but I cast around as though considering my options. Beside us, a man with a beer-moistened mouth showed a woman something on his phone. "Incredible view. Right in the middle of the woods," he said, and flicked the screen. "The only downside is that it was so hard to get to—heli in, heli out. We really need to figure out how to improve the UI of the wilderness."

My phone buzzed with a notification from Midas Touch. I assumed it was another rating, but it was Phil through the in-app messaging system: You were right. Porcupines don't shoot their quills. How's the party? 😊

I'd mentioned the barbecue to him at our last session, but I hadn't expected him to remember. Under other circumstances, I might have batted the text away, but here, in the slosh of strangers comparing their intermittent fasting schedules, it felt like a lifeline. I hesitated, wondering if Midas Touch monitored our chats, which were supposed to be utilitarian—to introduce ourselves and answer questions. But I was building rapport, I reasoned. This was good for business.

Patagonia vests as far as the eye can see, I typed. Please send help. As I looked up, I locked eyes with a man who introduced himself as Zephyr.

"That's an interesting name," I said. Out of the corner of my eye,

I saw my mother's friends huddle together, no doubt giving space to what they hoped was a flirtation.

"It's a Burner name, but I eventually decided to be myself both on and off the Playa," he said, and raised his hot dog in a toast. He nodded toward his friends, a balding man with stooped shoulders and a shorter, apple-cheeked man beside him. "This is Kenneth and Jed."

"I'm Kathleen," I said, and then felt the need to explain myself. "I'm Brian's future stepdaughter, I guess. Feels weird to say." As soon as I delivered the words, I sensed the converging vectors of their attention, as though a magnetic charge had been activated. It wasn't totally unpleasant, a heady cocktail of scrutiny and respect, and I wondered how it felt in my mother's shoes: Surely Brian's fiancée would command even more interest.

"Wow! So you're soon to be family. Good luck with that," said Kenneth.

"We know Brian from an incubator a whole while back," said Jed. "He was building a babysitter app called—what was it called?"

"OneSitter," said Zephyr, flashing a glop of half-chewed bratwurst.

"That's the one." Jed adopted an announcer's voice and a salesman's slick smile. "OneSitter—Go Out. Rest Easy."

"What did it do? Find babysitters?"

"Listed babysitters in the neighborhood, sorted by availability, rates, and reviews, accommodated special requests—the whole she-bang." Jed sucked something out between his teeth and swallowed the morsel. "It had such great promise."

My phone vibrated in my pocket, and I admired the timing. By so many degrees of separation, these were the people who'd connected me with Phil. It was hard to name a facet of life that wasn't controlled, in one way or another, by an app—an app built by someone like the ones currently flipping patties in Brian's backyard. The way some people theorized about the algorithms deciding their fate, connecting a constellation of digital clues to explain why they'd lost followers or been shadow banned, it was like deciphering the whims of a fickle god. It was funny now to face those gods in their determinedly bland footwear—funny and terrifying. I ferreted away the thought to tell Phil later.

Brian wandered within earshot, and Kenneth waved him over.

"We were just talking about you," he said. "She doesn't know about OneSitter."

"Most people don't," said Brian.

"What happened with it?" I was curious about his failures; he didn't talk about them. Even his past marriage seemed unimpeachable: He and his ex-wife had, after years of therapy and negotiation, realized that they'd grown to be incompatible—she pictured life in a smaller town, where she'd draw richness from routine, and he sought out novelty, speed, scale. They'd parted amicably, and still considered each other best friends. That had been his censored version of the story, anyway. In the brief pause after my question, I realized with a singe of panic that I didn't know him at all.

"It was the classic chicken-and-egg problem," Brian said. "I couldn't get enough parents on the site because there weren't enough sitters, and there weren't enough sitters because there weren't enough parents. I tried everything. We took no commission from babysitters for the first month—then we handed out vouchers to parents. But we couldn't get either side to balance out." He raised his beer at the other two. "What about you—how's it going over at Top Dog? I've been hearing great things."

"It's coming along," said Kenneth with a self-satisfied shuffle of the feet. "We're adding other species to the roster. Reptiles, fish. We might cross off fish, though. They're not very compelling—but we met a surprising number of fish lovers in user research."

"They run a pet influencer agency," Brian said, clueing me in.

Jed pulled out his phone and thumbed an app open. "We connect pet influencers with brands that want to tap into their audience." Then I was another woman being shown something on a phone: He scrolled through English bulldogs with distinguished frowns, Pomeranians peeping through milkweed manes, terriers with ears pert as sails. "These are some of the dogs in our lineup. Boris here just struck a deal with Home Depot. Huge get."

"Huh. You ever represent rats?"

He raised his eyebrows and flicked to another tab. "Why, you know of any good ones?"

"Look up @meetmilotherat. That's my friend's account."

He brought up Luke's page and hooted. "Kenneth, you said rats wouldn't take off, but check this out. More than fifteen thousand followers." He sped down the feed, maximizing and minimizing posts. I glimpsed a photo of Milo scaling a succulent in a glass terrarium;

Luke must have taken the photo outside my mother's apartment, just before he and Milo wreaked havoc.

Kenneth raised his head with a sharp inhalation. "Love the smell of fresh blood. Let's DM him—offer him ten percent off the membership, then push him to the smaller brands. He'd be a great case study."

"Hey, you're on the inside," said Jed, tapping me on the shoulder with his fist. "Let your friend know this is the move. As our flagship rat, we'll make sure he's in front of the right market."

"I'll tell him," I said, forcing a smile. My mother slipped beside Brian in the circle, and I took the opportunity to peek at Phil's message: Don't have much to offer, but someone once told me to always be closing. My insides squirmed. That was just what I was doing. I was networking, which I had loathed in graduate school, the waltzes we performed while balancing plates of crackers and cheese garnished with a respectable sprig of grapes. We laughed generously at each other's anodyne jokes, recounted our most charming stories, forgave the professor who made a pass at us in hopes of scrounging the tokens of success: a published paper, a powerful ally, tenure.

"What everyone looking at?" asked my mother.

"An app," said Brian, slinging an arm over her shoulder, "that apparently Kathleen now works for."

"What *do* you do, Kathleen?" asked Zephyr.

I faltered. It was a test, a way for him to gauge whether I had any value outside of my ties with Brian. Marissa rolled her shoulders back, a signal to say the right thing and cement our place in this society. Somewhere around us, a voice was saying, "I'm glad you mentioned Arcosanti. You should meet my buddy, actually—he's re-creating it, but in the water." Everything was transactional in nature, leading to embarrassingly naked displays of stature and worldliness, as it was now uncouth to be rich. Instead, you signaled your wealth and importance with ideas, innovation. Disrupting was the new currency. Every company mission statement couched making bank in terms of bettering society.

"Kathleen in a cognitive psychology PhD," said my mother. She tucked a wing of hair behind an ear, and the black band around her wrist—a literal tool of conformity—sent some mechanism whizzing inside me.

The voice continued, "A floating city that totally reimagines urbanism and ecology. The way the water's rising, we'll need it."

"Actually," I said, "I've been doing some gigs through this thing—not sure if you've heard of it. Midas Touch."

"Oh, sure," said Zephyr. "It's a cuddle clinic, right? I heard they just raised something like twenty million dollars. Are you a consultant?"

"No, I'm one of their professional cuddlers."

"What that mean, 'professional cuddler'?" My mother's smile wavered, an empty hammock.

"I hold and cuddle people who need touch," I said, laboring to stay nonchalant. "After a while, it feels pretty natural."

"And how long you doing this?"

"A little over a month now."

"These people, they are women? Men?"

"Both. Mostly men." I hadn't come across any female clients yet, but I threw out the lie to calm her.

The black of her irises seemed to deepen as she understood what I was saying, and I realized, too late, that beyond her disapproval there was fear, fear that I hadn't considered because she'd done such a good job of burying what had happened to her with one man in particular. In the years after, we'd hardly spoken about it, referred to it only obliquely—saying "that day" or "at that job"—and then not at all, her face threatening to cave whenever we got too close to the subject. A hinge door in my stomach swung open. Brian, sensing the sunset in her mood, cut in. "You know, Kathleen's just written a master's thesis on haptics."

"No kidding," said Kenneth, and the conversation lurched in another direction. Someone arrived at the party, pulling my mother into another orbit of introductions, and then I was left in the yard alone.

10.

I n high school, my extracurriculars carved a route around my
mother, whose nightly ritual after her shift at the restaurant was to
bathe in the crackling light of the television and drink until she
hardened to boulder, her features sediment in stone. Because I didn't
know how to help her, I escaped. I signed up for every club that
would have me: the Science Olympiad, National Honor Society, Key
Club, Amnesty International. I was the school treasurer and played
volleyball, rose before dawn to edit the student paper, and secured a
bit part in the fall production of *A Chorus Line*. That was how, in my
sophomore year, I met Andrew, a scrawny pothead I saw twice a day:
slumped in my morning journalism class, hammering lumber in the
evenings building theater sets.

It was two days before the show's opening night and we were on
our second run-through. The director, Mr. Baker, and the dance in-
structor, Ms. Sharif, had been growing shrill with panic, keeping us
until nine, ten o' clock. Jittery piano chords tumbled across the stage,
and we ran to our places.

"Step, kick, kick, leap, kick, touch—again!" barked the actor who was playing the choreographer. "Step, kick, kick, leap, kick, touch—again!"

In the second row of dancers, off to the side, I flung myself into the steps. My movements were broad and coarse, but I could at least keep up with the counts. Seated in the middle of the theater, Mr. Baker tapped his pen against the clipboard, then turned to shout at the control room. "Greg, are you sleeping up there? Lights! Lights!"

Warm, yellow light dawned on our faces. As I spun, I caught a glimpse of our bodies in the mirrored backdrop, a forest of legs sheathed in sheer nylon, sloughing off the sawdust that had settled on the black stage.

"God, I hope I get it," we sang. The lights swam from blue to red. "I hope I get it. How many people does he need?"

I wasn't nervous to perform. I was just a background dancer, and no one I cared about would see the show. I luxuriated in the anonymity of having a bit part the same way I would breeze alone through the city and feel as much a part of its choreography as the colored beat of traffic lights and trains screaming into the station. For several minutes there was nothing to worry about but keeping time.

After the opening number, I sat in the theater and started on my algebra homework. The others clustered around me, propping their feet on seat backs and ripping open bags of chips. A thud came from backstage and sent everyone into titters. There was a giddiness at dress rehearsal that had to do with the blaring music, the dark theater, the spandex costumes, and the loud makeup that projected our faces all the way to the back row.

"Devin has *such* a good voice," someone commented.

"He's been hooking up with Allison during intermission, you know," another girl answered, exciting a flock of squeals. I erased a bungled problem set and swiped the eraser shreds onto the floor. I tried to stay out of the gossip that embroidered the theater, the fawning over leading actors. I didn't want to assume any identity, drama kid or otherwise. I told myself that I was still half-formed, wet from the mold and refulgent with possibility, but in truth I was reluctant to excel in something my mother would be too drunk to appreciate.

Andrew rustled up the aisle in the red windbreaker he always wore, flanked by two other boys in the stage crew. He leaned across a chair back and said to the group, "We're going to get some food, anyone want to come?"

There were several takers. As they filed toward the exit at the back of the theater, he beckoned me with a swoop of his arm. We sat on opposite sides of the room in journalism and didn't talk except in passing, so I was surprised at his invitation. "I brought a sandwich," I said, kicking my backpack to indicate where it was.

"Okay. Don't tell Mr. Baker we left," he said, and winked. The gesture was as bright as a camera flash. No one had ever winked at me before.

I glanced at the director, who was massaging his chin and fixated on his notes. When I looked back, Andrew was already halfway up the stairs, taking them two at a time.

. . .

THE TELEVISION WAS on when I got home, but my mother was peering at something in her lap. I slung my backpack over a chair and watched her draw a threaded needle dangerously close to her face. Her yellow plastic sewing box rested on the couch beside her, and an empty glass and a bottle of wine were on the coffee table. When she glanced at me, her glasses stamped with reflected light, it was with the scowl she'd been directing at her project.

"What's that?" I asked.

"I tore my uniform." She held up the black collared shirt so that I could see the rip on the shoulder seam. The needle twitched on its black thread. "On a shelf in the kitchen."

I had been in the restaurant's kitchen before. The tiles were slick with grease, and dead insects studded strips of flypaper. The cooks had burns running in rivulets up their wrists. When she had first started working there, she'd said, "Well, it's tiring work, and the customers treat you like shit. No wonder your father went looking for comfort when he was waiting tables." And then she'd laughed and rubbed her neck.

My mother filled her glass and swallowed before craning back over her stitches. She was working by the lamp on the side table, but the rest of the living room was dark.

"Why don't you have this on?" I flipped the switch. Her body shot out of the shadow: hunched back, short hair dyed an oxblood red.

"Oh, it wasn't on? I was wondering why it was so hard to see."

There were pink blotches on her cheeks and her breastbone, the exposed skin a map of jagged contours. She shook her head and pawed at the stitches, mumbling, "This isn't right. This isn't right at all."

I sat beside her and took the shirt into my lap. The tear was the length of a finger. It should have been an easy fix, but her stitches were erratic and puckered the fabric.

"I can do this," I said.

She was silent as I snipped the threads and started over. The television cut from a grim anchorman to a commercial for furniture polish. I didn't know what was worse: her soggy presence after she'd been drinking, or the white fog that replaced her face when she couldn't get to sleep. She said that nighttime was when every anxiety came true, over and over, in her head. Alcohol was the only thing that could ferry her through the insomnia.

One night, while she was in the bathroom, I had emptied her glass in the kitchen sink. When she'd come back, she'd regarded the spent bottle and opened another, her eyes boring into me with every twist of the corkscrew.

"Was it busy today?" I asked.

"*Hai hao,*" she said through a yawn. "Not the worst dinner rush, but food was taking a long time to come out."

I wove the head of the needle back and forth through the fabric. On TV, a flurry of animated sparkles restored a dirty banister to its original mahogany glow. My mother drew a hissing breath and sighed. "Then I got into an argument with my boss."

"About what?"

Her head wilted toward her shoulder. "He said I was taking too many bathroom breaks."

I scoffed. "That's ridiculous."

"That's what I said." She twisted to lean against the armrest and drew her legs onto the couch. Her toes edged up to my thigh and stayed there. That was how I knew she was drunk—the easy affection, the unrationed touch. I tensed, stayed still to preserve the precious contact, though I also burned with self-consciousness.

"But I think it was an excuse," she continued. "He wanted to talk to me in the storage room. I was grabbing take-out boxes. He said if I didn't work harder, there would be consequences."

"You *do* work hard," I said. "What did you say?"

"Nothing. I left as quick as I could."

"Why is he trying to threaten you? Did he give you any actual feedback?"

She floated a palm through the air as though parting water. "I'm too tired to talk about it anymore."

I held out the mended shirt.

"Good. Now the overstitch." Seeing me pause, she put down the glass, scooted closer to me, and demonstrated how to run the thread over the top of the seam with slippery, but practiced movements. "See? You should know how to do this. Makes it stronger." She left the rest to me and returned to her previous position, closing her eyes. Her toes returned to my thigh with their gentle pressure.

I finished the stitch and trimmed the excess thread. Marissa's eyes were still closed as I latched the lid back onto the yellow sewing box.

The lines that pleated her slightly parted lips were stained red. As I watched, her face relaxed, and her fingers slackened around the wine glass balancing on the cushion. Fear roared past me like a freight train. What would become of us? Suddenly, she snapped upright. She peered at me and said, "Is it fixed?"

"Yeah." I folded the shirt and set it on the coffee table. Then I mustered my courage and asked, "Hey, Mom, do you think I could have ten dollars?"

This roused her. "What for?"

"For dinner tomorrow. At rehearsal."

"I'll pack you a dinner. I have leftovers from the restaurant."

"But we're all going, a group of us." This had worked when I was younger, conjuring the pack. Panicked about money as she was, she had nevertheless tried to keep me from feeling like an utter outsider. "We're celebrating the start of the show."

"Yes, the start of the show. Then you celebrate during the show and after the show." She rose and lumbered to the kitchen, slapping the glass on the counter. The skin between her eyebrows accordioned in irritation. "You can't just do everything you want to do. When I was your age I came straight home after school because I had chores. If I didn't make dinner, then we didn't eat." She gestured vaguely, swimming through the memory. "We didn't even have enough rice. We made *zhou*."

"Okay," I said. "Never mind."

"I don't think I'll ever see the day when I can rely on you," she spat. Her eyes were watery, the skin around them inflamed.

"I said never mind!" I clenched my fist to keep from spouting more. She dragged her purse across the counter and rummaged for her wallet. Sighing, she counted out the damp bills and left them doubled on the countertop.

"That's ten," she said. "If only I'd been so pampered by my mother."

THE NEXT DAY AT SCHOOL, Andrew's red windbreaker drew my attention as though he were north and I the trembling needle. Now he was tossing a pen into the garbage can (and missing), now he was smearing his nose on his sleeve. At lunch, as LB and I straddled a concrete bench in the quad, I wondered where Andrew was. Was he getting stoned in someone's car? Copying a friend's homework by the lockers?

"I've seen this before," said LB, picking up her soda, one outstretched finger capped with green gum. "It's the White Rabbit effect. He poked his head out of the rabbit hole, and now you're curious as hell what's down there."

LB, who had recently lost her virginity to a coworker at the frozen yogurt shop, was now an expert in dispensing boy advice.

"I feel dumb," I said. "I don't know anything about him."

"It has nothing to do with him. You could've been tapped on the shoulder by someone whose face was just one giant zit and you'd have the same reaction. You're totally jacked up on hormones." She poked the gum back into her mouth. "Don't even try to fight it."

After the last bell had rung, I reported to the theater dressing room. Girls in leotards were leaning over the makeup counter to fluff their eyelashes. I struggled into a turquoise bodysuit and turned to appraise my butt in the mirror before someone edged in front of me to twist her hair into a bun, her white hands flitting overhead like two attendant seagulls.

A breezeway separated the dressing room from the backstage area. Outside, Andrew and a couple of other kids knelt over the backdrop for the finale, when the dancers kicked in unison, doffing glittering top hats. He glued a plastic gemstone to a golden panel and looked up just as I passed, his lopsided smile making the earth tilt under my feet.

Our energy pulled the air taut, but there was something else besides the electricity: a graveness and reverence while we waited backstage and burst forth on our cues. Mr. Baker and Ms. Sharif sat side by side in the front row and whispered in each other's ears. After the first run-through, the cast sat scattered across the stage to wait for our notes. Mr. Baker always did this with gravitas, crossing each comment off with an extravagant swipe of the pen. Halfway through the notes, I saw Andrew and a gaggle of crew members saunter past the stage and out the doors, presumably on their way to dinner. I felt a beat of disappointment, sharp as a snare.

IN A DEFIANT MOOD, I set out for the strip mall alone, determined to spend the cash that I'd wrung out of my mother. It was a short walk. Early evening gave the houses a drawn and sullen look. I had tugged on a jean jacket, but beneath that I still wore a dance costume, and a car honked as it jiggled over the asphalt. "Hey, sweet thing," said the driver. Jerking to attention, I saw a carnivorous flash of teeth before he sped away. It made me feel mean, which was a break from disappointment. I kicked a soda can into the base of a tree and stretched my legs as long as I could.

The shopping center by the school had a smattering of fast-food restaurants with teenagers draped over the patio tables. I walked into Burger King and lined up at the register. As the seconds passed, the fluorescent lighting and the sound of hissing oil burned through my little bubble of confidence, and I grew self-conscious of my leotard. I watched myself shift from foot to foot in the surveillance video. Then Andrew in a gray jacket walked into the grainy footage, his face also turned up to the screen. I looked to my left and found him there in color, hands rammed into his pockets.

He gestured with a flap of his elbow. "They just started heading back to campus. You want some company?"

I shrugged. "You don't have to stay."

"No sandwich today?"

Masquerading my grimace as a smile, I realized how transparent my timing was. Now he would know that I'd arranged to come. "Nah, I ran out of time this morning."

"Yeah, zero period is killer."

I gave my order. "I'm used to it now," I said. I folded the receipt in halves until it was too small and dense to crease again. "So why are you taking that class? It doesn't seem like you're really into the school paper."

"Yeah? Where'd you get that from?"

"Um, I don't know, you seem to be asleep or in the bathroom most of the time."

He zipped up his jacket. "So you're calling me a slacker."

"Maybe."

He smiled, a cherubic effect. "Fine, you called it. I took it because I thought it'd look good on the transcript. My parents met at Stanford, and they won't shut up about me and my brother going there. I'm hoping he doesn't get in. That'll make it easier on me."

"Is that why you're doing stage crew, too?"

His head shrank back as though someone had yanked his hair. "No, I dig stage crew. I get to hang out with my friends and build stuff. I mean, same question—why are you doing theater?"

"Similar reasons," I said with a droop of shame at my omission. I didn't talk about my mother with anyone aside from LB.

When my order was up, Andrew carried the tray to a booth of padded puce vinyl. The gesture confused me. It was like the wink, bold and unequivocal. He watched me eat my burger from across the table, fidgeting with the paper wrapper of the straw. He dipped his finger into my cup of water and rained a single drop on the cinched body, making it worm in both directions.

"I've been wanting to talk to you ever since that one day in journalism," he confessed. "Remember when you almost made Sawyer cry? That ruled."

I squinted. "What are you talking about?"

"You were mad," he said, scooting forward on the bench, "because Sawyer made these cuts on your story. And you were standing over this desk, correcting his edits, basically making him look like an idiot. I don't think anyone's ever called him out."

I scraped a fry through the remaining ketchup. "I guess it was a little overdramatic."

"No, it was awesome. Sawyer's such a prick."

"I didn't think anyone heard me."

He made a bouquet of fries and swallowed it whole. "Well," he said thickly as he chewed, "I was paying attention."

IT WAS WELL PAST dark when rehearsals ended. The school parking lot, lit up in sickly yellow circles, held only a half dozen cars. Cutting across it toward the bus stop, hands tucked under my armpits against the chill, I was caught in a pair of high beams that flashed on and off. I heard Andrew's voice call, "Hey, Kathleen, need a lift?"

Suppressing a smile, I turned on my heels and walked to the passenger side of the sedan. Andrew was leaning out of the window, gesturing over his shoulder with a thumb. "My brother just got off work, you want a ride home?" A serious, square-faced version of Andrew waved at me from behind the wheel.

"That'd be nice, yeah." I slid into the back seat. The car seemed new: the stiff smell of leather, clean floor mats.

"Kathleen, this is my brother, Mike. Mike, Kathleen."

Mike nodded at me in the rearview mirror as he edged the car onto the street. His features were broader, reflecting their German side; later, Andrew and I would talk about what that meant in terms of moving through the world. Because the world read him as white, Mike floated on a cloud of esteem, found easy passage, fielded better opportunities.

"Thanks for the ride," I said. "I'm at MacArthur and Thirty-Fifth?"

"You got it," said Mike.

I held the backpack in my lap and toyed with the zippers. It felt important that I was in an upperclassman's car with a boy who was interested in me. I was fifteen and curious to see what would happen next.

When we pulled up to my building, I saw my mother's car parked diagonally across a spot, front tires gouging the strip of grass that separated us from the neighbors. Fear slid down my throat, cold as a slip of fish.

"Sweet parking job," said Andrew.

I rushed out of the car, swinging my backpack on as I shut the door. "Thanks again. I'll see you tomorrow!"

"Hey, what's wrong?" he said, but I was already at the stairs, bounding up to the apartment.

I thrust the key into the door and braced myself for whatever state I'd find Marissa in. This time, all the lights were on. The living room was empty, though my mother's purse sagged on the floor, and the shoes that were normally lined up against the wall were sprayed across the tile entryway.

I didn't have to go far to find her: Marissa was in the bedroom corridor, lying on her side. She still wore her work uniform of black dress pants and polo shirt, the one I'd repaired last night. Her face was hidden in the crook of her elbow. Pressing one hand to the wall for support, I leaned over her and said, "Mom?" When she didn't respond, I bent down and shook her shoulder. "Mom, go to bed."

Her tacky eyelids peeled apart, and her black pupils rolled back and forth across my face. There was no recognition; hers could have been the shrouded eyes of a rhinoceros. She propped herself up on an elbow and, with a slimy, croaking noise, released a stream of acrid liquid from her mouth.

"No, not here," I said. "*Qilai, qilai.*"

Pulling her up by the arm, I managed to get her on her knees before she lurched forward again.

"Hey, is everything okay?" said Andrew's voice.

I spun around and found him in the living room, my mother's purse at his feet. I couldn't control the look on my face. "Who said you could be in here? Fucking *leave*!" When he didn't move, transfixed by my mother crawling toward the bathroom, I stomped toward him.

"Sorry," he said, hurrying toward the door. "I shouldn't've—"

I slammed the front door behind him and turned the knob. No one had ever seen Marissa like this, not even LB, who had heard the stories. I kept from her the reality of my relationship with my mother, how close it felt to being unloved. A wet, unintelligible syllable escaped my throat.

In the bathroom, my mother clung to the toilet bowl, her choked breath and garbled retching ringing against the porcelain. I knelt on the tile and rubbed her back. Swaying, she tightened her grip on the toilet. A strand of mucus swung from her bottom lip.

After a few minutes, she muttered, "Go away." My hand stopped. I was surprised to hear her speak. "I don't need your help."

I resumed tracing a circle with my palm. Having a goal made the situation more manageable. "You'll feel better once you get it all up."

"I'll handle it—don't touch me." She threw my hand away.

"Just let me—"

"No!" She tried to pull herself upright by the rail on the shower door but only yanked the bath towel to the floor, rattling the frosted glass on its metal track. "Let me . . . let me be," she insisted, but I kept my hands on her shoulders and positioned her over the toilet. I thought of Andrew gawking in the living room and tightened my hold.

"Do it now, or you'll get it all over the bed," I said.

She clapped a hand against the upright toilet seat and said in a hollow voice, "I want to go home."

"You are home. You're right here at home."

"I want to go back," she said, and I understood she meant Shanghai. Kneeling over her, I could see the top of her head and the bright, waxy scalp under the dyed hair, flakes of dandruff caught in the follicles. "Why am I being punished? I do my work. I don't bother anybody." She drew a shuddering breath and growled, "Could you please just stop touching me!"

I took my hands off her back, but I didn't leave.

"There's punishment for an unmarried woman. You understand that, don't you? Listen to me," she said, twisting to look at my face. "It's going to happen. Sooner or later, someone's going to try to hurt you. You idiot, have you let anyone touch you?"

"What are you talking about? No one's touched me."

"Don't lie!" She gripped my forearm.

"I'm not lying," I said, trying to wrench it away.

"You don't listen. You don't come home." Her voice was a low croak, and her breath was sharp with bile. "You're bad, you're bad."

I couldn't pry her fingers off. Her nails dug into the flesh. "You're out of your mind," I said. "You need to finish up here and go to bed."

"You are the reason why I'm here, why I have to go to that restaurant and face that man every day." She was enunciating as best she could, but the effort only deformed the words. "Without you, I'd have a chance at the life I wanted. And look how you treat me. Like a pathetic child."

My eyes and throat filled with coarse salt. "You're an ugly drunk, Mom."

"I have an obligation to tell you the truth."

Finally, I tore my arm away, and her nails scored the skin. "If it's true, then you shouldn't have had me at all."

"How would I know I didn't want you," she said, "until I had you?"

I stared at her until her slack face swung back over the toilet and her back convulsed, neck straining with the vehemence of what came up.

• • •

THAT NIGHT, in a dream, I wove through the black woods, chasing a light that drifted between trees like a lamp on a passing boat. It led me to a clearing where an immense moon was setting. The luminous, cratered surface sank into the grass, making no sound, and I realized it was the backdrop from the musical. The stage crew had scraped off the cheap gold paint, the plastic gemstones. Invisible dancers began to project their shadows across the moon and the trees, deepening the darkness. Intent on stopping them, I pointed a gun at the ghoulish figures, but I couldn't figure out how to fire it; it was a weapon out of a science fiction novel, silver and gleaming, outfitted with impossible triggers and switches. Engraved on the surface, over and over, were the words *I say what I see, I say what I see.*

I woke to find my mother in my bed. She was sitting against the headboard, staring ahead with the comforter pulled up to her waist. For a moment she bled into the dream—inscrutable mother, unfathomable gun—and then I recognized my bedroom and remembered the contours of the night before. My mother looked down and saw that I was awake. I sensed that she didn't remember what she'd said.

"I quit my job," she said. She chewed the inside of her cheek. "I'm not going in today."

Light revealed the streaks on the window. I closed my eyes, wanting to slide back into sleep. After a moment, I dragged myself into a sitting position beside her.

"What happened?" I asked. "Did you drive home drunk?"

She nodded.

"Your shirt . . . you didn't tear it on a kitchen shelf, did you?"

She shook her head. Silence yawned between us, a sparse yellow landscape.

"It was your manager," I said.

My mother nestled deeper into the blanket. "He found me in the storage room, and he kissed my neck. I couldn't believe it. He'd always leer and make comments, but this . . . And when I snapped at him, he grabbed me by the shoulder. I almost couldn't get away." As she spoke, I imagined the manager, whose hand I had shaken once, who had seemed so innocuous and mute with eyes that drooped at the outer corners like teardrops—I imagined him folding himself around my mother and pressing his lips to her neck and felt horror jet through every capillary. She described the next night, how he had found her in the office and pawed her breast. "He threatened me by saying he knew about the drinks I stole at work—because, Xiao Mao, I do—" Abruptly, she stopped talking, as though someone had put her on mute. But her shoulders were shaking.

I leaned over to put my arm around her, and she gripped me for support. I couldn't remember the last time we'd embraced like this. I could feel her wet coughs in my own throat.

"I'm sorry," she said.

"Why didn't you tell me? Why didn't you say anything?"

"It's shameful. I'm supposed to be the adult." As if reminded of the fact, my mother nudged my arm away. She lifted the blanket to reveal her bottom half, clothed in beige briefs, and slid her feet to the ground. Then she retrieved her glasses from the bedside table and put them on, blinking at the window. A bird flew past the building, its shadow skating across the room.

MY MOTHER AND I spent the day on the couch. She scanned the classifieds for jobs while I flipped through a fantasy novel, absorbing nothing. When it got dark, she didn't pour herself a glass of wine, though I could hear her thinking about it.

It was Saturday, and I had missed call time for the musical; by this time, I should have been in costume and finishing with my warm-ups, alternating between lion face and lemon face. I hadn't expected to be missed, but an hour before showtime, Andrew rapped at the door. He stood on the landing in all black, the uniform for stage crew members.

"Hey," he said. "I said I'd come fetch you. Mr. Baker's pissed."

"Really? I didn't think he'd notice." I was elated to see Andrew. I couldn't believe he was here, after the state he'd seen Marissa and me in.

"Of course he would. You're essential up there!"

"I am not."

"Okay, you're strategically placed in front of Jacqueline, who has no idea what she's doing."

I laughed.

"Who is that?" My mother approached, stopping a few feet behind me.

"Mom, this is my friend Andrew."

She was too far away for a handshake, so Andrew rubbed his chest with one hand and then raised it in a wave. "Hi, Mrs. Cheng. Nice to meet you." He gave no indication that he'd seen her careening on all fours, and I felt a burst of relief and appreciation. No one knew what to say. Andrew broke the silence with: "Well, if you're coming, you got to come now."

"*Ni yao chu nali ah?*"

"I'm supposed to perform tonight," I explained.

"What! You not tell me," she said in English, for Andrew's benefit.

"My brother's waiting in the car," he said.

I scrambled to collect my things and then hastened down the stairwell. Andrew brushed my lower back with his palm and said under his breath, "Everything okay?"

I nodded, thrilling under his touch. There was such care in it, and tenderness. No boy had touched me there before. An echo of pleasure ricocheted around my body.

"Stop!" I looked behind me and saw my mother coming down the walkway. "So stupid, you not tell me about play! All you practicing for nothing."

"You don't have to come," I said.

She swatted away the suggestion and opened the car door.

Andrew's brother, Mike, had the radio tuned to a brash pop-punk song. As we pulled away from the apartment and Andrew pumped his fist in the air, I let out a laugh that sounded carefree but soured as it died. A great loneliness had broken for my mother and me, but I couldn't see what would come to take its place. I couldn't know that my mother would get a job at the perfume bar and quit drinking in tottering spurts over the next decade. Or that Andrew and I would kiss and squirm in the very back seat that I now kneaded with my palms. All I knew with certainty was that by the end of the night, I would be advancing upstage toward a dark and enraptured audience, bouncing against the golden backdrop with each high, exuberant kick.

11.

The **Double Straddle** is the way to go for
some mutual support, and it's surprisingly
comfortable once you find the right balance.
You'll both be seated for this one, knees bent
and feet on the bed. One person threads their
legs over the other's hips, and you both lean
forward into an embrace. It's not a position to
hold forever—as it's more active than most—
but can be a great way to close a session.

It didn't take long for me to acclimate to Phil's body—the dips and
swells, the patches of smoothness meeting fields of hair, the hu-
midity of his armpit and its pungent sweetness. Every so often, a
distant siren would reverberate through my body, as though my
mother's worry were searching for flesh to inhabit. I kept waiting
for something to go wrong. His body would change, maybe, the
muscles snarling with new intention, or his words would curl inward
and awry.

Once or twice, as we lay listening to each other breathe, I was surprised to feel a slip of desire unspool like a thin ribbon. It was easy to forget that touch was pleasure, that the body did not discriminate between sources of pleasure; it ensnared the stimulus like the searching arms of an anemone, passing the morsel from tentacle to tentacle into its waiting mouth. I thought about women who were aroused by breastfeeding, who masturbated with an infant at their nipple.

Phil and I never acknowledged it, however. Instead, I told him about the seams of my life coming loose and the utter strangeness of catering to my mother, the bride. I described the night we'd spent assembling the wedding invitations: the thick, dimpled paper collated with vellum and gold foil, the names *Marissa Cheng* and *Brian Lin* engraved across the cards. My mother had been in a good mood, hands deft as she chattered about choosing a song to accompany her down the aisle. The pile of envelopes had grown, each fat with ceremony.

"It was weird," I said. "It felt like I was helping her with a school project, like when I was little and she'd help me glue together a diorama." We lay on the bed facing each other, our bent legs stacked like logs. His khaki pants rode up on the ankles, exposing a copse of hair that prickled through my leggings.

"Is your dad invited?" he asked.

I laughed. "No." Our interlaced legs held us steady as I rocked back and forth. "I mean, not really out of any malice, but we have our own lives now, and him being there would just be awkward. But he congratulated her and everything."

"Do you see or talk to him still?"

I shook my head. It had been a long time since anyone had pressed me about Baba. Speaking aloud made me realize how far we'd drifted. Phil must have sensed my reticence because he continued, "It must be an interesting thing to witness, your mom falling in love. Not every kid gets to see that."

"What about your kids?" I asked. "Are you trying to fall in love? Are you dating?"

Discomfort rippled his face. "I've been on the scene off and on, but I haven't found anyone particularly interesting." He paused. "Are you?"

"Same," I said, thinking of the coffee roaster I'd met at a tiki bar, how he'd prattled about his motorcycle trip across the country and then slimed his tongue against my teeth at the end of the night. Then there'd been the data scientist, dashing and polite and irreprehensible except that I felt nothing for him at all.

"I used to be a sucker for love. You know, before Diane and I got engaged, there was a week that I walked around with the ring in my jacket pocket," said Phil. "Just in case inspiration struck. In retrospect I could've been mugged. But I ended up pulling it out at a construction site."

"Sounds a little less than romantic but on brand for you."

"I mean, it felt perfect. An easy metaphor for building a life together." It was nighttime, he explained, both of them limber after a few drinks with dinner, and they'd wandered into the wooden framework of a house, the air pungent with sawdust. They'd walked up the stairs to gaze through the skeletal rafters, the lumber a dim gold color in the streetlights.

"I know how I'm going to do it," I remembered Oren telling me one morning, his palm on the stem of the French press.

"Do what?" I'd asked.

"How I'm going to propose," he'd said, and pantomimed zipping his lips shut when I'd pressed him for a clue.

"I'm sorry," I said, swallowing the bitter memory. "You must miss her so much."

"It's lonely," Phil admitted. His eyes drifted, then returned to mine. "I did think of something I wanted to do, if you're open to it."

"Try me."

"What do you think about—would you mind putting on her sweater?" He rushed on. "It's just this thing she wore that feels homey to me. I know it's a weird request, so no pressure, but I thought it wouldn't hurt to ask."

The cradle of heat between our bodies seemed to intensify, the places where our skin touched excreting a gloss of sweat. A few seconds staggered past while I mentally scoured the Midas Method for the right response. There was a dress code of sorts for cuddlers and clients, but the rules dictated the minimum to be worn (a tank top and shorts), not what was to be worn. A crimp of anxiety deepened between his brows, and again I felt a pleasing shudder of power. Maybe that's why I agreed. After feeling so trampled and discarded by Oren, I wanted the feeling of control, even if control looked like indulging someone else.

"Okay," I said. "We can try it."

He smiled. "Are you sure? I have it here. You really don't have to if it makes you uncomfortable."

I nodded, and Phil slid off the bed to rummage through the black backpack he'd rested on the couch. His face glowed in the boyish way I'd glimpsed on our first meeting as he ferried the sweater back to the bed, sinking against the edge of the mattress. The folded sweater in his lap was a faded gray, the ribbed crewneck chewed by time, its weave speckled with lint.

"She bought this from a secondhand shop in New York," he explained. "We were out there visiting friends. It was cold out, and we had dinner plans, and there wasn't any time to run back to the hotel. I remember I was getting agitated about running late."

Diane usually didn't make a fuss about clothing, Phil told me. She wore neutrals, sober turtlenecks and wool trousers, sometimes a brass bangle or pearl studs. Her sisters, who had spent their lives straining to step out of her shadow, were the ones who wore clashing patterns and provocative shoes. That day, she was in a white cotton T and jeans, a blazer that didn't keep out the October damp. They'd had an argument that morning—something to do with scheduling and where to eat—and she'd forgotten to bring a sweater in the aftermath.

She browsed the circular racks in the small shop, which had the tang and musk of old things, unsure why she cared so much about finding the right layer. It would be a week later, when she peed on a pregnancy test and watched the pink dashes come to life, that she would understand her own anxiety, recognize the encroaching suspicion she'd had that her body was no longer hers only. When she finally lifted the gray sweater from the rack, she saw a second skin that she would later fill in.

It became a favorite of hers, during and after the pregnancy. Diane wore it so often that Phil could superimpose the sweater on every memory.

"I got rid of most of her things," he said. "But I kept this."

There was an artlessness to Phil's need that disarmed me. It was almost erotic, the tension between desire and fulfillment. When he passed me the sweater, I unfolded it across my lap. Then, like a diver tipping into a mute pool, I swam my head and arms through. Passing through the membrane, I thought I could smell her: a good smell, sweet and chalky, and something vegetal like a corn husk.

I looked at Phil, unsure of the effect.

For a moment, I worried that his taut expression would produce tears, but then he relaxed back into my arms. "You know, I can't tell you what a relief it is," he said, reaching out to caress the fabric, "just to see it on someone again."

PUTTING ASIDE THE FACT that it was my client's dead wife's sweater, it was the most comfortable thing I owned. Its fleecy underside had been eroded into an airy cocoon, and the material hung slack in an elegant, expensive way. I wore it to run errands, to grab coffee, to watch TV at LB's co-op, though I couldn't muster the courage to tell her whose it was. I knew what she would say: *Kathleen, that shit is creepy as fuck.*

The sweater made it easier to pretend to be someone else, someone less lonely and fallible. Sometimes, cloaked in the fabric, I performed being a good person, acting as I thought Diane would act. Kind, sociable Diane would usher the woman with just eggs and milk in her basket ahead of her in the checkout line at the grocery store; she would greet the neighbors as she passed them on the street, offer to help them with their bags. Ordering a sandwich, I gave the cashier Diane's name just to see how it would feel.

I wore the sweater to go cake tasting at Sugar Crush, a café and bakery at the edge of Golden Gate Park. Brian had had to fly to Denver for work at the last minute, and he'd asked me to take his place at the appointment. My mother and I hadn't spoken much since the barbecue, the silence between us like a scribble of radio static whenever we were in the same room.

The tasting room was tucked in the back of the shop, the perimeter marked by a glossy thicket of monsteras, rubber trees, and philodendrons. One wall was mirrored, a Rumi quote—*What you seek is seeking you*—plastered across it in white letters. A skylight above gently illuminated a long wooden table. At the far end were two tiered white cakes, exquisite with texture, as though blooming oleanders had rumpled the cream. My mother and I sat across from each other in silence, at a safe distance from the cakes, as though we could hurt them. Beauty was a menace, reminding us of our itch to own it and our ability to maim it.

It was not the type of place Marissa and I went to together. None of these appointments were. When we'd last lived in the same home, we'd shared McDonald's breakfast platters and gone to Costco for lunch, collecting free samples of cheese raviolis and chicken nuggets until we were full. We went to dim sum restaurants and ordered from a parade of silver trolleys, the dented tins of shumai fuming steam on the table. This place, with its staff strapped into denim aprons, would have been dismissed as *langfei qian*, a waste of money. Besides, foreigners didn't know how to bake cakes, my mother had always maintained. Their desserts were too sickly sweet, the flavors blunt, the dough coarse and dry.

"Marissa! It's so nice to meet you in person," exclaimed a woman approaching the table. She wore a flannel shirt under her apron with the sleeves pushed up to her elbows, and her walnut hair was loosely balled at the top of her head. She wrapped my mother in a hug and then turned to me. Her cheek felt warm and dry, like a laundered sheet. "I'm Shauna," she said. "We do hugs around here. Welcome, welcome! Big day! We have lots to try, so we'll bring the cakes right out. Can I get you girls anything to drink? Maybe a water or a tea, something light on the palate?"

"Tea, please," said my mother.

"Tea for me, too, thanks," I said. "How did you find this place?" I asked my mother in Mandarin as Shauna walked away.

She studied the cake specimens at the end of the table. "It was recommended by the wedding venue. And Brian knows them, too; it's apparently a very popular bakery on Wayfindr. People change their routes all the time to get buy-one-get-one-free cupcakes."

When Shauna returned, she was pushing a tea trolley. First she set down a speckled teapot and two matching mugs. Then she presented us with two dark slate slabs arranged with miniature cakes and a spray of berries, as though the pastries had been locally foraged. "Let me introduce you to the flavors we have here," she said. "On your far left, you have a classic white cake with taro frosting, topped with a hint of lavender. Here, you have a red velvet cake and vanilla buttercream frosting and gold flakes." She pointed to each dessert with a flat palm. "This is one of my absolute favorites: a lemon and blueberry cake with shaved candied ginger. And last but not least, a chocolate and espresso cake with salted caramel buttercream frosting."

"Look beautiful, thank you," said my mother.

"I'll let you ladies dig in. Let me know if you have any questions," chirped Shauna, and she rolled away.

I let out an involuntary snort. "This place is funny."

My mother glanced up from pouring tea. "What do you mean?" She filled my mug and set it down so gently that it felt padded with malice.

"I don't know. It feels"—I didn't know the word in Mandarin, so I switched to English—"contrived." I wasn't sure if she understood, so I picked back up in our language. "*Jia.* Anyway, I thought you didn't like American desserts."

"This one was recommended," she repeated, and picked up her fork. "And I don't like *cheap* American desserts." She paused, set down her fork, and pulled out her phone to take some portraits of the cake rounds, eyes narrowed as she calibrated her farsightedness. Somewhere above us, a cloud dissolved, stoking the light in the room so that things seemed to expand and sharpen. I could see the lucent hairs on her arm. She hovered the camera above each pastry. "Don't say anything until you've tried them all. I don't want us confusing each other."

I used the tines to slice into the first cylinder of cake. It was sweet but mild, the subtle taro frosting bringing buoyancy to the bite, the lavender both deepening and brightening the flavor. "What kind of cake does Brian like?" I asked.

"He's happy with whatever I pick," she said in a tone of dismissal. This marriage, I saw, was going to be on her terms. She jabbed at the air with her fork and broke her own rule. "This one is very good. Very light. And not too sweet."

Next was the red velvet. The deep red sponge collapsed as I carved into it, then mushroomed back up. This one was rich and moist, the frosting a satisfying paste. My mother's lifted eyebrows mirrored mine.

"Did you know," she said, swallowing, "that this was the first cake I ever had in America? Red velvet, I mean. I thought it was going to be strawberry flavored. I almost spat it out. And the frosting—I couldn't believe how thick it was."

"Really? Where did you have it?"

"It was someone's birthday, I think. Baba's classmate, when he was in school." She summoned it in her mind, the corners of her mouth weighed down in concentration. "I didn't speak English. It was early—my first month here or something like that." She peered at her fork in silence again as though seeing the scene reflected in the tines. "I was very young."

It was rare for her to bring up my father and that era. Even though I had been there to witness them, her first years in America were unfathomable to me. It struck me that now, at twenty-eight, I was three years older than she'd been when she'd had me. It seemed shameful to be paralyzed by indecision, unable to imagine my life beyond the summer while my mother's past trials suddenly loomed with mythic vividity. She had raised an infant on her own and boarded a plane for the first time, daughter shitting and hollering in her arms, to speed toward a distant continent. She contorted her tongue to fit a new, barking language and resigned herself to foreignness for the rest of her life, endured disdain and hatred from strangers. She forfeited a sense of home in either country and bore the relentless loneliness of being a housewife in an alien place, and then the wild fatigue of being a single mother. And it had all happened over my head.

What was it like, I wondered, to be suddenly robbed of language and legibility? It felt too intimate to ask, the answer too hard to bear. Plus, the conversation required better Mandarin from me, which was already a step removed from her native Shanghainese. That had been the price of her success: Because she'd worked herself ragged to make me an American, we would never truly know each other.

I tweezed, with my fingertips, the pilled fibers on the sleeve of Diane's sweater. I wondered how much Diane had known about her mother's journey. Probably she had been mature enough to treat her with respect. Probably she had been more appreciative.

"Do you remember the cauliflower truck?" I asked.

"The cauliflower truck?"

"Baba was driving. And we were following this truck, a farm truck, that hit a bump in the road and dropped cauliflowers all over the road." We had hurried to gather the knobby heads. It had felt like a windfall, a tender sign from the universe. By recounting this I meant to say *I know things were hard. I know you went hungry so I could eat.*

She gave a short, shocked laugh. "I can't believe you remember that! You were probably around five years old then."

"I remember because I hated cauliflower, I found out."

"You were a picky eater. But you loved Spam. That's how I got you to eat anything—I'd put Spam in it." She took a bite and pulled the fork out of her mouth, clean and glistening. "You were too young to know we were suffering. Sometimes I think I shouldn't have protected you so much, so you don't think things come so easily."

This was the undeniable force that sucked all conversations back to the core: her sacrifice, my ingratitude. Our feelings fluctuated, but at their most extreme, they were cruel and reductive: To her, my pursuit of happiness was lazy and wayward. To me, her insistence on stability was materialistic and myopic.

"I'm not giving up on school because it's too *hard*," I said. "I just don't know if it's the right program for me."

"Didn't I warn you? You could've chosen any field—"

"You mean I could've chosen computer science or bioengineering."

"Other mothers may be like that, but not me. Don't lump me in with them. I let you do whatever you wanted. All I'm saying is, Ingrid—"

"Will you please stop comparing me to Ingrid?" She was the perfect cousin: respectful, obedient, delicately feminine, and on the business track with a boyfriend in corporate law.

"She's just one example. Don't you want to be like the others? Don't you want the freedom of a secure job, the warmth of a husband and a family? You're not eighteen anymore."

The others, meaning the other immigrant and first-generation children I'd grown up being compared to. "It's not that I don't want those things," I pleaded, throat tightening, "but it's not the only way to be happy." We had had this conversation hundreds of times before. Neither of us could find a new way to speak, a new path to travel, so we circled the same grooves until our feet wore furrows in the ground, furrows that deepened into canyons, gouging out a mountain with our failures of imagination. Now I would say the ugly thing, unable to admit that I was scared she was right: that I had been wasting my time.

"Not everything is about money. And if it were, then you should be relieved that Oren's out of the picture. He was never good enough for you. No one is! No woman can be thin enough, and no man can be rich enough."

Her face, until now made of stone, seemed to waver. Her voice warbled. "For someone who grew up without money, you sure do think you're above it. But it's my fault. I made sure you never felt the worst of it. You didn't see me faint in the morning because I was so hungry. You didn't see the jewelry I sold." She chewed her bottom lip. "You don't know about rigidity. Me, when I was young—we didn't get to choose our careers. There was a set path, and you either went down that path or died on it. Food, books, music, clothes—everything was controlled. We lived under the government, and we did what was best for the family."

Those were the untouchable themes I was scared to ask about and that she rarely shared—Waipuo joining the Red Guard, Waigong being stoned as a counterrevolutionary, my parents growing up in a rationed world. Diane, whose presence had been drowned out by my irritation a moment before, seemed again to step into the room as I deflated. "I just don't know what you think I should be doing," I said.

"Something other than using your body for money!" she said. "Maybe that's why Oren left—you don't know how to see something through."

I shook my head. "You don't know us."

"You think Baba wouldn't have rather done something else? You think I didn't want to go back home? But we got through it. There will never be a perfect life. But there can be a safe one, a comfortable one." She kneaded a napkin in one fist. "I meant what I said. If you weren't my only one, I would let you go. But my whole life, my whole heart depends on you."

We loved each other too much. That was the vise that crushed us. We would never agree on how to build a life, which was another consequence of her having delivered me into another world. "My life depends on you, too," I said. "I don't know what to do." Suddenly conscious of our surroundings, I clutched at my tea, tasting nothing, registering no temperature. I glanced over my shoulder, but the other patrons seemed unconcerned with our drama. A woman in an off-shoulder sweater fed her labradoodle a scrap of croissant.

My mother shifted the slate trays around. We had barely touched the frilly cakes. "It's not your fault. Maybe I care too much about what people think. It's hard, you know, when Tiffany keeps asking about you, when Meredith wonders how you're doing. I can't tell anyone about your job. Just tell me: Are you safe?"

I looked at her, at the device on her wrist. She was so strange, so infuriating, and so precious to me. She was the only family I had in the world. I nodded. "I'm safe," I said, and shoved up the sleeves of the sweater to feel fewer fibers against my skin, lessen the tactility of the lie. "I promise I'm in control."

12.

What we love about **The Cuddle Puddle** is how reciprocal it is. In this O-shaped position, both cuddlers are on their side facing each other, lying head to toe with slightly bent knees. The bottom knee slides forward, forming the perfect pillow for your partner. It's a good one to melt into, and you can even hold hands for a better connection.

Dolly's was having a midsummer rave, and the theme was techno circus. When LB met me at the entrance, she was partially done up—her choppy bob was slicked back into an oiled helmet, her fishnet tights visible beneath an old Star Wars hoodie she'd thrown on.

"That's a good look," I said as she unlocked the gate.

She posed, one arm thrown over her head. "We're a work in progress. I'm thinking, like, cyborg lion tamer. You want to be the lion?"

"Sure. Can we raid the Free Pile?" This was, by LB's account, the source of half her clothes: a utility closet filled with discards from the co-op members, the Dolls.

"Can we raid the Free Pile?" she said with exaggerated glee. "I *live* in the Free Pile."

We crossed the courtyard, a cracked concrete expanse with a grid of raised garden beds. The other half was occupied by a metal sculpture, its rusted architecture suggesting the coil and flare of a cobra, and a corrugated steel fire ring surrounded by tree stumps. Under the sculpture, someone lounged in a hammock. The low sun on her wide-brimmed hat scattered sequins of light across her shoulders. As we passed, she lifted her hand in a lazy wave, and I saw that she was sunbathing nude.

"That's Baby Shirley," said LB when we were out of earshot. We wound through a back stairwell where someone had painted a mural, a translucent skull sprouting a spectrum of colors out of its sockets. "I think she might be, like, seventeen, eighteen, but her older brothers both manage Dolly's—they're, like, DJs—so she gets a room. She's always hogging the hammock trying to get an even tan."

The door clunked as LB heaved her body against the handlebar, leading us to a concrete corridor and the Free Pile. She flicked the light on in the utility closet, revealing the chaotic heap. Aside from a few garments still clinging to a clothes rack, everything lay in a calf-deep tangle on the floor. A plastic orange snow saucer leaned against a nightstand with a missing drawer, its maw stuffed with mangled books.

I waded farther in, stepping on a pair of python-print jeans. "Wow, I didn't realize this would be so daunting."

"You kind of just—" LB plunged her hands into the jumble and extracted a slip of red satin, shaking it until it resolved into an unhooked corset. "Voilà."

I plucked through the musty items: a single striped knee-high sock, a bicycle helmet plastered with stickers and lined in pockmarked foam, an old Boy Scouts uniform, a Christmas sweater with a hole at the armpit, a souvenir mug from Grand Teton National Park. Stirred up, the pile emitted a dank smell, like wet earth, rot, morning breath. "I don't know if I'm going to find anything," I said.

"Not with that attitude. Here, what about this?" She held up what looked like a clump of fur.

"Ew. What is that?"

"Try it on." She tossed it at me, but the material was so light that it arced to my feet. I picked it up and made out that it was a faux fur vest, the fibers tacky in one area but otherwise intact. "I have a pair of leggings that could go with it. It's all about the makeup and hair, anyway. We can tease it out hella big. No, without that. What is that, your depression sweater? You're wearing it all the time."

For a beat, I considered coming clean, but I was afraid of rooting out the pitiable truth.

I peeled it off and said, "Just something I thrifted recently."

"Well, it's okay to give it a wash every once in a while."

I hooked the vest closed over my torso. "How's this, then?" Surprisingly, swathed in fur, I did feel wilder, more potent. I imagined the hairs growing out of my chest and strutted around the room, mashing the items underfoot.

"Much better," said LB.

ON THE BED she'd raised on shipping pallets, I sat between LB's legs so she could tease my hair with a comb. The wooden slats protruding past the edge of the mattress formed a shelf for a mug and its damp sachet of tea, an orange peel mounded with gray ash. Succulents lined the windowsill, which stretched the whole length of the wall. Light scythed through the loft and bathed her bike, which leaned next to a floor mirror draped with scarves.

"How's Towers going?"

"Good! We actually recorded last week. Wanna hear?" She paused in her work, stretched to retrieve her laptop from the floor, and typed something in. A song sauntered out of the speakers, a catchy riff with a wandering bass line. "We're pretty stoked." She beat the air around my body in time with the exuberant drumming that ushered the vocals in.

"You guys sound great."

"Thanks," she chirped, using my shoulder as a hi-hat, then scrunching up her eyes as she mouthed the words. "That's the great thing about living at Dolly's—it's free practice space. Hey, where are you going to live when your mom gives up the apartment? Go with her?"

"What, and move in with Brian? No, thanks." I'd avoided thinking about it. There wasn't much I could afford. I was still paying rent on a one-bedroom apartment in a pink-and-yellow row house in Baltimore, a couple of blocks from the university. With Oren's things gone, the place looked like it had been pillaged in a frenzy, and I hadn't had the strength to sort through the flotsam before I left. The plants would be languishing by now, withered and crisp. The lease was up in September. "Or who knows, maybe they'll buy a house together. Maybe they'll renovate something. We haven't really talked about it."

"I wouldn't've pegged your mom for the renovating type."

"I bet she is now. She drinks kale smoothies and takes spin classes and probably knows a thousand names for white paint."

LB snorted.

"You think there'll be openings here?"

"At Dolly's?" LB lifted a fistful of hair and dragged the comb backward in rapid strokes, sending tingles through my scalp. "I mean, there's always a room somewhere, at least short-term. But is this really your scene? A seventy-person co-op?"

The back of my neck warmed under her gaze. "What do you mean?"

"I mean, are you sure you don't want to finish school?"

I stiffened. "Okay, Brutus."

"No, I mean, I support anything you do, obviously. If you've already thought it through, great. And if it means you're not going back, also great."

I felt a pinch as she yanked a hair out of its follicle. "Hey, can you take it easy back there? That hurts."

"Sorry." The scratching of the comb resounded in my ear. I

wondered if she could feel the flush of my skin. My mother was getting married and pursuing a new career, LB was going on tour with her band, Andrew was heading for law school, and I didn't know where my bed would be in a couple of months. My best friend pointing out that fact made me feel stupid and childish, and my annoyance at her only underscored the truth of it. After a few moments, she continued, "I just think this is a chance for you to do things on your own terms. Your mom has always wanted a certain kind of life for you, and Oren made you feel inadequate for not being just like him. But what do *you* want? You've hit pause to think about it, right? Which means it's worth thinking about."

An ember leaped up behind my eyes. "Can you drop it, please? If I knew the answers, don't you think I would've told you by now?"

Her legs stiffened around me, and her hands stilled. I didn't need to see her eyes to know they were dark with reproach. A car drove by, dragging a few bars of pulsating bass. "Sorry," I said. "I know you're just trying to help."

She continued her work, gentler now. "It's okay. You'll figure it out."

AN HOUR LATER, my hair was a mane, crisp with hair spray. I had painted a lion's face over my own, tracing my eyes with a black crayon until they were shaped like leaves, coloring the tip of my nose. I wore LB's brown velvet leggings with the Free Pile vest, ignoring the chemical smell that clung to its fibers.

"It's probably just poppers," said LB, scrunching her nose as she whiffed the air. She'd peeled off her Star Wars hoodie and stood in her bra and fishnet tights, considering the pile of clothes on her couch before extracting a pair of black leather shorts and shimmying them on. Then she pulled on a red bustier with industrial buckles at the shoulder straps and pinched at the ensemble, twisting in the mirror. "What do you think? We like?"

Before I could answer, the door swung open and Andrew stood in the doorway. "Why isn't anyone answering their phone?" Then he noticed our costumes. "Damn, I am severely underdressed."

"Let's put some glitter on you," said LB, giving him a kiss that detonated something in my chest. "Glitter solves everything." She squatted to rummage through the makeup bag at her feet. "Here," she said, passing a tub of iridescent paste to me. "Would you mind doing the honors? I still need to put on my face."

"Sure," I said.

Andrew cleared a couch cushion by shoving the mound of clothes onto the rug below and landed on his side across the orange uphol-stery. "Make me pretty," he said. His hair had been recently cut, and he wore a short-sleeve button-up that I recognized, black with a squiggly '80s print. "I was thinking cheesy magician vibes," he said, "in case that changes your approach."

"Cheesy it is," I said, and sat on the edge of the couch. He re-moved his frames and hung them from the collar of his shirt.

"You know that app you told Luke about?" he said, loudly enough for LB to participate in the conversation. "It's already matching Milo up with brands. He's talking to a pet food brand and—get this—a skate shop in Venice."

I dipped the pad of my middle finger into the goop. "Oh, yeah? That's awesome. He did text me to say thank you."

"He's stoked about it. He was running laps around the apartment."

"Now he won't shut up about this pet expo that's happening in Vegas," said LB, who was standing before the mirror flicking her eyelashes with a mascara wand. "Supposedly it's like the who's who of celebrity pets, and it's where you go to meet brands in the industry. He's trying to get us to go with him."

I snorted. "Why am I not surprised."

"I mean, it's a free trip to Vegas, so . . ." LB turned, smirked into her shoulder.

"What? He's paying for you?"

"Technically his dad is," said Andrew.

"It's in a couple of weeks! Isn't that when your mom's bachelorette is?" said LB.

"Yeah, actually," I said through a wave of panic. I had yet to book the hotel rooms. I tapped around the outside corner of Andrew's eye and down the slope of his cheekbone, leaving a shimmering wake.

He chuckled, his breath warm on my hand. "It'd be so funny if we were all there."

"It would be *spectacular*," said LB. "Promise you'll come to the expo if you're there."

I laughed. "Okay, okay. I'll look at the dates tomorrow." The staccato tapping of my finger grew more insistent. "There. All done."

"Thanks." He put his glasses back on. "Hey, you guys think it's time to dose?"

"Oh, yeah." LB spun theatrically around to face us, her chin tucked so that her eyes gleamed through her lashes. "I have this new connect, and his stuff is impeccable." She pulled open a dresser drawer and held up an Altoids tin, then smiled as it rattled sparsely.

"What'd you get?" I asked.

"Molly." She pried open the lid and came close to show us the nest of translucent pills, the gel caps dusted with white powder. "Super pure, gentle comedown." She placed one on her tongue and swigged from a Nalgene bottle.

Andrew took his pill and then offered the tin to me. I took one of them and held it up to the light, watching the crystals fall from one end to the other. In these moments I always considered my mother, whom I'd watched pad her sadness with substances, and felt a pang of guilt. *I am not my mother,* I told myself. Andrew whooped as I downed it with an overzealous drink of water, wetness dripping down my chin.

THE COMMON ROOM of Dolly's had been decorated to look like the inside of a circus tent, with red and gold swaths of fabric radiating from the ceiling. A fan of green lasers swept through the fog that obscured a writhing thicket of bodies, and a periodic fusillade of strobe lights revealed hands raised in worship, napes of necks glossed in sweat, teeth bared in rapturous rictus. The DJ was on a dais above the crowd, aerial silks cascading behind the booth. She bobbed her head to the music, a manic beat and a sinister dribble of bass, an electronic wobble weaving between them. Skin suctioned against skin as a train of people coursed past us, clutching drinks, and LB took the opportunity to draw a mouthful of smoke from the cigarette she held overhead.

A lull of submerged sound. Desperate energy milled in our bodies, horses hoofing at the gate. Shapes shifted from side to side in the dark, riding the low thrum until it exploded into a missile of noise, hard and massive against the chest. Cheers and whistles rose from the crowd, all feeling and muscle, and we threw our bodies into the music: Andrew, a pop of shoulder and curl of arms; LB, hips tracing long ellipses; and me, bobbing and tossing my hair. Spliced by the strobe, Andrew hooked his arm around LB and caught her mouth in a slow, ravenous kiss that I saw in lightning flashes, but I was too feral to care. I closed my eyes as the sound surged through me, delivered me into a dark and vaulted bliss. I sighed with a bone-deep shudder of relief and wiped the sweat rolling down my temples. When I opened my eyes again, Andrew and LB were fused together, their many hands tracing the swerving planes of their body.

"I love you guys," I shouted.

"What?" they said.

"I love you guys!"

"Really good!" said LB.

I grinned. It didn't matter that they hadn't heard me. It was all the same conversation, tender and inane. The beatific faces of strangers drifted in and out of sight, trailing a wake of identical faces all smiling holographically at the ecstatic ritual. I couldn't keep my eyes open. Heat was a wet rag in my mouth. Someone wrapped themselves around me from behind, and their hands massaged the tops of my thighs, the outer corners of my ribcage, every touch reminding me where I was real. I traveled along the stranger's body, riding its taut waves as every nerve crackled and stretched toward pleasure. Their mouth tasted like smoke and spent gum. When the beat retreated, coiled into itself again, they held a key with a mound of powder to my nose and I hunched over it, inhaled, drawing breath and clarity deep into the lungs.

"Thanks," I yelled into their ear. "I need to take a breather."

I wasn't sure if they'd heard. Relentless sound obliterated all other meaning. I fought my way back out to the courtyard, where the steel ring now held a lashing fire. The figures around it flickered and laughed, phantasmic, producing a canopy of smoke that obscured the metal sculpture. The night air laid its cool, merciful palm across my forehead. Beside me, a woman with a shaved head dipped her cigarette into a cupped flame. She scanned the crowd as the end pulsed orange. I tasted the chemical slick at the back of my throat.

"It's like a sauna in there!" It was Andrew, fanning the soggy collar of his shirt. He took a crumpled carton out of his pants pocket and fitted a cigarette between his lips. Then he tilted the pack my way. "You want one?"

"Sure, thanks." I plucked one from the dwindling stash. "Where's LB?"

"Getting another drink," he said, and flicked a flame into being. I took a drag, smoke expanding my chest like an auroral dawn. The world seemed to twitch and refocus with a new strangeness, as though everything had rotated an inch in the time it had taken to blink.

Andrew laughed at my apparent euphoria. "How are you feeling?"

A broad smile lazed across my face. "Good. How are *you* feeling?"

"Fantastic." He disappeared behind a fan of smoke, then emerged like the moon. The steam that had clouded over his glasses was clearing in irregular shapes. "You look good as a lion. You ever think about making this a permanent look?"

"Basically nothing I'm wearing is actually mine."

"No way. I really had you pegged as a velvet pants, fur vest kind of girl."

"How's the glitter holding up?"

"You tell me. I got some in my eye earlier and it felt like fucking gravel. Pain is beauty, or whatever."

A cheer went up around us, stripping away the blanket of hoarse chatter that had fallen. A troupe of women dressed as trapeze artists were clearing a space in the courtyard, sashaying in widening circles. One by one, they ignited their fire poi and traced long arcs of light through the air with the flaming orbs, a mesmerizing dance of suns.

"Hey, you want to sit for a sec?" Andrew tapped my arm and indicated the couple vacating the couch behind us. I hadn't seen the deflated, graffiti-covered thing in the dark.

"Sure." We sank into the cushions, which were so worn that they folded around us like enormous slabs of white bread, pressing us thigh-to-thigh. I let my head fall onto his shoulder, relieved to put down the sudden weight of my skull. "You know, you predicted this," I said. "When we broke up, you said that at least we're not the type to just disappear completely, that we'd be friends."

He took one last sip of his cigarette before grinding the butt under his shoe, and I did the same. Having moved, it didn't feel right to put my head back on his shoulder.

"We didn't do each other wrong," he said finally. "You were an important part of my life. *Are* an important part. Why do we have to throw that away?" His arm was draped across the couch behind me, and his gesturing hand coaxed goose bumps from my bare shoulder.

Sometimes I wondered what would have happened if we'd tried to stay together through college, but even in theory it seemed far-fetched. As serious as we'd been about our love, in the grave and sentimental way of teenagers, we'd also known that committing to each other would be giving up a spectrum of experience. When Oren left, he'd said that he hoped we could someday be friends. I couldn't imagine it—being around him and not wanting to be gathered into his arms. Or worse, not wanting it and feeling the heft of that absence like a phantom limb.

"We're locked in," I teased. "Friends forever."

"I think that, honestly. It's crazy, isn't it? It couldn't've happened if I didn't have genuine admiration for you." Andrew scooped me closer against him and squeezed my shoulder for emphasis as he talked. "You've always been such a steady, reassuring presence. Long as I've known you, you've just been doing your thing, figuring it out, taking the hits as they come, you know. Fuck what's cool—you're just going with what you believe in. And sometimes you get lost, but never for long. You're like this quiet, unstoppable force."

It was an unfamiliar version of who I was, but one I wanted to believe in. I nodded, letting the idea dilate around me, become environment. It was such a relief to feel like I could like myself. "Thanks," I said, and exhaled a long breath through pursed lips. "That's really nice to hear."

"Hey, let's go to Vegas together." He had turned his head so that his mouth was by my ear, the voice dense and humid. "Come on, just book the bachelorette for the same weekend. We'd all be there at the same time! When is that ever going to happen? Imagine this, but in Vegas, kicking back with Milo." He leaned away, angling for the proper distance from which to pin me with a smirk.

"You're ridiculous," I said, but my thrumming heart was already longing to alight on yes. "Fine. Fine! Let's do it." He threw his body on top of mine in celebration, making me squirm against the disintegrating cushion in a tangle of glossed skin, smoke-tinged breath. For a moment, I remembered how our hips had moved together, how the spine arced and sprouted glistening new vertebrae. Then I laughed and said, "Get off, you're squishing the pee out of me!"

We had sunk so low in the cushions that it took two tries to dislodge myself. I staggered back onto the dance floor, where bodies were thrashing to a dungeon beat and lasers beamed through a tropical fug that was fragrant with cigarettes and sex. I followed a current down a corridor and into the bathroom, where the fluorescent lights seemed to throb and drone over the people in line for the stalls. When was the last time I'd had a drink of water? Stepping over wads of disintegrating toilet paper, I rushed to a sink and slurped from the faucet. The water was sweet and cold, and I sucked at it lustily until someone said, "Hello? Some people need to wash their hands."

A girl was standing behind me, a silver star drawn around one brown eye. She was radiant in a silver halter top and earrings that skimmed her shoulders. "Where do I know you from?"

One of her shoulders rose and sank, making the earring tremble. "I'm Baby Shirley."

"You were in the courtyard," I said, remembering. "You were totally naked, and you made it look so glamorous, even though at the time I was judging you a little bit. But that's just stupid internalized misogyny, the way we've been programmed to undermine each other."

"Wow, you're on one," said Baby Shirley, tearing a length of brown paper towel from a warped cylinder propped up on the sink. "I hear you, though. Like, fuck the patriarchy, I want to have my tits out. Hey, you're in the way." She herded me away from the sinks and back into the hall, where someone in harlequin pants sat passed out against the wall. One of the doors was halfway open, revealing a panel of red light.

"That's my room," she said, noticing my fascination with it. "We're hanging out in there if you need a place to lie down for a sec."

"Sure," I said, the thought of it filling my bones with lead.

"Hey-ey-ey," sang Baby Shirley as she sauntered in. A mesh of people covered the bed, couch, and floor like netting, their limp bodies packed three deep. There was ambient music playing, and everything was awash in a red light from the neon tube propped in a corner. Baby Shirley shut the door behind us and insinuated herself in the human heap.

"There's a seat here," said a guy in a leather harness. He was sitting up on the bed, and there was no room around him, but he patted his pale stomach and its scrawls of hair as though beckoning a cat. Gingerly, I crawled across shifting planes of flesh until I reached his lap, breathing a sigh of relief as I laid my head against the warmth and strength of his body. My weight pooled around him.

"What's your name?" I asked as he ran a palm down the front of my vest. From my vantage point, his face was long and benevolent with dark, bean-shaped nostrils. He introduced himself as he pulled the hair back from my face, giving it a firm and delicious tug.

"Is it okay if I play with your hair?" he asked, smacking his gum.

"Oh, please. That feels great."

His hands burrowed into my scalp and combed through the tangle, picking knots out of my hair as though undoing bad thoughts. I closed my eyes, feeling somebody's legs flex and relax under me, someone else rubbing the length of my arms. I had the languid resolution to suggest cuddle puddles to the higher-ups at Midas Touch and smiled at how the Method would read. *When navigating a cuddle with three or more people, be sure that no one is in danger of falling off the bed.* Glimmers of conversation hung like a canopy overhead, words and phrases falling into my ear like the drifting sparks of fireworks. When I looked up again at the circle of strange, seraphic faces, it felt as though either a second or an hour had passed.

"Better?" he asked.

"So much better," I said, buried deep in a mud of contentment. "You guys are so nice, wow."

"Party favors, anyone?" The mattress rocked as Baby Shirley climbed on holding an oval platter. She searched around for a flat surface before placing it on my stomach. Ungluing my head to look down, I saw that it was a mirror arrayed with dashes of powder. I could see the shape of each granule, each speck reflected in the glass like ice floes breaking over nacreous water. She looked at me and warned, "Don't laugh, and don't sneeze."

"What is it?" I asked.

"That one's ketamine." She pointed. "That one's Molly. These are coke, and we're not sure what this is, but we've been calling it lollipops. It's mildly psychedelic."

As I pondered each portion, someone stirred from the armchair they'd been curled up in, and I recognized what was draped across the seat back—Diane's sweater. My intestines clenched in alarm. Had I left it in the Free Pile earlier in the evening? I couldn't imagine having lost it. Now that it was in sight, I yearned to crawl back inside its weathered skin. Suddenly, as though a layer of gauze had been lifted, I saw how out of place I looked. Everyone seemed so young, baby fat swelling under porcelain skin.

"Hey, where'd you get that sweater?" I asked.

"What sweater?" Baby Shirley swiveled around to see where I was looking, then snorted and turned back. "*That* sweater? I copped it from an ex. Why, you cold or something?"

I struggled to sit up. "No, I'm just—I'm just pretty sure it's mine."

"Why would it be yours? You've never been in this room before."

"No, but I accidentally left it in the Free Pile earlier today."

I focused on the eye she had drawn the star around. Its pupil glistened and twitched slightly from side to side. "Okay, well, it's probably still there."

"It's got history, that sweater."

"I mean"—she contorted to retrieve a curled bill from her desk and rolled it on the top of her thigh—"if it looks anything like that thing, trust me, no one's taken it." She bowed over the mirror and neatly vacuumed up one of the lines before tossing her head back, sniffling and flicking the end of her nose. "Marco."

"Polo," said a girl, her voice seemingly directed at me, soft and sneering. She took the mirror, snorted her line, and smeared the crumbs against her gums with a fingertip.

"Give it here," said someone lying on the floor.

"It was a gift," I persisted. "From a friend. I can see it from here—same holes in the collar and everything."

"Can you please shut up about the sweater? I'm telling you, it belonged to Johnny Beckman, and now it belongs to me." Her brows formed an inverted peak. "I don't know you, and you obviously don't know me, so let me tell you right off the bat that I don't take any bullshit. If you're going to fucking lay on my bed and whine, you can get out right now."

I became cognizant of the hardness of bone under the meager blanket of flesh I had been lying on. The world was losing its dimensionality. Things were regaining their hard, unremarkable surfaces.

"Ugh, you guys are giving off such bad vibes. Can you talk about this outside?" said the guy in the leather harness.

"No need," said Baby Shirley. "She's leaving."

"I'm not leaving," I said, "until you give me what's mine."

She raised her middle finger. "Oh, you mean this?" She threw her head back and cackled. It was a grotesque, childish taunt. I must have looked wild, my makeup swamped around my eyes and my hair a matted tumbleweed, as I lunged off the bed and snatched the sweater.

"Stop that," growled Baby Shirley, pouncing off the bed and gripping a sleeve. I heard a thread pop and tried to pry her fingers open, but she yanked me across the bed. I felt other hands clench around my body, voices clashing unintelligibly, but I stayed focused. Finally, she pulled her arm back and struck—a bright clap of pain landed across my cheek, and I let go at the shock. Baby Shirley was breathing heavily as she found the tag inside the collar and thrust it into my face, too close for me to see clearly.

"See those initials? JB. John Beckman. I've had this since middle school."

I didn't look. I didn't apologize. I held her gaze for an excruciating moment before clambering out of the room, feeling everyone's eyes trained on me in hostile silence. "Who the fuck was *that* crazy bitch?" I heard someone exclaim as I crossed the threshold, followed by a chorus of laughter.

In the bathroom, I skipped past the line and dove into an empty stall, ignoring protests shouted from people waiting their turn. I planted my ass on the wet seat just as urine gushed out of me. I was holding back tears of humiliation, and my knees trembled under the weight of my forearms. I read the graffiti in the stall, chanting the phrases in my head until I could draw a regular breath: *ACAB. Kevin Mullen drinks momsauce. Save the Ents.*

There was no toilet paper, so I pulled the leggings over my damp thighs. At the sink, I lathered up my hands with soap and rubbed away what was left of my makeup. Rubbed raw, lips swollen from gnawing, my face looked pink and distended in the mirror. It was a face I couldn't let my mother see, though I ached to be home. Too often, I'd confronted her vacant, glass-eyed stare, watched her marionette movements slurring and jerking as she tried to pour a glass of water. I didn't want to terrify her in the same way.

Heading for LB's room, I pinballed through the dance floor again, which seemed to have grown even more hysterical in my absence. Upstairs, I tried the knob on LB's door. It was locked. I jiggled it back and forth before beating the heel of my palm against the door. "Hey, I need to crash, let me in." I pressed my ear to the cold metal and heard a truncated giggle, a clang. My body went heavy and hollow at the same time. The insides of my cheeks were ragged and sore, tangy with blood. "Come on, guys," I said, pounding with my fist now, but for what reason, I wasn't sure—the last thing I wanted was for the door to swing open, for LB to greet me, flush and sheepish, her chin stained with lipstick while Andrew stood out of sight long enough to pull his pants on.

I swore, spun around. Avoiding the common room, I took the stairwell down to the basement floor, where the Free Pile was, and lurched from door to door until I found a storage room. I palmed the wall, unsuccessfully, for a light switch, but a thin band of windows allowed enough light to limn a labyrinth of discarded furniture. The drum kit that LB must have practiced on gleamed in one corner.

The rustling I was hearing, I realized, came from two people who were making out on a loveseat, one straddling the other. A curtain of hair obscured their faces. I lay down as far from them as I could on a couch that smelled of mildew. I was thousands of miles away from sleep, but I stripped off my vest and folded it under my head. Scenes from the night began their broadcast on the backs of my eyelids, bright and lurid as billboards; the lovers' shaky exhalations, the clinking of a belt buckle, resounded in my ear. I sighed and coughed to signal my presence, but they didn't hear or didn't care, their earnest fumbling creating its own perimeter.

I lay awake and miserable. I massaged my jaw and tongued the tears on my lip while the couple's noises filled the room like a persistent rain. Trying to steer my thoughts somewhere comforting and safe, I leapfrogged over Diane's sweater to Phil, and to Phil's curiosity about Baba. I'd flinched at his questions, but now in the restless dark I allowed myself to feel the winnowing cold of the truth, which was that I missed my father but didn't want to give him the chance to reject me another time. Turning to face the back of the couch, I held up the memories that had begun to disintegrate from handling: Baba getting a haircut in the bathroom, dark clippings collecting on his collarbone and landing on the tile like snow. Baba running a knuckle down the length of my nose. Baba laughing. Baba changing a light bulb, wrist turning and turning until the filament burst into life and his face came on, aglow.

13.

Getting into **The Sweater** is like crawling
into your coziest hoodie. One person sits with
their legs parted, creating a backrest for their
partner to lean against. The cuddler in the
rear wraps their arms around the other's
shoulders, warming them up like a favorite—
you got it—sweater.

The sweater had been in LB's room all along. Having retrieved
it, I watched it sway on a hanger in my closet while I dialed
my father's number. I hit the green button before I could
second-guess myself, heart banging against my chest. I'd thought
about him all night, it seemed, until the darkness thinned to a solemn
blue. What if something had happened to him? I couldn't remember
the last time I'd heard his voice.

As the phone rang for the third time, however, I fought the urge
to hang up. I had nothing important to say to him. It would be

awkward or, worse, it would be sad. But the trilling stopped short, and there he was, sounding bemused: "*Wei?* Kathleen?"

I'd been pacing beside the bed and now froze. "Hi," I said in Mandarin, mustering cheer. "I was just thinking of you, so I decided to call." I dug into the pad of my thumb with the nail of one finger, then the next, then the next. "What are you up to?"

"Oh," he said, trailing off, and chuckled hoarsely in a way that I couldn't read. "I'm taking Sesame to the groomer's. We're in the waiting room." Sesame was his and Leslie's Siberian husky, a dog they'd gotten when it had become apparent that they weren't going to have biological children.

"Yeah? How's Sesame?"

"Good, good. She's tired from running around the dog park. She has a lot of friends there." I heard him mumble something, probably to Leslie. "What about you? How are you?"

"I'm good. Just, you know, at home and helping Mama with wedding stuff."

"Yes, I know. I'm very happy for her. I worried about her being alone all the time."

The thought came reactively, like a bitter spray of venom: *Then you should have stayed*. But all I said was, "You would like Brian. He's very nice."

"I'm sure I'll meet him soon. Sesame. Sesame, sit." He cleared his throat. "What about you? Your boyfriend, is he going to propose? Maybe you'll let me come to that wedding." A wry laugh.

I rubbed the side of my face. "Who knows what'll happen?" I said, falsely bright. It wasn't something I wanted to talk about right now. I started pacing again. It seemed like the end of the conversation. "Well, I'll let you go. You probably have errands to run."

"Okay, Kathleen. We're taking Sesame in now." I heard the jangle of dog tags. "I'm really glad you called."

"Me, too. Bye."

"Bye-bye."

I tossed the phone onto the mattress and sank down beside it, cupping a palm over each eye in mortification. Speaking to Baba only reaffirmed the distance between us. Why had I put myself in that position? I dropped my hands and stared at the hanging sweater. I could imagine the barely perceptible shifts in fabric as the specter of Diane slowly filled the void. Perhaps I'd been possessed, urged into something I hadn't been ready for. The moment I'd seen the sweater in Baby Shirley's room, things had gone downhill. I would get rid of it. I would give it back to Phil. I would give it back to him right this moment.

He had floated the possibility of us meeting outside the clinic, which was verboten according to the Midas Method—ostensibly for the safety of cuddle practitioners, but realistically for the sake of company revenue. "Coming to the clinic can just feel a little . . . well, clinical," he'd said. "What if I just want to hang out?"

I was wading through muddy ethics. Therapists, of course, could not befriend their clients, but what about masseuses or hairdressers? It was easy to justify having a cup of coffee after you'd cradled the person in your arms. I was thinking rashly, I realized, reeling from my brief exchange with Baba, but I didn't care. Besides, it was Phil, not just any client—and there had been some problematic clients, men with whom conversation was a political minefield or whose roaming hands I had to stay. After a sour session, it was always a relief to see Phil.

It's nice out, he had texted me earlier, because that was another boundary we'd crossed—exchanging numbers.

It is, I wrote back. What are you doing right now?

IT WAS A searingly beautiful day and the grass around Lake Merritt was a patchwork of picnic blankets. People lazed in the lacework of dappled shade. Food trucks and vendors lined the sidewalk, and dogs pranced at the end of their leashes, sniffing at jettisoned chicken bones. Phil and I lay on a striped throw. He was on his side, angling toward me, and I was propped up on my elbows as I recounted my attempt to steal Baby Shirley's sweater. He had a dry, galloping laugh; every new detail released another cavalry. Every so often, his hand cupped my shoulder to underscore a reaction or it lounged on my thigh. Free of the clinic's transactional context, his touch carried the frisson of mysterious intent.

We lay amid a cornucopia of crackers and dip, prosciutto, hunks of cheese, strawberries. We sipped from plastic cups of white wine, using our shoes as cupholders. Someone vaulted toward a Frisbee floating over our heads and apologized, her eyes pinballing between us as she calculated our relationship, the age difference. I knew what it looked like. I knew what it *felt* like. Despite myself, I'd enjoyed the chore of buying groceries with him before scouting our spot by the water. Even the banal felt meaningful with another person. The worry I harbored about what we were doing had been barely detectable under the comfort of it, and I'd reasoned that I deserved this: the small pleasure of discussing cracker options with someone you knew just well enough.

"Ah, whatever," I said, draping a tissue of meat over one of the fig crisps we'd chosen. "I had fun still. I drunkenly agreed to line up the bachelorette party with this pet convention that's happening in Vegas."

"A pet convention?" He peered at me from under the brim of his cap.

"Yeah. My friends are going. Remember I told you about Milo the rat?"

"Milo the rat," he repeated, nodding slowly. "When's the convention?"

"The nineteenth and twentieth."

We watched a teenager swerve around pedestrians with each foot planted on a Lime scooter as though they were skis, music blasting from the speaker clipped to his belt.

He turned back toward me. "So it's, what, people showing each other how to express their dog's anal glands?"

I laughed. "Yeah, plus, exhibitors and competitions and all that."

"And how many exhibitors are there?"

I shrugged. "You're full of questions, aren't you?"

"I'm just—I'm fascinated by the whole concept, that's all. I have some buddies who work in Vegas. I've done a fair share of projects out there, too. Mostly hospitality. I did a rainforest-themed bar with seats that swing on vines."

"Maybe we'll go," I said through a mouthful of food. I thumbed away the crumbs at the corners of my mouth and considered the sailboats drifting across the water rumpled by wind, asterisked by sun. On the other side of the lake was downtown Oakland, its buildings emerging from behind a band of trees. "What about you?" I asked. "How are things?"

Phil sat up, peeling himself off the blanket. "Oh, things are largely the same. Aster backed his car into a pole and has been bugging me for cash, but I refuse to capitulate. Nothing wrong with driving with a dented bumper."

"They really trade off with their crises, don't they?" By this point, I knew the headlines of his twin children Aster's and Ada's lives. Last month, Ada had lost her passport in Nice, and Phil had had to rush documents to her through the mail. "But it makes sense—they've competed for attention their whole lives."

"One hundred percent," said Phil. "Diane and I used to rock, paper, scissors when something came up. Now it's just me, I guess." A halfway grimace cracked his lips open as her name dropped like a stone. "You know, it means a lot that you fought for her sweater, even if it wasn't the right one. It's the thought that counts."

"Sure. I know it's important to you. Actually, that's partly why I wanted to see you today." I reached into my tote bag and held the folded sweater in both hands. "I don't think it's right for me to hold on to it. I've gotten a bit too attached to it, to be honest, and I can't imagine the guilt if it got lost or damaged."

Phil was quiet, his expression muffled by his heavy brows and beard. His eyes were on the sweater, which I held up like an offering. Then, as though he'd made a decision, he looked at me and shook his head. "No, no, you keep it." He palmed it back toward me. "It doesn't do anyone any good being stuck in a drawer."

"Phil—"

"Do it as a favor," he insisted. "Please. It gives me comfort to think of it being out and about. And if it gets ruined or stolen, so be it. That's part of life, isn't it? I like to think of Diane's things as being part of life. Oh, come on, that's not as sad as it sounds. Come here. You're hungover. Just relax a bit." He shifted to face the water and patted the space between his bent knees.

I tucked the sweater back into my bag and sat down with my back resting against him. His arms encircled my shoulders, and we fell into a silence as we watched the activity around the lake like a mural unscrolling endlessly. It wasn't surprising that I had given in. To put the sweater on was to slip under a cloak of love and devotion, and the longer I wore it, the easier it was to pretend that I was the object. At the same time, I was wary of what I was doing: once again acquiescing to someone else's version of me. It was best not to examine that too closely. It would be simple to remain in denial. The mind was weak and fallible.

"You know that your brain is always subconsciously working to weed out the bad stuff?" I said to Phil. "There was a study where they showed people two spots of light and asked them to compare their brightness, but there was a word embedded in each spot that was too dim to actually see. Some of them were neutral—*apple, book,* whatever—and some were like *bitch, penis.* And people reported the spots with vulgar words as dimmer, even though they were actually the same."

"That's wild."

"And if you ask someone on a witness stand, 'Did you see *the* stop sign' versus 'Did you see *a* stop sign,' you can completely insert a stop sign into their memory."

"Is there something you're trying to tell me?"

I bit my lip, reached up to clutch his forearms closer to my chest. "No," I said. "Just thinking aloud."

14.

As a child, one of my most precious possessions was a miniature koala bear I'd gotten from a garage sale. It had a demented, melted face with patchy gray felt, and I called him Lucky Frank, though he never brought me any luck. He fell out of my pocket somewhere in Las Vegas during a family vacation, and my parents, who had all day nursed an injured silence between them, united to teach me a lesson.

Baba, Mama, and I occupied a booth at the Emperor's Buffet in the Imperial Palace Hotel, a monumental pagoda on the Vegas Strip with eaves outlined in blue neon and the name written in tapering strokes meant to resemble Chinese calligraphy. I stabbed at the depraved meal I'd made of orange chicken, french fries, enchiladas, beef stroganoff.

"If something is important to you," lectured my father in Mandarin, using a fork to pry a length of meat from a crab leg, "you need to take better care of it."

My mother used the back of her hand to push up her glasses,

fingertips gleaming from peeling shrimp. "That *polan* bear," she said, grimacing. "You have nicer toys than that."

Most of my "nicer" toys had been fished from the garbage bins at our apartment complex or donated by Brianna from apartment 2G, but I was too devastated to argue, picturing a toddler retrieving Lucky Frank and putting him in their mouth.

"Maybe I left him in the hotel room," I said. I wanted them to agree, to make it so.

But they were intent on making their separate, conflicting points. "You should have left him at home, like I advised you to," said my father.

"Frank's never been to Vegas," I reasoned.

My mother smacked her lips, swallowing. "It's about developing a better taste in things. Look at your plate. That's all cheap stuff." She pointed to her dismantled shrimp, her sliced ham—a beige slab coated in slime. "We paid to sit down, you know."

"Well, we half paid," said my father.

When we'd first gotten to our room this afternoon, he had taken a shit in the bathroom and called the front desk to report the outrageous stink. He had left the door open while he strained on the toilet, his thin face growing taut as something rotund plunked into the bowl. The concierge, after he'd assessed the situation, had upgraded us to a suite and left us with coupon books that included two-for-one buffet vouchers.

The turd had punctuated the argument that my parents had carried on in the car, which was something about money, as it always was. My grandfather, Baba's father, needed to fund an operation for his heart, I gathered, and Mama begrudged him the money on the grounds that it was the man's own fault for eating so much pork fat, and anyway, where had he been when Baba had needed him? My father was not usually a crass man, but his dump had done a spectacular job of reminding us that he was in charge, that it was his money to spend.

"You're wild," said my mother now, and her lips suggested a smile, though she had screeched at him in the hotel room while he shat. She had not put on the weight of anger and abandonment yet, though her body was pleasantly round, her hair a series of brown loops from her spirited perm.

Playing along, my father grunted and gnawed on the crab leg like a mongrel, and she came up with a few buoyant notes of laughter. Work had chiseled his face into sharp gleaming facets, and I was relieved that my mistake struck his lighthearted side. He could have a carefree charm that was positively boyish, which in turn made my mother girlish and me an infant for whom the world was dim and diffuse, the space between each particle dilated so that something marvelous could pass through.

SHORT OF BREATH with the Herculean task of digestion, we stood near a blackjack table, getting our bearings. The dealer was a blond man wearing a silk tunic with a mandarin collar. When he saw us, he angled his hand toward the empty stools.

"Let's play a couple of rounds," said my mother. "I'm feeling lucky."

"*Hao*," agreed my father, cracking his knuckles in mock determination. They looked at me as though waiting for me to excuse myself. "Kathleen, why don't you go to the arcade while we finish a game?" With his chin, he indicated the dark cave of the arcade nearby. He passed me a fistful of quarters, instructing me, "*Guai*." Be good.

Begrudgingly, I went in. I was used to the arcades at Treasure Island and Circus Circus—expansive playgrounds filled with children clutching bales of yellow tickets—and this one, a perfunctory size and occupied by one preteen girl zapping zombies with a plastic gun, was an insult. I watched the lurching corpses explode in bouquets of blood until she sneered at me, "What are you looking at?"

I shrugged. I went to the change machine, which alchemized quarters into game tokens. It was next to a claw crane, and I gravely checked its contents in case Lucky Frank had traveled through a miraculous Rube Goldberg contraption and landed in the bin, where his doleful eyes would be peering out from behind a stuffed dolphin. At the back of the machine was a mirror, multiplying the sea of prizes and reflecting my frown. Considering the dozen quarters in my hand and the coin slot flashing red, I deemed it an omen that *this* game took money instead of tokens. I hadn't spotted Lucky Frank, but I could conceive of a world in which the claw jostled the toys in such a way that they would reveal his body, like shaken leaves allowing the passage of sun.

I relinquished one quarter. The claw trembled to life. I guided its three prongs to the center and let it drop; it grazed the head of a penguin before retracting, shivering with the effort. I put another quarter in, and it made another half-hearted grab, this time dragging a clear vinyl backpack a few inches in the air before letting go. I groaned.

"Hey, stupid. You're gonna run out of quarters before you get squat out of that machine," said the girl. "It's rigged."

I looked over my shoulder to find her still fixated on the screen, one hand in her pocket while the other fired. It occurred to me that I was in the perfect setting to duplicate my remaining quarters. I left the arcade.

At last, I could examine one of the slot machines up close. I ducked under a garland of smoke that trailed from a woman's cigarette and wandered down the aisle, watching the adults in their rapt observation of falling cherries, sevens, crowns. It wasn't so different from the claw. One man, hunched to scrape the shower of quarters into his plastic bucket, looked up from the din as I passed and pretended to swallow a coin, a magic trick I dimly believed back then. He next held a hand to his throat, eyes white and fluttering in mimed death. I hurried past him and climbed onto a chair at a carousel of abandoned machines. Above them, a spinning neon sign spelled 25¢ in pink tubing. The game was called Genie's Cave, illustrated by a woman festooned in jewels and a gauzy pink top that revealed her cleavage. Her body evaporated from the hips downward in a spectral trail that led to the spout of a golden lamp.

I looked around, slumping to hide in the vinyl seat. Gingerly, I inserted a quarter and listened to the metallic digestion of it before punching the illuminated button. The digital reel spun and blurred. One by one came the unintelligible runes: camels, gold coins, an elaborate letter *G*, gold lamps, a ponytailed genie. Mysteriously, the machine spat a clatter of quarters into the trough. I straightened up. I slipped another quarter in and set the reels in motion, feeling like my pupils were spinning on their own axes. This time, the payout was even more generous. I laughed and squeaked at the magic of it.

The man who had pretended to choke on a quarter was walking away from his machine. He paused beside me. He was wearing a green windbreaker with athletic stripes over a yellow polo that seemed yolkish with his belly. White curls sprouted around his ears, though his hair was otherwise black. Slinging his arm around the back of my chair, he used the resting hand to point at the reels. "That's pretty lucky," he said. It sounded as though he had a cold. "You're a pretty lucky little girl. What are you going to do with the money?"

I knew I wasn't supposed to speak to him, but shyness made me pliant. I was also pleased that I had a witness to my escapade. "Probably use them at the arcade."

"The arcade?" He seemed astonished, hanging on to the chair as his knees dipped. "That's just a con. You never win enough tickets to get the doodly-wads and what-have-yous. You throw basketballs and whack moles all day and what do you get?" He rubbed an imaginary marble between his fingers and stiffened his upper lip. "You get a little green pencil eraser. You get that, and you know what? It's useless. 'Cause pencils, they already come with erasers."

I nodded.

"So what you do is you get yourself something you *don't* have." He pumped the plastic bucket in his hand so that the quarters clanked once. "For me, that's a car. My last one didn't work right—drove clear into a fence and gave me this." He pressed a thumb into the side of his nose, which had a disjointed look. "You got your license?"

I shook my head.

He laughed, the pink body of his tongue undulating like a seal. "You're real earnest. I can tell you're going to be an honest person if you're not already. You're probably going to tell just five lies in your life—but they'll be awful, nasty ones, I'll bet. Yeah." Something behind his face rearranged itself, and he leaned close enough that I could smell the rot of the food between his teeth. "What's your name?"

"Ingrid," I said, using my cousin's name.

"Where are your parents, Ingrid?"

I pointed vaguely at the blackjack table. We couldn't see it from where we were. I was still having a hard time drawing breath and I couldn't tell whether it was because this man's presence was oppressive or because my body was dense with food, like a blow-up clown tilting on its weighted haunches.

"Go on, then, Ingrid. Play your quarter. Nothing to do here but win."

I slid the coin in, pulled the lever. He called out the symbols as

they dropped: "Oh! Genie lamp! Gold! Gold! What's it gonna be—?"
I couldn't see how I would win anything with him crowding my luck,
and I was sure that his keening would draw attention to me and place
me back under sensible adult supervision, but I tried again. "Yes,
there it is," he said, clenching my shoulder and letting it go. I looked
down at it, imagining that it would bear the imprint of his fingers as
though my body were made out of clay. "Genie lady, genie lady, genie lady. Oh, out of luck!" His mouth leaked a green smog.

"I'm going to try another one," I said, and slid down the seat to
gather my winnings from earlier. I couldn't fit all the quarters in one
hand, so I shoveled them into the cradle of my shirt.

"That's a wise idea, Ingrid." He reached into his jacket and
scratched his side. "I know all the hot spots. I can tell just looking at
'em which ones are ready to blow. It's like clockwork, you see. It's
a . . . a science. It's all been built by engineers, and they put in this
fancy carpet to make you forget where you're at. But I always got my
feet pointing north, so to speak."

Now that I was standing beside him, I realized how tall this man
was, and how real. I glanced around, but no one had noticed us. I
began walking toward the blackjack table in hopes that the direction
would discourage him, but as I approached, I realized that my parents
were gone. Only a couple in matching aqua fanny packs slumped at
the table now, with the dealer standing over them beaming a deck of
cards from one hand to the other. I held the corners of my shirt, the
thin fabric sagging with quarters.

The man clicked his tongue. "You're not telling me those are your folks, Ingrid—those Ohioans?" He blew a blubbering sigh through his lips. "From now on, until we find your mom and dad, you're my ward and I'm your responsi-billy-buddy." His voice descended into a register of exaggerated grown-up concern. "You sure they were here? You sure this is the table?"

I skimmed the floor, remembering how it felt to recover my mother in crowded department stores, the warm bath of relief, and willed the divine faucet to run now.

"This is exactly what the bigwigs want!" continued the man. "They create this maze—this . . . this pinball machine that gets you pinging from corner to corner and spending your hard-earned money. Hey, Ingrid, what is it you do for a living, anyway?"

"I'm just a *kid*," I told him in exasperation, tired of his games.

"Watch out! She bites!"

I approached the blackjack table as though at a certain distance the strangers' bodies would warp and dissolve, revealing my parents underneath. I got a better look at the couple and scowled at the man, the oily bulb of his chin, until he felt the heat from my gaze. The anger was for my parents, however: It was they who had left me in the casino, who muttered their adult secrets, who dismissed the loss of Lucky Frank. They had always taught me to stay put if I got lost, but I was going to teach them a lesson. I would find them in some huddle around a gambling table, and this man with the distended stomach and fractured nose would be in tow.

A solid red swath of carpet delineated a path. I merged into traffic, marching alongside a woman whose bag, hooked in the crook of her elbow, knocked against my shoulder. The unfamiliar faces parading past seemed something other than human, piscine with indifference.

"What do they look like?" asked the man, following behind me. "Are they skinny, fat, tattooed, three-legged? Who are the suspects here?"

"They're normal," I said, aggravated at his cheerful tone. "My dad's tall and he has black hair, and my mom's short with permed hair. They both wear glasses."

"Okay, that's a start." He snickered. "You've really narrowed it, narrowed it down now. Now, do you remember what they were wearing?"

I rewound the evening until my parents and I were back at the buffet. Their heads floated above the banquette, fed by two disembodied hands. When I tried to imagine their clothes, the man's yellow polo and green windbreaker hung on their translucent frames.

"I'll know them when I see them," I said.

"You know what you should do? You should dump your coins in here, and I'll take care of them for you." He rattled the bucket. "You look a little loopy, walking around like you're picking them off the . . . the bushes."

My arms were growing tired with the coins' weight. I said, "Okay, but we're counting them."

"Fair enough."

We stood to the side and dropped them, one by one, into his bucket. Each coin I surrendered deepened my anxiety, and there were eighty-eight quarters in all.

"Now, do your people play poker? Could they be playing craps? Or would they be at the slot machines like the two of us?" He twisted the white tuft of hair behind his ear and gestured erratically with his other arm.

We had wound up near the glass doors that opened to the Strip, and each time they swung open they let in new air, marinated in the sounds of music, traffic, conversation. I was tired. My parents and I had spent the day wandering through different hotels and fondling cheap souvenirs. At this point in the night, they usually deposited me in the hotel room and returned after I had fallen asleep to something on the television. Had they forgotten that I was in the arcade? I seethed with fresh anger and something more rancid, like fear.

"What do you say?" prompted the man.

"Craps," I answered, only because I remembered my surprise at my father pronouncing what I had thought was a bad word.

"I once saw a woman roll eighty two times in a row," he said. "One after another after another. It's this way, darling." He indicated where the carpet branched in another direction. "I wasn't kidding— I know my way around this place." His warm, meaty palm grasped my own, the calluses an alien topography. I jerked my hand into my chest.

"Come on, Ingrid, you got to take my hand. Minors in a casino get thrown out like day-old bread around here. You want to end up in some lost and found with a load of . . . of crunchy swim trunks and twerpy sunglasses?"

He stuck out his hand and quickened his pace so that it was a challenge to reach up and grab it. "You can call me Frank," he said. His firm, curt handshake morphed into a guiding hand as he led me to the craps tables. The radiant name that he'd pronounced gave me renewed hope. This was part of the mandalic plan of the universe.

But it was clear, and became clearer as we got close, that my parents were not there. A sour pressure built behind my eyes, and a pebble of desperation clogged my throat as the tears came.

"Hey, okay, don't be upset." He waggled our joined hands and bent his knees so that his face drifted toward mine and I could see the thin red veins threading his nose. "They're around here somewhere. One thing I'm one hundred percent certain of—and that's a conservative estimate—is that they didn't poof into thin air."

We were drawing other people's eyes, the small white movements like bulbs flickering on.

He idled, emitting a nervous, puttering energy. "Forget it, I need to visit the john," he said. We made for an illuminated sign that red MEN.

"Well, I *don't*," I snapped. "I want to keep looking."

When he laughed, his mouth was wrenched awry as though he was crying. "Miss Ingrid, you didn't have six scotch and sodas like I did."

His hand, which had been gripping my four fingers, now forced its digits between my own, and I understood that he meant for me to accompany him inside. The carpet seemed to thicken under my feet, becoming plush enough to sink into with each step. I was too young to fathom what might happen, but I could sense its large, jagged contours. I forfeited my indignation toward my parents and wished I had stayed near the arcade, where the girl would now be playing Skee-Ball, lifting one foot behind her like an ice-skater as she lobbed the stone.

"Let go, Frank," I whined. I tried to twist free, but he only tightened his hold, wringing pain from each of my fingers.

"Can't have you running loosey-goosey through the place," he said.

Now we were at the dark threshold, and the trash can outside was topped with a brass ashtray with a fungal growth of cigarette butts.

"There you are, you rascal. I have your drink." It was a cocktail waitress, and she was trotting toward us in a snug casing of blue satin and fishnet tights, trailing plumes of dark eyeshadow. Her lips spread in a wide, glossy smile as she switched her gaze to me. "And who are you? You're cute as a button."

"She's my four-leaf clover," said the man. He seemed exhausted. "Watch her for a sec, would ya, Jill? I need to take a leak." He waddled into the bathroom.

"What were you doing with Frank?" Jill set her tray of drinks on the carpet and used a black cocktail napkin to dab at the hot tears caught in my lashes, which had come as suddenly as a sneeze. "Are you lost? What's your name?"

The dark line of her cleavage and the spice of her perfume embarrassed me. I said in a shuddering voice, unable to shed the situation, "In—Ingrid."

Her brows twitched. "Okay, Ingrid, don't you worry. I'm going to help you find your parents, okay? This happens all the time. Let's go get my manager and sort this out."

I nodded. Frank emerged and bent over the water fountain, noisily sucking at the faucet before claiming his drink from the tray table.

"Fiend," said Jill, but with affection in her voice. "You've been dragging this poor girl around the casino?"

A dark veil descended over his face and lifted just as quickly. "Just doing my duty as a Good Samaritan."

"Come on, to the office we go. Let a real adult handle this."

We followed her through a door marked EMPLOYEES ONLY. The other side of the threshold was bare and corporate, lined with gray lockers that gleamed under the fluorescent lighting. Frank seemed comfortable here, tipping the glass into his mouth and placing it back on the tray, landing an echoing smack on Jill's ass with the other hand. It was a fearsome, thrilling sound that resonated down the hallway. She laughed and said, "I'm on the clock, you know."

"You never let me forget it, Jilly."

"Spare me the dramatics," she said over her shoulder. Seen in profile, her false lashes obscured her eyes, lifting and closing like the wings of a black moth. She made me aware of my eyelids and the weight of each blink, a thing I had never considered before.

Her heels clapping with metronomic precision, she led us to what appeared to be a break room. A square table held a cluster of empty beer bottles and a box of doughnuts, and there was a kitchenette with a coffee maker and a microwave.

"Oops," said Jill, placing the tray on the table. "He must have gone home."

"Oops, my ass," said Frank, pawing her closer. "This was your plan from the beginning. Admit it, Jill Marie Reynolds. You wanted to get me alone."

"My middle name," she said, placing a hand on his chest so that her back arched, "is Ramona."

"Like I give a half a damn what your middle name is." He slid a hand over her ass, lifting the lustrous fabric just enough to reveal the swell of flesh through the webbed tights. "Ramona, Ramona," he said in a low voice, his face angling toward hers in the fashion of a seedling twitching toward the sun in a time-lapse video, all jerk and quiver on its pale green stem. When they met, their mouths made slow, suckling sounds, and the breath hissed out of them as though they were angry. I recognized some of these noises from my parents' bedroom. It was an association I did not want to make. Watching them grip each other with a sidelong gaze, I felt a desirous muscle tense and twist in some unknowable corner of my body. I envied Jill, though I never wanted to be touched in that way—I envied and pitied her.

"Frank," she gasped, as though just remembering, "there's a *child* in this room."

Frank halved his eyes with his lids and said to me, "Young Ingrid, this is where we part ways."

Despite everything, I still remember that his dismissal had hurt my feelings. I felt strangely inadequate, for what, it was unclear. As the adults returned to their groping, I grasped the pail of quarters where it sat on the table and ran out the door with the bounty outstretched between two hands.

"Little bitch!" I heard him shout as the door shut. I ran back the way we had come, the quarters clapping against one another like bells on a sleigh. I heard his thudding footsteps behind me as I barreled back onto the casino floor, clipping someone's arm as I cut through the slot machines. I kept on going, tracing the frenetic path of a housefly, until a hand caught my upper arm. Panting, I looked up into the disapproving face of an older woman.

"Slow down," she said. "You're going to hurt somebody. Or yourself."

"Do you know which way the arcade is?"

The edges of her frown stabbed deeper, and she indicated a direction with her head.

"Thank you." It couldn't have been more than forty feet away. Taking long strides, I made for the sign. Now that we were on the cusp of night, women in treacherously short dresses multiplied on the casino floor, bare legs lofted on dagger heels. In the space between passing bodies, I saw my parents waiting by the door.

My father spotted me first. "Where have you been?" he barked in Mandarin. His eyebrows seemed to grow denser and darker with anger.

"Why weren't you in the arcade like we told you?" said my

mother. "And this!" She ripped the bucket of change out of my hands. "Where did you get this? Did you steal this?"

"*Ni tou de?*" echoed my father.

It was impossible to explain. I shook my head desperately. "I found it," I said. "I had to go to the bathroom and I found it there."

Frank had been right on one count—I rarely told a lie, but the daunting truth made me believe this one. I could picture myself working a dollop of soap between my palms, tiptoeing to peer into a bucket that someone had left on the countertop. I let my face reflect this version of events; my eyes project the flickering image.

My mother grabbed my father's arm and said slowly, as if trying to tease out the truth in pronouncing it, "She found the money!" I noticed then the splotches of heat at her throat and realized that they had been sipping cocktails, the same cocktails that had wavered in their cheap glasses as Jill and Frank had struggled against the table.

"If she found it, then she should turn it in," said my father.

My mother clicked her tongue, smiling deviously now. "Look at you, always trying to be the hero when it comes to cash. Why can't you take this as a sign from *shangdi*? He's trying to reward you for helping your old man." She pressed the bucket into his chest. "You earned it."

"All right, all right," he relented. "Don't overdo it with the flattery." It pleased him, however, to think that the universe had repaid him kindness for kindness.

Maybe they recognized that they needed this to quiet whatever restless thing they had aroused between them, but they said nothing else. We rode the elevator, rising with the feeling that we had really won our share. In our hotel room, the curtains were drawn, revealing the brightly freckled city. I fell asleep as soon as I rested my cheek against the pillow. I only woke once, in the desaturated hours before morning, and I could just make out a hump in my parents' bed, evolving by the second, forming and melting as if trying to escape the burden of shape once and for all.

15.

Sometimes you need to take a breather, but you've still got your partner's back. Take it to a literal level with **Back to Back**: Lie on your sides with your behinds touching as the name suggests, creating a strong pillar of mutual support.

After perusing one too many bridal magazines, my mother was determined to get crafty. Spools of lace and heaps of pressed flowers were strewn across the kitchen table, and the bachelorette party sat elbow-to-elbow as we collaged the scraps between gold-framed panes of glass. There were stationery cards for table numbers, tender photos of Marissa and Brian, signs that burbled the cocktail menu and chirped SWEETS FOR THE SWEET.

It was a torturous endeavor, but I was clearly the only one who thought so. Assembling the materials only made me aware of how badly I'd botched planning the bachelorette party. Last night, I had finally tried to book our rooms in Vegas and found virtually no block available on the Strip. We would have to stay farther away, pay an exorbitant amount for a suite, pack into a smaller room, or split up. None of these were good options. Overwhelmed by the decision, I had shut my laptop, stared at the wall. Pried it open again and pulled up Netflix. I had been ten minutes into a reality show before I remembered that Phil had mentioned connections in Vegas and I'd sent a frantic text, to which he'd answered, I'll see what I can do.

"Those colors don't go together," my mother admonished, plucking a purple sprig from Tiffany.

Tiffany, hairline pearled with sweat, swatted her away. "*Bu yao fan.* I know what I'm doing."

"What about this?" asked Joyce, one of my mother's coworkers, as she sat back from her arrangement. She spoke in a childish, lilting voice, and her eyes blinked and shifted expressively even when she was just listening. She looked to my mother now for approval, her wide-set gaze slipping between pride and uncertainty.

Marissa hummed in approval.

"Where was this taken?" Meredith, another coworker, held up a black-and-white image of my mother lifting her face to Brian's for a kiss, light trumpeting between their profiles.

"That was the proposal," said Marissa, softening. "We asked a stranger to take that on the beach, right after it happened." I remembered getting the call, my mother unintelligible on the phone, rattling off all the happy details I'd thought I was soon going to recite to her.

"It's romantic," said Meredith, and she placed it gingerly on the glass plate as though it would flake away. The oldest of the group, she had silvering, close-cropped hair and a long, mournful mouth with a slight underbite. I'd always found her to be a comforting presence. She was stalwart and rational, but warm and easily moved.

Tiffany's eyes raked over my work. "Kathleen has an eye for this stuff. Look how her little hands are working," she said. It was a compliment, but it made me furious. I'd already been feeling incompetent for not reserving the rooms; I didn't need to be patronized by Tiffany, to whom I would always be a pitiable child, which was what I'd been in her home. Her voice burrowed lower. "You know who I heard from? Luo Yuan. She went to go see the house in Los Angeles."

My mother froze, lace trapped between two scissor blades. "Not the old house?"

"The old house. I told her not to do it, but you know her. *Xin tai ruan*. She was destroyed, of course. Nothing good could have come of that."

"Which house?" I asked.

"The one she lived in with her ex-husband when they first came to the States," my mother explained. Tiffany pursed her lips in distaste, the pink flesh swelling like paste out of a tube.

Even I knew that it was a bad idea. My mother and her friends worried over Luo Yuan's life as if it were a discontinued soap opera whose ending they still hadn't digested. Over the years, I'd absorbed most of the details.

Luo Yuan had been one of Tiffany's childhood friends: a reticent girl, but kind and generous. She would buy a bag of roasted chestnuts on the way home from school and peel open the steaming shells, give you half the sweet, chalky meat. She was always at the top of her class and led the athletic drills in the morning. After college, she managed operations at a shoe factory and fell in love with the owner, a glamorous man who soared from California to Hangzhou so effortlessly that it was like moving from room to room. He was the only man she'd ever met whom she respected, who seemed like he could show her a different kind of life. They married, and she prepared for a new beginning in Los Angeles. Before she left, she saw a doctor to abort a pregnancy that would have jeopardized her immigration—something they would mourn for years.

The house was something out of a fairy tale, a pink layer cake in the Hollywood Hills. The pool cast its rippling net of light over the living room, making the paintings swim, and an endless series of palatial doors led you deeper into the gilded labyrinth. Luo Yuan had one miscarriage, and then another, and then another. He was a perfect husband through it all, and eventually she let go of her dream of having a child. Then she discovered that he had a three-year-old son with someone else, an employee from the factory back in China.

He needed someone to carry on the family name, he said, gripping her wrists when she tried to strike him. The boy's mother was poor and uneducated. She had agreed to let the child come to America; the boy could be theirs to raise and they could finally be a family, like they'd wanted. When Luo Yuan recovered her voice, she said she would only consider it if he promised to never speak to the mother again, but this he couldn't do. He had a responsibility to her, he explained, though he assured his wife that it wasn't about love—he didn't love anyone but her. In a way, he'd done this out of love, out of desperation to be with her and still have an heir.

The divorce dragged on for years and left her with nothing. Trust shattered, Luo Yuan never dated again. She often thought of the child she'd briefly carried, the daughter who might have survived if only she'd been a son.

"I don't get it," I said, smoothing the hem of a yellow poppy. "Why didn't they adopt? Why didn't they try a surrogate?"

"How many times do I have to tell you?" my mother snapped. "It just isn't done. Surrogacy isn't even legal in *Dalu*."

"You look back now and you wonder what her life would have been if she'd forgiven him," said Tiffany. "Can you imagine? Seeing the lights on in that house, knowing another woman lives there—"

"*Forgiven* him?" My voice leaped an octave. "I'd rather gouge out my own eyes than spend another minute with that man. She would've been miserable."

"When we first found out, we were all fuming. But life is long, you find," said Meredith.

Joyce swept floral crumbs into her curled palm. "It's especially hard for her during the holidays," she said. "Even though she always has a seat at our table." In the silence that ribboned outward from her statement, I remembered that she had a younger brother who was not her father's son. Everyone in the family knew except for Didi himself, though it was never discussed. Growing up, Joyce had wondered why her father was so cruel to her and so doting on him. It was because Didi's face wasn't his, she realized much later; the boy's angled cheeks and hooded eyes gave face to his wife's betrayal: a hurt he couldn't bring himself to hurt back.

"Time smooths everything," she continued. "That was something we couldn't understand back then—time. When you're young, you see everything through a magnifying glass. When you're our age, it's like the other end of a telescope."

Their hands floated over the table, ruffled through the mementos. No one wore a wedding ring, I noticed for the first time, out of separation or practicality.

"*Aiya*," said Meredith. She'd snapped a desiccated blossom in half. Something indecipherable passed over her face, but when she caught me looking, she gave her head a tiny shake and said, "Kathleen, are you ready to hear this kind of talk for an entire weekend? You sure you won't get tired of us?"

"*Buhui, buhui*," I said dutifully. Then, recognizing the opportunity, I added, "But I'll probably see some friends who'll be in town at the same time."

"Ah? Who?" asked my mother.

"LB. Andrew. Andrew's roommate. They're staying the weekend for an event."

She glared across the table at me. "So now we're working around *your* schedule?" She appealed to her friends. "*Ni kan. Zhe zhong nuer.*"

"It won't interfere with anything we're doing, I promise."

Meredith clicked her tongue. "Let her have her fun. You're lucky to have a daughter who would come in the first place—never mind plan it! Mine would never have agreed." Her daughter was often bemoaned, a poet who wore her hair half-shaved and had twice gotten arrested at protests.

My mother latched a gold frame into place, shunted it aside. "It's not their fault," she said, sighing with resignation. "They grew up here. They don't belong to us."

"Send us the booking details, will you, when you can?" asked Joyce in her gentle tone.

"Sure," I said, straining to sound lighthearted. Out of nervous habit, I checked my phone and was surprised—elated—to find an update from Phil. The Venetian okay with you? It was hard to keep from cheering. I turned the phone over and assured them, "I'll send it all over tonight."

16.

The Half Spoon is second only to The Spoon
in popularity, and for good reason—it's a huge
dose of comfort and support. One person lies
on their back with their arm outstretched to
welcome their partner, who rests their head
on the other's chest, arm and leg draped over
their human body pillow.

The lobby of the Venetian was a lavish marble colonnade. Frescoes covered the arched ceiling, each tableau riotous with figures draped in red cloth, sherbet-tinted clouds, gleaming equine musculature. Another bachelorette party bobbled in a circle with their hair piled in blond twirls. The bride-to-be wore a white tank top that read I GOT THE HUBBY, the loopy script distorted over her breasts, and her entourage sported pink versions that said WE GOT THE BUBBLY. They seemed to be waiting for a straggler to join their party, content to trill and stamp their cowboy boots on the polished floor, which had a dizzying geometric pattern that seemed to drift when I looked at it too long.

Our party stood between black velvet ropes waiting for the receptionist to check us in, essentially the opposite of the Southern belles now crouching in front of a lofted phone to take a group selfie, jostling to get their toothy grins in the frame. Our clothes were wilted by the plane ride and the onslaught of desert heat, skin tightening in the cool, sterilized air. Only my mother looked fresh, her sculpted arms and shoulders set off by a black tank top, her face with its bright, uncomplicated beauty framed by a baseball cap.

When the receptionist signaled us over with a practiced smile, I handed him the credit card that Brian had given me to use for our Vegas expenses. My mother had been unperturbed when I'd told her about it. "*Yinggai de*," she had said, as though her life had always been pillowed by cash.

We rolled our suitcases past the other bachelorette party as they huddled to compare photos. The route to the elevators skirted the edge of the cavernous casino, a golden cast to the light over the card tables. Everything seemed lubricated—cards wafting across tables into the players' hands, the wheels of our luggage quieted by the deep red carpet. In the mirrored elevator that lifted us to our rooms, I watched my mother trace her thumb along the edge of the room key and wondered if she hoped to seal her destiny here, record over our ill-fated family vacations with this new version of her life: healthy, prosperous, lucky in love.

. . .

WE GATHERED IN my mother's suite, which had a living room in addition to two queen beds lofted on a kind of dais, and an immense bathroom lined in large-veined marble. As we toured the suite and fondled its extravagances, I felt a deepening sense of indebtedness to Phil, who had convinced someone—a former client of his—to let out a few of the rooms reserved in case a VIP arrived. We drew the curtains to a landscape that had the precise beauty of a machine, far from the cartoonish theme park I remembered, the fantasy of Excalibur with its Technicolor turrets. From up here you could see clouds reflected in the glittering towers, parking structures encrusted with cars, dormant billboards waiting to flash and whirl like the innards of a pinball machine. The palm-lined Strip was a river of light and glass, and where the Imperial Palace had been now stood a gleaming metal compound.

"And now," declared Tiffany with a dramatic sweep of her arm, "it's time to decorate!"

"Decorate?" my mother repeated, changing into hotel slippers.

I unzipped my suitcase and revealed what I'd packed without her knowing: tinsel streamers, confetti-filled balloons, paper fans, pink garlands. It was unexpectedly cheering: What had been garish baubles going in now sprang forth like spools of luminous silk, and we stood bathed in its light as though we'd lifted the heavy lid of a treasure chest. My mother gasped and hid her astonished laughter behind her hand.

"I don't need all this fuss," she protested.

"You only get one second wedding," said Meredith. She drew a mass of tinsel into her arms like a magician pulling knotted scarves from a hat.

Joyce huffed a balloon into being, the rubber pulled taut to reveal the sequins inside.

We dispersed, taping the decorations on the walls, smacking the balloons across the room. We were giddy as girls—we *were* girls, and as my mother shuffled forward in her slippered feet to smack one just before it hit the carpet, I realized how rarely I'd gotten to enjoy being one with her. "Up a bit more on the left side," she directed Tiffany, who tiptoed to pin a banner to the wall, and I wondered why I'd been so doubtful of Marissa's joy—of her capacity for joy.

When we'd decked the room, we draped gold feather boas over our shoulders and poured champagne into plastic flutes—sparkling cider for my mother—and saluted her as the bride-to-be.

"To Mama," I said, raising my glass, "who deserves all the happiness that's coming to her."

EFFERVESCENT WITH champagne, we were fifteen minutes late to our appointment at the spa downstairs. As we stripped in the diffuse light of the changing room, I felt a strange sisterhood with my mother's friends. Maybe it was the luxuriant pace with which they put away their belongings, at ease with their bodies, the thrilling terrains that swept into tangles of dark pubic hair. There were heavy breasts capped by brown nipples, thin veins marbling thighs and calves, dimpled knees blooming yellow bruises. None of them shaved their armpits, and it wasn't a statement the way LB or I meant it. Their bodies had simply transcended the conversation.

Joyce, whose slight build swelled at the hips and thighs, latched the door on her wooden locker and took in my mother's hardened physique. "Marissa, when were you going to tell us about your modeling career?" she teased.

"*Nali!*" My mother pinched the skin under her arm. "Does a model have flaps like this? I've been working out for the wedding, that's all." Her muscles were softly traced by shadow, her skin baked gold. Her breasts had grown smaller, the pale weight of them drooping on her chest. When was the last time I had seen my mother's naked body? I remembered brushing my teeth as a child and my mother raking back the shower curtain to reveal her raining skin, gesturing for me to pass her the towel. Or it might have been one of those nights when she was a smear of booze on the mattress as I tried to swap her work uniform for her cotton tank top. I had loathed the unfeeling flesh, the bloat of the eyes with its sunken intelligence, like that of an octopus. I had always been tempted to leave her in her dingy underwear on top of the covers, but I had been too ashamed, mortified by the thought that come morning, we would both have to confront the way I'd left her.

In the main room, a long pool slowly pulsed green, blue, purple. In a hot tub off to the side, other nude women were steeping. Two stone angels replenished the pool at the far end, water streaming from the jugs they shouldered. Undulating wooden benches and spindly plants accented the space, and underneath our party's chatter I heard ethereal vocals and birdsong playing through the speakers.

We filed into a room wrapped in rosy Himalayan salt, each opaque brick gleaming as if lit from within. The heat was strong and dry, dense as stone. Stalagmites jutted upward from a bed of pink gravel, and a curved ledge had been carved out for seating.

We fitted ourselves, shoulder-to-shoulder, on the bench. My mother was pinned to my left, her thigh smashed against mine, and to my right was Meredith's ropy arm. Lulled and massaged by the heat, I slumped against the wall, creating an accordion of fat on my abdomen. If we had been alone, my mother would have critiqued it. Going through puberty in sixth grade, my body had tapered around the waist, and during that slender era my mother had exclaimed in delight, "*Mei la!*" as in, *You've disappeared. You're no more.* Now I was here.

It took a few minutes for the heat to cling. We were quiet, waiting to be ferried out of discomfort, dilated into bliss. I looked at everyone's feet and the pale lattices left by sandal straps. The places where our skin touched grew greasy with sweat, and when Meredith moved to wipe a meandering droplet from her temple, her oiled biceps rolled off mine. It felt familiar, her body, though the Meredith I was accustomed to wore black blouses and pearl earrings, and spritzed fragrance testers with prim decorum, so far from the wiry length of flesh that hunched beside me.

"I needed this." Joyce sighed, closing her eyes. "I can't remember the last time I sat down and did nothing for ten minutes straight."

"That's too bad," said Tiffany. "I make time for nothing every day. At the very least, I take a bath with this magnificent oil. It smells amazing—remind me to send it to you."

My mother huffed through her nose. "You must have been a peasant in a past life, to be so lucky now."

Tiffany waved her off. "Haven't I paid my dues? Wasn't my marriage enough suffering to last a lifetime?"

"I think Chen Yu has a *xiao laopo*," Meredith said suddenly, her voice steady and matter-of-fact, as though she was reading a recipe aloud. Chen Yu was her husband. We sat aghast. I shifted against the slick salt slab.

"That's nonsense," scolded Tiffany after she caught her breath. "Chen Yu? He can't even lie about the color of his shirt."

"How do you know?" asked Joyce.

"I've been having this feeling. I can't explain what it is. He's just different. I can tell when we're talking that his thoughts are somewhere else. He's been good, kind, more loving, but at the same time, more distant." Meredith winced as she pinpointed it: "He's *polite*."

"Oh, that could be anything," said my mother.

Meredith shook her head. When she spoke I could feel her muscles clench and unclench under her sweat-greased skin. I remembered the look on her face when we were talking about Luo Yuan's sadness, her devastation after the divorce. "The other day I thought I heard him talking to someone in the closet. At first I thought maybe he was just talking to himself, but then it went on a little too long. There would be a pause, like he was listening, and then he would answer in this quiet voice. Every hair on my arm was standing up. I said his name, and he immediately shut up. He must not have thought I was home— I'd just come back with the groceries. And he came out of the closet, smiling, holding a shirt he hasn't worn in months, saying, 'I found it. I thought I lost it.' And he walked right past me."

The women made low, sympathetic sounds.

"How long do you think it's been going on?" asked Joyce. She added, forcing an optimistic tone, "If that's really what's going on."

"Who's to say? It could be a month, it could be years."

"Well, you have to get the truth out of that *wangba dan*!" said Tiffany, slapping her thigh. "Let him know you're not as stupid as he thinks you are." She rocked forward and back in agitation as she spoke. "I really thought highly of Chen Yu. Out of all the husbands, he's the most even-tempered—the most willing to help around the house. When he brought me that plate of sliced oranges! I thought, *This one's well trained.*"

"You're right," said my mother. "Chen Yu *is* different. Meredith, you have to think clearly about how you approach this." She leaned past me to look her friend in the eye. "We're not young girls anymore. I'm not saying he deserves your forgiveness, but you have to decide whether this is powerful enough to destroy everything you've built together. Think of Luo Yuan, how miserable she is!"

Meredith nodded at her knees.

"Mom," I muttered.

"Paying off the house. Raising June. Taking care of your mother. He's been a dependable man."

"Mom," I said, a little more loudly, "don't you think you're being a hypocrite? You weren't so clearheaded when it was Baba."

She waved my point away. "Baba was different. I allowed the girl-friend, but I couldn't allow it becoming public."

"I've been too nauseous to think about what I'm going to do," said Meredith. "I haven't told anyone else."

"You have to sit with it," said my mother. "You have to decide: What is bearable and unbearable to you? That's all life is—"

"What do you mean, 'I allowed the girlfriend'?" I interrupted, still reeling from her statement. I gripped the edge of the bench.

My mother let her shoulders fall and looked at me. "I never told you? I knew about Leslie."

Her words shucked the heat from my body. The walls of the room seemed to vanish, the pink bricks receding into blustery darkness.

"You *knew*? How did you know?"

"He confessed."

"And you were okay with it?" I gawked at her. "I can't believe you never told me this."

"I wasn't okay with it, but I needed to live with it, do you under-stand?" My mother looked around the room. The other women al-ready knew the story, apparently, and sat in silent reverence. Her voice softened. "We were still living in Shanghai, and Baba had been gone a year. I could tell that something was wrong, so I pressed him until he told me he'd slept with someone. With her." I studied her profile, the damp hair scrawled on one cheek. Her features, glossed in sweat, seemed like simulations of the real thing. Holding her gaze was an Olympian task. "I had never heard him cry like that. I cried, too. I went completely numb. I didn't sleep or eat for weeks. Waipuo and Waigong took care of you. I lost fifteen pounds. I wanted to leave him, but I couldn't bring myself to do it. Then someone— actually, my best friend's mother—she asked me, 'Do you love him any less?' And I said, 'Well, yes—I hate him!' But it wasn't really hate. Pain, maybe, and anger, but I loved him just the same. That's the idiotic thing about love. And after I admitted that, she said, 'Do you believe him when he says he loves you just as much as before?' Today I might have come up with a different answer, but at the time I believed him. I believed *in* him. She told me, then, not to raise you on my own. She'd been through it herself, being a single mother. Besides, back then, getting to America was what everyone wanted. I couldn't do that without Baba."

I glanced at Meredith, who was bowed over her knees. "But now don't you regret it? Staying with Baba?"

She shook her head. "*Mei neme jiandan.* We could have gotten past it. I was ready to forgive him. I told him if it happened again, I didn't want to know about it. He worked hard, you have to understand. He worked himself to the bone and sent money home. And it was lonely, lonely work. I thought, if he can suffer through two years in a strange country, then I can suffer through a night or two with a strange woman."

Joyce hummed a note of recognition, and I remembered what she'd said about the magnifying glass, the telescope, how your per- spective elongated with age.

"The most painful thing—and I figured this out much later; it wasn't clear to me then—the cruelest thing was the fact that he let it get so out of hand that he couldn't control it. That he was so stupid and reckless about it, leading her on. We had an agreement. Leslie was supposed to stay a ghost, an idea, not come knocking on the door. That was the true betrayal." My mother threw her hands up. "That he chose a life with her afterward—that was easier for me to swallow than if he'd married someone else down the line. At least it led to something real."

I tried to follow her logic. "So Baba's mistake was promising Leslie too much? That's what bothered you?"

"If he promised her anything at all, it would have been too much. Who knows what he told her all those years ago, but it was enough to make her desperate."

I consulted the faces of the other women; again, they confirmed that this was the truth. I felt dumbfounded, naive.

"People expected me to be heartbroken, and I was, but not because Baba had chosen Leslie over me. Baba always chose me. But I did what I thought I was supposed to do—I cried, wailed, behaved as though I'd been blind to the whole thing. Then I figured it out. I was grieving something else, something harder to explain. I could forgive his mistakes, but I could not forgive his weakness. Weakness is part of the character. It's what allows a mistake to determine your life, to become a decision. He should have been clear with her. He should have been clear with himself. That's when I understood what he had really done to us. That's when I finally left."

"If what I think is happening is happening, how could I trust Chen Yu again?" asked Meredith.

"That depends on how he acts," said my mother, shifting her gaze back to her. "Whether he respects you. What kind of life he's invested in. But like I said, what you're willing to bear is up to you."

The conversation drifted on without me. The heat bore down with renewed intensity, and I could feel sweat coursing like pebbles between my breasts, down my back, along my arms. I would never have believed that my mother was capable of such agonized, self-sacrificing love in exchange for what she considered a better life.

As far as I knew, Oren had never been unfaithful. But he had eroded me in other ways: with his patronizing tenderness, his narcissism, his willful refusal to acknowledge that anything was wrong until it was too late. He wanted perfection, a laminated existence; I wanted to stop proving that I was worth being with. Hadn't I borne it all? Even loved him for it? A relationship could be a kind of hypnosis. It hadn't occurred to me that I deserved to be happier—or rather, it had occurred to me so constantly that it had become like the weather, an infinite drizzle, and to act on it would have involved too much risk and pain. Of course, we could have limped along, made a decent life. In the end, Oren had given us both another chance at joy. How powerful my mother had been to know her own limits, to give this to herself.

LB, ANDREW, AND LUKE arrived the next day. I left Marissa and the others wandering above the chlorine-scented canals of the Venetian, shopping bags dangling from the crooks of their elbows, to meet my friends at the Caesar's Palace pool. After the spa, my mother had said nothing else about my father's affair, and I'd been too stunned to bring it up again. All night, in the room that intermittently hummed with air-conditioning, I'd lain awake and tried to imagine the aftermath of Leslie's appearance.

I navigated the throng at the pool party. The unflinching sun gave everything a kind of digital superrealism, every taut physique impossibly smooth, reflective with oil or sweat. Some of the women were topless, baring pale triangles where their bikinis had cupped their breasts. The perfect upholstery of skin over muscle, the neat curves of waistline and calf, seemed bland in comparison with the bodies I'd seen yesterday at the spa.

Somewhere, a DJ was playing, adding a soundtrack that thrummed incongruously with the prim landscape of the pool deck, which was lined with Mediterranean trees and classical elements—white Corinthian columns that supported nothing, winged lions resting prostrate above miniature arches.

I got halfway around the pool before spotting LB stretched out on a chaise longue in a black one-piece swimsuit, sunglasses perched over her eyes like the wings of an enormous moth. I thought she might be asleep, but as I approached, her lips formed the drowsy smile of someone who had already had several beers.

"What took you so long?" She scooted over so that I could share the seat with her. The lounge tipped from side to side as I settled in, each of us hanging one leg over the edge. "The boys are getting drinks."

"Sorry. I'm moving slowly. I got, like, three hours of sleep."

"Wow. Wild night at the spa?"

"I mean, kind of." I told her the revelatory news. As I spoke, a girl started twerking in the pool, her pulsating ass slapping the surface of the water while her friends yipped encouragement.

"Holy shit," said LB when I was done. She circled the air with an open palm. "Give me a second to process all that."

"I know, right?"

"Props to Marissa for staying true to herself. I can't imagine." Her sunglasses slid down her nose so that I could see her eyelashes batting in shock. "Is there a part of you that, like, resents her for not trying?"

"Not trying?"

"For not sticking it out. With your dad."

Now it was my turn to reel. "I don't think that's even crossed my mind, her staying with him. Why would I want her to be miserable?"

"I just mean . . ." LB used her dangling leg for leverage to get higher on the seat. "You used to say, 'Oh, at least you have both your parents around.' You've never stopped loving your dad, in your complicated way. Now you know that Leslie wasn't exactly the homewrecker you always thought she was. Does a part of you wish they'd worked through it?"

It was true: I had always envied the Hinmans' full house, even though LB's mother was often in her backyard studio, assembling her grotesque sculptures. In the early years, I'd yearned for Baba to come through the door again with a rattle of keys. I would have searingly vivid dreams of the way things used to be, hallucinate the sound of sunflower seeds cracking between their teeth as my parents sat watching their favorite show. But that was a lifetime ago. Now it was painful for us to even talk on the phone.

"I can't even imagine a world where that was the reality," I said.

LB nodded. "That's fair." She adjusted the strap of her swimsuit. "I used to resent my mom for always choosing art over us. I thought of it as her choosing herself. But now when I picture what it would've been like if she'd been a quote-unquote perfect, doting mother, I just feel a sense of loss. Her work sustains her, you know? It just makes me think that families are where we first learn how cruel love can be. How every decision you make is a decision that'll affect someone you care about. I think it's pretty fucking brave, knowing that and still wanting to make new connections, date, whatever. Anyway." She gave me a wavery smile. "You can tell I'm a little lubricated."

"No, you're completely right," I said. I threaded my arm under her shoulders. "And it wasn't a bad question. God knows I resent my mom—just not for that reason."

She laughed, her breath hot on my skin.

"Getting cozy, I see." Andrew and Luke appeared, hands dangling several beers by their necks.

"I accept your offering," I said, and took a bottle.

"Sorry we took a while," said Andrew. "Luke wanted to, uh, grab something from the room."

Following his gaze, I saw something twitch in the pocket of Luke's swim trunks. The tip of Milo's nose appeared with its trembling fan of whiskers.

"Are you serious, Luke?" demanded LB. "Just—why?"

"We're definitely going to get kicked out," I said.

"That's precisely the strategy," said Luke, shielding the rat from view with his hand. "My agent says that having some Vegas posts gain traction is the best way to woo sponsorship deals. We have to prove that rats *are* on brand. They're mischievous, you know. Rascally. They capture a certain reckless joie de vivre. All I need to do is get a couple shots of him before security escorts us out."

"Sorry if you were counting on a pool day," said Andrew, and swooped down to kiss LB.

"Everyone here is out of control," she said, resettling her sunglasses.

Out of his other pocket, Luke produced a yellow patch of cloth, which he laid at the pool's edge. He scooped Milo onto the rat-size towel. I glanced at the woman in the adjacent chaise, but she was too absorbed in plucking a hair out of her mouth—pinching her flat tongue and missing—to notice anything.

Luke pulled out a Cheerio and brought it to Milo's nose. "Sit," he said, and the rat tilted back onto his haunches, gripping the treat. As he nibbled the edge of the O, his miniscule jaw working at a throttle, Luke dropped to his knees and took a series of photos with the pool in the background.

"This is what portrait mode was made for," he said, mouth hanging open in concentration.

Hearing a splash, Milo paused, protectively lowering his snack. His nostrils trembled as though following the ghost trail of a scent in a cartoon. The bright sun stroked his eyes into slits and glossed his fur, illuminated his delicate pink ears. Then the yelp I had been anticipating came from the woman who'd been cleaning her tongue.

"Oh my God, oh my God," she said, scrambling to get up from her seat. "That is a fucking *rat*, oh my God."

"Keep it down," hissed LB. "He's not hurting anybody."

"Let's wrap it up," said Andrew, looking over his shoulder.

Luke returned Milo to his pocket, where the rodent squirmed and strained against the blue camouflage fabric.

"Ew, what are you doing?" The woman whipped her head around in search of an audience. "This guy has a *rat* in his shorts."

"He's not just any rat," Luke announced to the small perimeter around us that had gone quiet. He struggled to contain Milo, whose paws now scrabbled at the top of the pocket. "He's @meetmilotherat on Instagram—check him out."

Andrew tossed back a final swallow of beer, planted the empty bottle on the table, and said, "Let's go."

The four of us gathered our things and wove through the nonplussed crowd, ducking past the phones that had extended to record our exit. "This motherfucker brought his rat to the pool," someone narrated, his voice cinched with delight. It wasn't until we entered the casino that we were stopped by a sneering security guard, who demanded that we put clothes on over our swimsuits. "Everyone thinks just because it's Vegas, anything goes," he said.

17.

We all deserve to take a load off after a long day of pounding the pavement. For **The Lap of Luxury**, one cuddler sits on the couch while the other leans against the armrest and stretches their legs across their partner's lap, conveniently positioning themselves for a foot rub (hint, hint).

Outside the convention center, Luke passed around a stack of business cards that read LUKE WINCHESTER, RAT AMBASSADOR with an embossed silhouette of Milo on the back. "Pass them out like candy," he instructed, flashing his silver card holder. Milo, in the flesh, preened himself on his owner's shoulder. Luke was endearingly overdressed in a blue collared shirt and khaki trousers, insisting that he needed to maintain a veneer of professionalism. "Every single person in there has the potential to build Milo's brand," he said. "Don't write anyone off. The owner of a parakeet store in Milwaukee can turn out to host the most popular pet podcast in North America. A dog groomer can photograph a pet calendar that sells out at Barnes and Noble. We want them to think of Milo as cute, mischievous, and relatable. A rat they'll want to align themselves with."

"How much did you pay for these?" asked LB, turning a card over and over in one hand. Around us, conference attendees ambled through the doors, many of them with dogs in tow. A woman walking a Pomeranian wore a shirt with the same Pomeranian screen-printed on it, the image pale with washing. The last time I'd been at a conference, I'd given a presentation on how glabrous (smooth) and nonglabrous (hairy) skin processed tactile information. It was liberating to be here, a witness instead of a participant, at an event that didn't intersect with anything I knew.

"Don't leave an interaction without asking to follow them on Instagram," said Luke, ignoring the question. "Make sure you're logged into @meetmilotherat. Pull out your phone, ask them what their handle is, see if they'll follow you back right then. Any questions?" he asked in a schoolteacher voice. "Okay, let's go."

We parted the membrane between the heat of the sidewalk and refrigerated commerce. The main exhibition floor was a sprawling maze of booths, some of them crude constructions of plastic tables and sagging vinyl banners, others built like professional storefronts.

"Shall we divide and conquer?" suggested Luke. He nodded at Andrew and LB. "You guys take rows one through fifteen, and we'll do sixteen through thirty. Let's meet"—he consulted the glossy program he had stuffed into his back pocket—"at one-thirty for the dog-grooming competition. By the Nationwide stage."

Andrew gave us a two-finger salute. "Good luck out there," he said.

"Where should we start? Glamorama?" I indicated a spacious booth stocked with rhinestone dog collars, the encrusted bands glitching under the corporate lighting. A slender attendant, dressed in black with a platinum-blond bouffant, busied himself with tidying a display of harnesses. At his feet was a small vanity, proportioned for a dog, with warm bulbs gleaming around a pink arched mirror. As we approached, he snapped his features into an expression of effusive welcome, eyes narrowing into arcs of pleasure. "Welcome to Glamorama, folks! Can I help you find anything today?"

"Got anything that would fit this tiny pup?" Luke indicated Milo with a bob of his chin.

"What a little cutie!" The man walked closer to give the rat a perfunctory tickle. "And who do I have the pleasure of meeting?"

"This is Milo," said Luke, forcing a business card into the exhibitor's hand. "He's cute, he's fuzzy, and he's got tons of personality. I think he'd look great in a tiny collar—we'd love to collab. He knows tricks, too. Want to see?" He straightened his arm, prompting Milo to amble from his shoulder to his palm. "Clap!" commanded Luke, and the rat touched the pads of his paws together in tiny, brief applause.

My attention drifted to the other side of the carpeted aisle, where a vendor hawked samples of organic dog treats containing CBD oil. A sign read CANNABIS? MORE LIKE CANINE BLISS! From somewhere on the exhibition floor, a loudspeaker blared the syncopated synth line from the *Space Jam* theme song, causing a red-and-blue macaw to beat its wings as it rolled past us in a giant cage.

"You get a plain pink background, right?" Luke was saying. He was standing too close to the attendant. "Then imagine Milo walks in front of the camera with a tiny rhinestone collar. And the voice-over comes in: 'Glamorama. Bling for pets of all sizes.'"

"Actually, we recommend them for dogs and cats—"

"Yeah, yeah. It's not literal. But it gets the point across, see? These are not just everyday collars and leashes. They're full of personality, they're custom *made*. Check this out." Luke pulled out his phone and replayed a story he'd posted to Milo's Instagram account. In the five-second clip, Milo yawns and stretches his paws against rumpled hotel sheets before accepting a shred of scrambled egg. The caption reads: *Room service? Don't mind if I do.* Luke thumbed into the analytics. "More than thirty-eight thousand followers, more than three thousand views in five hours. That's a great ratio. Forty-eight profile visits, sixteen replies. Huge engagement. These numbers don't lie—rats get attention. Or should I say, *this rat.*"

"Impressive," said the exhibitor, sounding entirely unimpressed.

Two women with stiff, flattened hair sauntered into the booth and began fondling the collars. "These are just too cute," declared one, angling her palm so that the merchandise winked with light. "I have to get one for Junebug."

"Good eye," said the exhibitor. "That's our bestselling mood collar. It changes color in response to temperature."

The women cooed in harmony.

"Let's stay in touch," said Luke.

"Let's," said the exhibitor, who was already drifting over to his potential customers. "Thanks for stopping by!"

"Come on," said Luke to me. He was checking his phone. "They only have six hundred followers anyway."

We wandered away and spoke to two founders, self-identified Theta Chi brothers from the University of Virginia, who had designed a smart robot—Fetcher—that could lob tennis balls up to forty feet away, amble over grass to seek them out, and suction them back into its body for "slobber sterilization." You could record your own voice saying "Good boy," they demonstrated, or "Leave it," or "I love you, Sparky." The next generation would have a motion-activated camera that sent photos to your phone while you were at work and a pop-out head scratcher. They gamely followed Milo on Instagram, though we could hear one sniggering to the other as we walked away, "Yo, what if we shot that rat through Fetcher? How sick would that be?" I patted Luke's tense biceps, oddly sympathetic to his crusade for Milo's fame.

Next we met a caricaturist with purple cat's-eye glasses who was doing portraits of owners and their pets. For the sake of getting into her good graces, Luke sat for a drawing. The finished result was all jaw and cheekbone, Milo with elephantine ears grinning on his shoulder. Still later, we watched a woman squirt an organic cleaner on a loveseat, demonstrating how it lifted odors and dried instantaneously.

"Are you sure this is the best use of our time?" I asked Luke as we approached the booth of a tick medication company. "Maybe we should look at the map and see who it makes the most sense to talk to." Someone spun the prize wheel, the clacking arrow slowing to point to FREE PLUSHIE. The toy was shaped like a giant tick and squeaked in the jaws of the wagging labradoodle that had won it.

"It's a hustle, Kathleen. It's a hustle." Luke presented his card to the man sitting behind a table cluttered with pens, stickers, pins, and brochures. "How are you doing today, sir? I wanted to introduce myself and my rat, Milo—"

"Didn't your friend just drop off a card? A minute ago. A young lady with black hair." The man frowned at the card. "Ah, no, a different rat."

Luke and I exchanged a glance. "Was her name Charlotte?" he asked.

"I don't recall. . . . She gave me this." He handed me a card. It was thick, matte black, with silver lettering. The front featured an ornate rat illustration, wreathed with flowers, and the back was an Instagram handle—@nightshade_andnymph.

Luke stalked away without saying goodbye to the man, bringing up the account on his phone. I recognized the raven-haired woman and her two rats as the competition he'd complained about on acid.

"You've mentioned her before," I said.

"Yeah," he said, thumbing in and out of the images in agitation. "She's been doing sponsored posts like crazy. Like, look at this." *Lately I've been feeling uninspired*, she'd typed underneath a selfie taken in bed, camera angled down from above. You could see two rats huddled at her collarbone and the lacy trim of a black cami. *I've gotten so lost in work, family obligations, and friend dramas that I haven't taken any time for myself. I haven't written a song in too long—coming from someone who used to rush to the keyboard every day. But you have to trust the process. Feeling blessed to have my furbabies to keep things in perspective, and trying to take a page from their book and greet every morning as curious and carefree as possible, which is honestly so much easier to do after a good night's sleep in my new Lemon Baby pajamas. Big love to all. Never lose your spark! #ad*

Luke turned one palm up in disbelief. "This is such bullshit. You can hardly see the rats. It's essentially a vanity account."

"Luke, have you seen Instagram? Personal branding is what it's for."

He darkened the screen and shoved the phone into his back pocket. "There's no integrity left in this world."

I bristled. "I didn't realize your mission to make Milo America's sweetheart was rooted in integrity," I muttered.

Luke stared into the middle distance and didn't answer. Maybe he hadn't heard me, and that was just as well. I didn't feel like having a debate about whose bid for clout was more legitimate or how infuriating it was to be a woman online—scrutinized for perfection, but crucified for inauthenticity.

"You want to take a break?" I asked. "Are you hungry?"

"Yeah," he said in a defeated tone. "I want a corn dog."

The pet carrier we retrieved from the lockers had a fleece interior and mesh windows. Milo seemed relieved to be sheltered, and part of me wished I could crawl into a dark, plush room of my own. I was tired of canvassing the exhibitions, and my feet were feeling tender. When we reached the food court, we discovered Andrew and LB seated at a table, sharing a banana split. The paper canoe between them held a mangled log of fruit and a deflated skirt of whipped cream.

"You want a bite?" LB waved her plastic spoon at us.

Luke was too impassioned by the emergence of his nemesis. He showed them the account and spat, "She's good-looking, that's all it is." I let his tirade fade into the background and listened to the convention drone on: the blur of overlapping conversations, an announcement reverberating over the floor. I watched a black poodle stop in its tracks to indulge a shimmy that passed from its hind legs to its head, all blur and jingle. I was struck with envy for its little life, its few desires—a snippet of praise, a twist of rawhide—that induced waves of uncomplicated joy.

The television screens mounted above the concession stands, which had been displaying local advertisements, turned blue and then twitched again, displaying footage of a row of dogs onstage. They were fancifully groomed and dyed, panting on pedestals as their handlers finessed their diaphanous tails.

"The grooming competition!" said LB. "Can we go watch?"

Most of the folding chairs were taken by the time we reached the stage, which was presided over by another giant monitor. The emcee, a woman wearing glasses on a thin gold chain, introduced the contestants. Poodles and bichons masqueraded as zebras with black manes and dyed stripes or as circus clowns with strap-on hats. One was a convincing camel with a hump of fur and bright tassels hanging from a braided muzzle.

"And here is Disco Danger and his mom, Karen," said the emcee, "coming to us from San Diego, California!" The groomer, who wore a bright yellow caftan, a floral crown, and heart-shaped sunglasses, leaned into the emcee's ear. "Sorry, from San Clemente, that is! Karen, what inspired this look today?"

"Well, as you can see, Disco here is all about flower power," cooed Karen. The bichon wore an exaggerated brown 'fro, and its chest had been colored to form a tie-dye T-shirt. Poufs of fur ringed its ankles, which had been rigged with LED lights. "He preaches peace and love—and most of all, he loves to dance."

"And I hear you have a little presentation for us," said the host. "Let's see it!"

Karen said something, the words too faint to be picked up by the microphone. Bringing out her phone, she tapped the screen and "Shake Your Groove Thing" began playing through a speaker on the table. She skipped ahead a couple of times until she found the chorus and then she bounced on her heels, waving her hand to encourage Disco Danger to trot in place and wag its tail. I traded looks with LB as the dance grew too long, the shoddy audio sabotaging the effusive spirit of the song. The host and contestant persevered, however, with cemented smiles.

"Show 'em how we do it now," the host sang along tunelessly. "Thank you! Karen and Disco Danger, everybody, from San Diego, California!" The groomer spoke into her ear. "I mean, San Clemente!"

I leaned forward through the applause to snicker to LB, but stopped short, confused. Phil was standing among the spectators at the end of the row. I did a double take, so mystified that Andrew had to physically stay my hands from clapping after the rest of the crowd had gone silent.

"What's wrong?" whispered LB, reading my face.

My eyes were still glued on him: black T-shirt, jeans, the unmistakable gray-streaked hair and beard. "That's one of my clients," I spat out. "That's Phil."

"What the fuck? Why is he here?"

I shook my head and sat back in the seat, heart ricocheting in my chest as the initial shock gave way to a cold, seeping fear. I searched for a reason for him to be here but came up empty. I remembered his volley of questions, our picnic by the lake. His curiosity about the pet expo. He'd done research, then. It still made little sense: He'd bought a ticket, booked a flight, checked into a hotel, idled at the convention until he found me? Every realization wrenched my insides into a tighter knot. I stared at the stage, comprehending nothing of the manicured dogs, the emcee's banter. When I finally glanced at Phil

again, something shifted. I sat up straighter in my seat, fortified by a
bolt of anger. I'd trusted him, batted away my doubts in hopes that it
could be true: a man offering up his vulnerability with no expectation
of anything in return. I felt stupid. He'd made me stupid.

"Want me to get rid of him?" said Andrew under his breath.

"No, it's okay," I said. "I'll go talk to him. I want to figure out
what's going on."

"Isn't it obvious?" hissed LB. "He's *stalking* you, is what's going on."

"I'm going to go talk to him," I repeated.

"Please don't."

"What do you want me to do, hide in a corner?"

She groaned. "No. But be careful."

I heaved a breath, bracing my hands against my thighs, and then
willed myself out of the chair. Phil was laughing as I approached, and
as his chuckle subsided he turned toward me, betraying no surprise
or sheepishness, only pleasure. My hands felt clammy and useless. I
scrabbled for something to say as I got close.

"Hi," I said. "It's—I'm surprised you're here."

"That's the point," said Phil, wrapping my stiff body in a hug.
"Surprise!"

I looked around at strangers' faces, each one facing the stage in
rapt attention. "Can we step aside for a sec?"

"Sure, sure," he said in his slow, genial way.

We walked to the back of the auditorium. "I'm going to be honest," I said, my words clipped in frustration. "This is freaking me out. What are you doing here, exactly?"

Confusion pinched his face for a moment and then he gestured vaguely at the booths around us. "I have a buddy who was contracted to design the Purina exhibit. He had an extra ticket, and I knew you were going to be here, so I thought I'd come."

"The Purina exhibit."

"Have you seen it? It's all about health and better design for dogs. They have these midcentury-inspired beds—"

"Why didn't you tell me you were coming?"

"It was a last-minute decision, to be honest."

I stared at him with my arms crossed. "Why are you pretending that this is a normal, perfectly okay thing to do?"

"I didn't think—" His cheerful tone finally cracked and he fingered his beard in agitation. "I knew I was going out on a limb, but I didn't think you'd be angry. I only got the ticket because I was calling on old friends, trying to hustle up some accommodations for you, if you remember that request." A sandbag of guilt and regret punched into my stomach. "Look, I know we've been operating in a gray area. Here, this is white space. Standing here right now, I'm not your client." He paused, eyes darting back and forth. I studied the texture of his skin, the widening pores of his nose, the shape of his mouth as it twitched toward the words: a face I knew so intimately in one context that had become frightening in another. "It's just me. You know me."

His words conjured a great distance between us, his body receding into the blank, liminal, nameless country he described. His shrinking figure made it clear that I didn't know him, really. I'd only seen him up close, huddled in fantasy. Being cocooned in his arms had made it easy for me to confuse him with somebody else. I remembered how I'd woken up beside him at Midas Touch with no memory of the slow sink into sleep. I was confused, the room illegible. For one blissful, lilting moment, I thought that I was in the apartment Oren and I'd shared in Baltimore, and that it was Oren's arm clutching me to his chest.

"What time is it?" I had murmured, expecting to hear a leisurely morning hour—9:45 or 10:15 on a Saturday, time enough to twist ourselves into a knot of bleary kisses and half-dreamed sex, yellow light from the sun making our skin gleam, time enough to rock each other into oblivion. Then, as we cooled and grew tacky with drying sweat, we'd begin to crudely shape the day, map its boundaries, savor the possibilities. We could visit the new place for brunch if the wait wasn't too long. Or we could put our names in and spend the intervening time at the farmers market. We were out of tomatoes, we could get some fancy mushrooms, we could each pick out a type of mushroom we'd never had before.

But it wasn't Oren that day, of course. Phil said, "Four fifty," which meant we had ten minutes left in the session, and that I'd slept through nearly the entire thing. I hadn't known I was so tired. The Midas Touch bedroom was exhausting to look at, to exist in. I turned to Phil, meaning to apologize for falling asleep, but he began to trace the contours of my face, lashes downcast, fitting a fingertip briefly in the Cupid's bow of my lip before outlining my chin. It had been so quiet, so gentle, that it had brought hot, sudden tears.

Now, adrift in this new space, I understood the vast sweep of Phil's loneliness. I couldn't, I knew, do anything to really help him, or I was in the wrong kind of work to help him.

"Phil, I think we're in over our heads." The next words brimmed in my throat before I spoke them. "I think it's best if we don't see each other anymore."

His head fell forward as though his neck had been cut. "Not even at Midas Touch?" His voice sounded high and far away.

I shook my head. "There are lots of other cuddlers."

"Let's take a second, okay?" He sighed, regrouped. "Look, I get it. This is weird. There's a lot of unanswered questions. Maybe we can get a quick drink and talk things through."

"I'm not—" I threw up my hands. "I don't have time to explain this to you." I gestured at us, the stage. "Clearly, this has gotten out of hand." Pivoting, I caught LB's eye and signaled that I needed help with wide eyes. "This is way over the boundary of what's safe or acceptable."

"*Safe?*" He frowned. "What do you mean, 'safe'? You think with me being here, you're in danger? Do me a favor and at least tell me the truth, which is that you're a coward. You weren't talking about things being safe or acceptable when we met at the lake, or when I drove you home and listened to you complain about school and your ex and the wedding. Or when you asked me to fix your mistake with the hotel rooms." He grasped my shoulders. "We were getting some-where. We're good together." He paused, his eyes glossy and amphib-ian. "But as soon as I make a real gesture—well, you're a consummate professional."

It was my turn to stare at the floor, unsure of my footing. I couldn't deny the fact that it was my fault that Phil was here, holding my hands and pressing his thumbs against my knuckles while purebreds with baroque haircuts promenaded across the stage. I'd been reck-less, selfish, willfully dumb to what had been happening, and I couldn't come up with a suitable defense.

"I'm sorry," I said, all of a sudden remembering the way Leslie Fang had appeared on my family's doorstep, announcing her existence in flesh and blood. I saw now how easy it was to lose control of a situ-ation, how two people could convince each other the mirage was real. For the first time in my life, I felt a wisp of what Baba must have felt that night. "It's my fault. I didn't mean for any of this to happen."

18.

> **The Stargazer** is simple and sweet. Both
> cuddlers lie on their back with elbows hooked
> and legs crisscrossed. True to its name, it'll
> make you feel like you're lying on a picnic
> blanket counting the stars—or counting sheep
> while you drift off to sleep.

Back in the hotel room, I sat on my heels on the crisply made bed and stared at myself in the mirror. Then I bowed forward, letting my forehead rest on two fists. I heard text messages dinging, their steady insistence marking the cadence of Phil's speech. The yellow broth of light thinned to a husk of blue, and then I got up to get dressed for dinner.

I'D HAD TOO MUCH to drink at the sushi restaurant—we all had, with the exception of Marissa. To dull my anxiety, I had saturated myself in Japanese highballs and now I moved with the giddy bloat of a balloon. We squealed as we entered our private karaoke room, its dimness pierced by a fan of lasers that pulsed from green to red to blue. Red leather benches padded three walls and on the table was the carafe of lychee-flavored soju we'd ordered beforehand, along with the props of our evening. Tiffany swooped up the tambourine and began beating it against her thigh, drowning out whatever she said next. Collapsing onto the bench, Meredith picked up a microphone and said, in an announcer's baritone, "Ladies and gentlemen, please welcome our lovely Marissa Cheng to the stage!"

"No, no, I'm not singing first," my mother protested, scooching around the table until she was as far from the TV as possible.

"Fine—I'll pick a song." Meredith drew a tome of a binder into her lap and began flipping through the plastic-covered pages.

Tiffany poured the soju cocktail into four glasses and pushed them into our hands. Then she gripped the other microphone and took a deep breath, holding her drink in the air, the creamy liquid catching the colored beams. "Marissa," she said, and released a gust of giggles. "I don't have anything to say. I just wanted to hold the microphone." Her eyes narrowed into mischievous slits. "I promise I'll be more prepared at your wedding. *Ganbei!*"

We drank down the sweetness and tartness, and my mother took a swig of her sparkling water. She was being a good sport about the tipsy chatter, the blustery, red-cheeked commotion. Her smile stretched like a hammock, long and easy, and she wore a white eyelet sundress that skimmed her body in an expensive way. She'd bought it yesterday and snapped the tag off as though performing a magic trick: *I wanted it, and voilà—now it's mine.*

"I've got one, I've got one," said Meredith, and punched the numbers on a remote. A pert disco beat started, joined by a blithe synth as the camera pulled back to reveal a young woman with a wave of blond hair pedaling along a beach boardwalk, ass straining against frayed jean shorts. Her knees pumped, liquid with leisure, then faded out to swaying palm trees. "Gotta make a move to a town that's right for me," crooned Meredith, bouncing in her seat. I cackled.

"Town to keep me movin', keep me groovin' with some energy," joined Joyce in high, precise tones, her shoulders bobbing up and down.

"Well, I talk about it, talk about it, talk about it, talk about it," we sang. I heard my mother's voice, coarse and flat, beside me. Her lumbering notes were like an alligator's stiff-backed advance through the marsh, magnificent and prehistoric. I'd always loved to hear her sing, but this song was foreign to her, I realized, as she struggled to keep up with the lyrics careening neon across the screen.

"Let's sing something we all know," I yelled into her ear. I was aware that I was trying to manufacture something—a memory, an anecdote I could tell someone who asked about the bachelorette party. I wanted proof that I'd done a good job, made her happy, that our confused roots could still produce petals of joy.

I leaned over the pages of the binder. The first half was all in Chinese, characters that I recognized but that were as mute to me as the neighbors I watched through glass. I used my phone to illuminate the pages and gestured for my mom to pick. She pored over the text, and I listed from side to side, singing snatches of song. Finally, she called out the numbers. I punched them in the remote, interrupting the video as the blond woman danced in the surf, ankle-deep in foam.

The screen went blue, prompting screeches of protest. Then rose petals crowded the screen, dewdrops stippling the pink folds. A high, breezy flute melody began, and the women cooed in recognition. I hadn't heard it in years, but it was deeply familiar to me—a song that had seeped into my childhood landscape. Perhaps it had played on the Chinese radio station or been sung during Chunwan, the New Year television special that riveted my mother each February. She'd squawk for me to sit beside her during a particularly impressive performance—ribbon dancers undulating in hypnotic synchrony, silk unfurling around prancing legs—and declare, "Look how *zhengqi* this is. Americans could never be this precise. Only Chinese people know how to suffer and work this hard."

The women crooned the lyrics, which I'd never paid attention to before. *Dark nights then bright days, dark nights then bright days. How much joy and sorrow does one life hold?* Their voices jostled one another's, wavering in their separate keys, but they burst into the chorus as one triumphant chord. *Spring goes, spring returns. Flowers wither, flowers will bloom again. As long as you're willing, dreams describe the tides of your heart.*

By the last chorus, I was singing along. It felt strange and exhilarating to sing in this tongue, the unfamiliar sounds rising from my throat a kind of incantation. It was so rare to feel like my mother and I had come from the same place. Our bodies swayed in the darkness, pinpoints of blue light on our skin like stars sunk in a deep pool. I remembered the New Year's spectacle on CCTV, the dancers' limbs exploding with sheets of red fabric, the supple lengths like leaping mountains.

I WOKE IN THE DARK hotel room and slumped into the bathroom, clipping the edge of the bed, and kept the lights off as the toilet bowl resounded with pee. The floor rocked like a cradle. There was a knock at the door—probably not the first, I thought, a soft, dumb realization in a sedated state. I padded to the door and opened it a sliver, squinting at my mother's face.

"Mom?"

"I couldn't sleep," she said in a timid, childish voice. "Can I come in?"

I yawned, nodding, and let her in. She got into my bed, shimmied under the covers. We lay face-to-face, her expression vague in the dark. "What's wrong?" I asked, feeling the irresistible weight of sleep collect on my eyelids. I could taste my own sour mouth.

"It's nothing," she said. "Probably just too wound up from all that singing."

"Mmm."

"I might not have a voice tomorrow."

"Mmm." I tried to ignore the nausea awakening in my stomach. "Did you have fun?"

Her cold toes brushed my legs. "I had a lot of fun." She brought an arm over the comforter. "These beds are so nice. My mattress at home dips down on one side, you know. The side I sleep on."

A clomping in the hallway announced a drunken group heading back to someone's room. Someone was trilling about ordering pizza; someone else was violently shushing the others, cutting through the giggles and hiccups.

"I can't stop thinking about the future," she said after they'd passed down the hall. She kept prodding me with her cold toes and then our feet wove together, our calves stacked one over the other. "With Brian."

"In a good way or bad way?"

"Mostly good," she said. "It's not like when I married Baba. Back then, I was wondering what it would be like to be a wife." *An American, a mother,* she might have said, too, her hushed voice filling my delirious head.

"Now you know what it's like," I said.

"But I don't know how to be me." Her head shifted on the pillow. "The new me. Who I'm supposed to be."

I had visions of her body morphing, melting down to her ankles like a candle. "That's okay. Me neither."

As the seconds ticked past, the bed seemed to grow, the mattress creeping forward in all directions.

"Do you miss Oren?" she asked.

I answered from a foggy, faraway place. "All the time."

"That will pass. Grief is a long train, but eventually it will pass."

"Mmm."

"*Hao. Ni shui ba.*" The last thing I remembered was how strange it was to be drunk in a listing bed while my mother lay awake, being comforted by her small, tender words, when so many times it had been the other way around.

19.

If your cuddle partner is in low spirits, **Sleepyhead** is just the thing to get them riding high again. Sit cross-legged on the bed, then guide them onto their side so that their head falls in the cradle you've made. Pro tip: Now's a great time to incorporate some gentle head or back scratches.

The second day of the conference attracted an even denser crowd that was now wearing the swag they'd collected the day before: baseball caps embroidered with company logos, buttons pinned to tote bags, cheap sunglasses with neon-green arms. I scanned the crowd, but Phil did not appear.

Luke was in low spirits and had returned to his uniform of T-shirt and drooping jeans, leaving Milo in the care of the convention's pet sitters. Though we'd tried to talk him out of it, he was adamant that the four of us attend a panel featuring Charlotte—@nightshade_ andnymph—as one of the speakers. I'd agreed to come as moral support before meeting my mother and the others for lunch.

Far removed from the pomp of yesterday's grooming competition, the panel was being held in a nondescript side room. It was half-full of attendees slumped in their folding chairs, leafing through their programs. At the front of the room, three speakers sat behind a table, water bottles placed at neat intervals. Charlotte was easy to identify. Her black hair was straightened to a prismatic sheen. She wore a black choker and an emerald lace dress with voluptuous bell sleeves. Seated between a man in a bowling shirt and a teenage boy in a backward cap, she looked decidedly out of place.

"Come on," said Luke, marching down the aisle. "We need to be in the front row for this shit."

It was strange, being able to anonymously study the face of someone, like sitting behind a one-way mirror. Charlotte used the camera on her phone to check her makeup, pivoting to examine one cheekbone, then the other. When she set it down, her eyes fell directly on us, the gaze easy and unknowing.

The moderator walked onstage wearing a loose linen tunic, her gray hair plaited down her back. "Good morning, everybody, and welcome to Rats, Snakes, and Spiders—Oh, My!, where we're going to talk about the popular narratives surrounding these less favored pets, and whether or not they're truly deserved," she said, smiling at the crowd from her tall director's chair. "By a show of hands, how many of you in the audience have, or *have had*, a rodent, reptile, or an

arachnid pet?" Her voice was warm and full-throated, the last conso-
nant a gentle percussive into the microphone. I looked around in the
dim room and was surprised to see that the seats had filled up; the
majority of people were raising their hands.

"Excellent," she said. "I can tell this is a topic that's close to home
for many of us—myself included." She raised her hand, wiggled
her long fingers. "I'm your moderator, Julia Kurtzman. Before we
start, I'd like to introduce our panelists. Here on my right, we have
Tyler Keane, whom many of you know from YouTube." A chorus of
hoots rose from the room. Tyler, hunched over folded arms, tucked
his lips and gave a short wave. "Tyler has had more than forty tarantulas, starting at the age of twelve, and is currently taking care of
seven.

"Next we have Charlotte Raines, who is the mother of rats Nightshade and Nymph, as well as the grandmother to a healthy litter of
growing pups! Last year, Charlotte and her rats appeared in a docu-
mentary about a close-knit group of rat owners in Portland, Oregon,
and since then her furry family has become an Instagram sensation."
Charlotte used the back of her hand to push a length of hair over her
shoulder and smiled coyly as applause peppered the room. "And last
but not least, you have Michael Rodriguez, otherwise known as the
Snake Man. Michael has been breeding snakes in Michigan for the
past six years and has lent his expertise to television programs like
Animal Planet and *Good Morning, America*." Michael grinned and
winked at the front row, nodding through the clapping as though as-
suring us his biography was correct.

"My first question is for Tyler," said Julia. "How do people react when they find out you keep pet tarantulas?"

Tyler reached for the microphone lying on the table and considered before drawling, "You know, the immediate reaction is, like, being surprised and grossed out. They're, like, 'Whoa, dude, I can't believe—of all the pets you could have, like, cats and dogs and whatnot, you have a pet tarantula?' You definitely get some funny looks."

"And how do you respond?" asked Julia.

Tyler pulled at a cord on his hoodie, cinching the fabric around his neck. "Well, I tell them to check out my YouTube—Spider Tyler, hit that Subscribe button—or I try to explain, like, depending on the breed, tarantulas are super friendly, they're easy to take care of, don't take up a lot of space, plus they're fuzzy, so, like, for me it's, like, why do you have a dog, bruh?"

Julia shifted her gaze. "Charlotte and Michael, have you faced similar reactions when you talk about your animals?"

Michael leaned forward and intercepted the microphone. "You know, my experience is different because most of the time if you meet me, and it's a small town where I live, you already know I'm the Snake Man." He had a hoarse voice and rocked back and forth as he spoke. "So there's a lot of curiosity—the usual 'Is it dangerous?', 'Have you ever been bit?' kind of thing. And I'm always happy to answer. The more I can educate people about snakes, the better. I get kids, schools, to come to the facility and tour, and they get real excited."

It was Charlotte's turn. She held the microphone limply, far from her mouth. Her voice was airy and high-pitched. "Yeah, I've gotten some weird looks. People are a little taken aback that a woman would keep pet rats. But to me it makes a ton of sense. I consider myself a modern-day witch, you know"—Luke groaned beside me—"and my pet rats hold a lot of meaning for me in that sense. Rats and witches have been tied together since medieval times, when rats embodied plague and, like, disease, and witches were seen as pests. I think it's powerful to be able to reappropriate that history and celebrate feminine power and its ties to nature."

"What bullshit," muttered Luke, this time loud enough to draw Charlotte's eye. Her lips bowed in a subtle frown, and she wrenched the neck of her water bottle to break the seal. I pinched the skin above his elbow, and he jerked his arm away. "Ow. What's your problem?"

"That's a fascinating history," said Julia. "Speaking of which, I'd love to hear about each of your firsts. Who was your first rat?"

"My first rat was a dwarf named Jasper. He was an absolute sweetheart. I was maybe twelve or thirteen, and my mom was not pleased with having a rat in the house, but she warmed up to him. I learned so much through Jasper—that male rats mark their territory with urine, for example. I got peed on a lot." She laughed, a series of squeaks and wheezes.

"That's a fake laugh," said Luke, even more audibly, attracting more eyes.

"Luke, shut the fuck up," whispered LB.

His comments continued, however, for the rest of the talk, though Charlotte betrayed no further sign of hearing them. Finally Julia said, "Let's open it up to the audience. If you have a question, please line up at the mic in the center aisle."

"Luke, I forbid you," LB said, her voice thick with warning. "Let this poor woman post her selfies in peace."

"If she can't handle a little heat," said Luke, half out of his seat, "then she shouldn't be in the public eye."

"What are you going to ask?" I said, but couldn't wait for the answer because, just beyond Luke, there was Phil, sauntering down the aisle and coming to a stop at a respectful distance from the person at the microphone, hands tucked into his pockets. Though we were no more than ten feet apart, he kept his eyes trained on the stage as though he knew that as soon as he looked in our direction, we would scatter. For now, the shock of seeing him again rooted us all in our chairs.

Then it was his turn. "This question is for Charlotte," he said.

She accepted the microphone from Tyler, lace sleeves brushing the table.

"My friend here has a rat named Milo, and Milo, like you, has a sizable internet presence." Phil indicated our row with a raised hand, causing Luke to deflate in his seat. "You might know him, actually. He's @meetmilotherat on Instagram."

"I'm not familiar," said Charlotte. If she felt any hostility toward her heckler, she kept it out of her voice.

"Well, I suggest you give him a follow," said Phil. "Anyway, my question for you is, do you have any tips for growing an online audience and reaching other rat aficionados on social media?"

Charlotte drew a breath and rolled her shoulders down her back, holding the microphone with both hands as though it were a bouquet. "I have lots of tips," she said, looking not at Phil but directly at Luke, who sat frozen. "I'll skip over the basics, but something that wasn't immediately obvious to me in the beginning was the importance of having a color palette—like, a family of colors that become part of this visual language and ultimately part of your brand." She went on, but the words shed their meanings, like insects walking out of their crisp shells, as I stewed in quiet panic. I kept my eyes trained on her, knowing that the longer she spoke, the more time I would have between now and whatever happened next.

I turned to LB and whispered, "I'm going to go." She nodded vigorously.

Clutching my tote bag, I crab-walked out of the row and hurried out of the room into the echoing main hall. I trotted across the polished floor tiles toward the exit, hoping to become just another body in the crowd, but as I leaned my weight against the push bar of the door leading outside, I heard my name.

"Please wait," he was saying. "Kathleen."

For a few paces, I waded out into the relentless heat and brightness, squinting at the palm-lined street and the air boiling above the hoods of cars. Then I stopped.

"Can we just talk?" he asked, now at my side, screwing up his eyes against the light. "Are you done running?"

I agreed with a half nod. He cast around for a place to sit and indicated the jagged shade of a white-tipped shrub. We settled down on the concrete edge of the planter.

"What was that in there?" I asked.

He shrugged. "I was just trying to be helpful. I knew you guys would be there—I mean, stuff like that is what you came here for, isn't it?"

A scrawl of ants traced a crack in the pavement. "And what did *you* come here for?" I nudged the line with my foot and sent them scattering like beads. "Like, best-case scenario, what was going to happen?"

He blew air past his lips. "I don't know what I was hoping for. I wanted to see you; that much I had figured out. I wanted you to see me in the crowd, I guess, and smile and wave. I wanted to do this." He closed the few inches between us and reached for my hand, meshing his fingers with mine. It felt bulky, foreign, obscene. Like something humans didn't do. I sat with it for as long as I could out of a sense of obligation—even now, I felt like I owed him something, both as a client and as someone with whom I'd become embroiled— and then withdrew my hand.

"And then what?" I asked. "We'd go for a drink on the Strip? We'd get drunk and go to a twenty-four-hour chapel?"

"Don't make this a joke."

I rolled the ball of my foot over an ant. From underneath, it crawled out, quivering.

"Listen, you think any of this computes?" He gave a short, mirthless snort of laughter. "You think I don't know how ridiculous this looks, how desperate? I don't know what's going on either. I just wanted to be here. It sounds stupid, but it's as simple as that."

"But to what end?" I insisted.

"You keep asking me that. As if I knew the future. Do you know where you're headed now? Are you making decisions with absolute clarity and intention?"

"I'm not indulging a shared delusion." Even as I said the flinty words, I tasted their falseness. I meant to rebuke myself as much as him, but I was diminishing things. Whatever distorted ideas we'd harbored about the situation, whatever private narratives we'd concocted, our bodies had been undeniably real. The way he'd grazed my arms with his fingertips had been real, and the weight of his leg over mine had been real. Those glimmers of arousal had been real.

"A delusion." His voice stiffened. "I may be just some weird, lonely man to you, but I think I know the difference between what's transactional and what's authentic." He held my gaze, jaw clenched, ready for more unkind words, but when I couldn't muster any, the hardness gave way. He said in a depleted voice, "Are you telling me you're not the least bit happy to see me?"

I ached for a breeze, for a small consolation in the sweltering heat, but the air was still and stifling. I scoured myself for signs of happiness and perhaps a version of it was there: the blunt satisfaction of being wanted and being known. It was a relief to confront my affection for Phil—a relief, even, to see how situational it was. It existed in the roles we'd assigned each other when we clung together in bed. Here, in the sun-bleached clarity of the desert, I felt the urge to split, like a roach thrown into the light.

Encouraged by my hesitation, he pressed on. "Think what we

could be outside the clinic. We could go out for a drink, see a concert. Take a trip up the coast, even. Spend a weekend in a cabin somewhere doing nothing. You can read in bed in that old sweater while I make breakfast."

I saw what he saw—the wood hut and split logs stacked by the stove, the windows filled with redwoods, a bleary figure in the sweater—a scene I'd cruelly helped him stage. I'd allowed myself to be a conduit, regurgitating memories that he'd fed me, animating the husk of his relationship with Diane.

"Phil," I said, putting my hands on his knees, "I'm not the person you want."

"What are you talking about? Did you not just hear me?"

"Who you want is Diane, and I can never be her."

He jerked his face away, as though shaking his head but freezing in motion.

"I think we were both trying to take the contents of one relationship and pour it into something else." There had been so much lost between me and Oren—a whole irretrievable universe we'd assembled out of private rituals—and I'd used Phil as a surrogate for that intimacy. But hadn't it been mutual? It was hard to parse where the power lay; he had paid for my time and touch, but I had encouraged him past the platonic with the authority of the professional. And now, I realized, I was ready to stand alone, while Phil was more entangled than ever. "I let things go too far," I continued. "It was selfish, and I'm really, really sorry." The words were flat and clichéd, but they were all I could muster.

Phil made no response, but after a few minutes of devastated silence, he tipped onto his side and put his head in my lap. I threaded my fingers through his hair, felt the grease on his scalp as I raked through the folds. Sour pressure gathered behind my eyes as I palmed the warmth of his head. Despite everything, I would miss this sweetness and goodness. There would be shame going forward, I knew, and grisly realizations of how we'd used each other, which was also a strain of love. For now, I sat with him. People crossing the plaza outside of the convention center lassoed us with curious looks, but the only one who disturbed us was a panting retriever who huffed the planter and smiled at us with a spit-flecked tongue.

Then I saw my mother stepping out of the rental car several feet from where we sat. I waited until the last moment to stir, raising Phil's head out of my lap as though rousing a child.

"I have to go," I said, and he nodded, avoiding my mother's eye.

I waited, but she asked no questions as we drove to meet her friends. I was grateful. What could I have said that she didn't know already?

20.

Though the temperature was forecast to reach 110 degrees on our last day in Vegas, my mother convinced the four of us to drive to a trailhead in Red Rock Canyon, the air conditioner cranked so high that we had to strain our voices above it. Crouched in the middle seat, I watched an Instagram story that @nightshade_andnymph had shared and that Luke had reposted on Milo's account. Apparently, he had stuck around after the panel to talk to Charlotte. Service grew frail as we left the sprawl of tract homes and adult superstores, making the video stutter and blur.

"Hey, guys," said Charlotte in a bubbly tone. The camera was held high, angled downward to fit her and Luke's faces in the frame. She looked radiant, all crisp eyeliner and accentuated cheekbone, while Luke looked dazed. "I'm here at Petopia in Las Vegas, and guess who I just ran into—my friend Luke, who runs the account over at @meetmilotherat." As she spoke, she moved the phone around to capture the background, pivoting to stay in frame, though Luke kept drifting out of view. "Milo's a total cutie who will steal your heart—definitely go check him out. Always love running into fellow rat geeks!" She'd tagged Milo in the video. When I clicked on it, I saw that the rat had gained another two hundred followers since yesterday. Shortly after, my screen stopped loading, the ouroboros indicator stuck in mid-swallow.

I dropped the phone in my lap. Phil's question must have forced Luke to introduce himself. I pictured a mortified blush on his cheeks, the resentment softening to repentance during the conversation. I admired Charlotte for being able to endure the life of an influencer, being the subject of so many parasocial relationships—some of which, I imagined, were hateful. She seemed self-assured or maybe hardened. I wouldn't have wanted to read her direct messages.

Buildings and billboards lagged and then gave up, replaced by desert scrub that swelled toward the red jag of mountains in the distance, the hazy blue peaks beyond. Wisps of cloud textured the sky; it looked just like the painted ceiling inside Caesar's Palace. As often as we had come to Vegas in my childhood, my parents had never taken me this far, and I stared at the otherworldly forms, the deep, sensuous grooves of rust-red rock.

Eventually, we had to enter the roaring heat, dragging our bodies out of the car. I spotted a small lizard bobbing its head on a rock. Someone got too close, and it flickered underneath into a thin crescent of shade.

"Does everyone have a full water bottle?" My mother held up her container and, as if to demonstrate the proper way to drink, unscrewed the lid and started gulping. Out of all of us, she looked the most prepared, greasy with sunblock and vacuum-sealed in a spandex tank top whose straps crisscrossed her back. Her hair had been pulled into a short ponytail that protruded from the back of her baseball cap, and she carried a turquoise pack full of clementines and granola bars. She swung her arms around in their sockets, stretched a hamstring. Her black bracelet flashed silver in the sun.

"*Hao le, bu yao zhe yang le*," said Tiffany, feigning exasperation. Bent over a shoelace, she revealed the sweat-mottled fabric stretched across her back. "You'll be miles ahead of us by the end. How about you let us get a head start?"

"I'm going to faint, and I haven't even moved a muscle," said Meredith, her long face panning disapprovingly across the landscape, the eroded towers guarding the horizon.

"You girls are so dramatic," my mother said, laughing, though the words carried the brittle edge of annoyance. "It's good to get the heart pumping, especially at our age." We followed her lead onto the trail, footfalls crunching on blanched twigs.

"I feel like I'm on another planet," said Tiffany.

"Any place that's not a Prada store is another planet to you," Meredith pointed out.

I brought up the rear, following Joyce, who wore leggings, long sleeves, and a black visor that covered her entire face like a welder's mask. A modest woman, the one thing Joyce took pride in was her skin, creamy and poreless, lunar in its glow. She used to give my mother facial cleansers that purported to be skin lighteners, the pearlescent bottles wrapped with smiling Asian women whose features had been obliterated by Photoshop. Marissa forced me to rub the milky goop on my cheeks each night until it became obvious that my color would not wash away.

As we wove past the striated boulders, I reached out to feel the gritty sandstone. Sometimes the burnt earth soared upward to form a shaded canyon and sometimes it simmered close to the surface in petrified waves. Dribbles and stabs of color formed the landscape: orange cliffs, pale rose, bronze dirt. Mesquite and creosote bushes fanned out from the trail, and the occasional Joshua tree, that revelatory sentinel, raised its furred mitts.

"This reminds me of the Stone Forest in Kunming," said Joyce, meaning the city where her mother had grown up. "Have you ever visited? Gray stone jutting out of the treetops like skyscrapers. We used to go a lot as kids, and my brother would always wander off and get lost. I have a memory of my mother finding him and twisting his arm so hard that they both began to cry, and there was an engagement shoot happening behind them. They were in traditional clothes, the bride and groom, and the colors were so bright, and they were laughing at something. I remember that so vividly. Two people laughing, two people crying."

"Yes, *Shi Lin*. It's incredible, how ancient it is," said my mother. She uncapped her water bottle. "Brian hasn't been back to *Dalu* since he was Kathleen's age, can you believe it? He has family in Nanjing. And he's never been to Shanghai at all."

"The last time I was in Shanghai, I felt like a peasant," said Tiffany. "Imagine—me! The rate it's developing, it's like a city on the moon. Girls in professional hair and makeup, like perfect dolls. Trains arriving on the second, and so clean you could eat off the floor. Coming back to the U.S. was so depressing."

They reminisced as they went, their stories a kind of birdsong. We didn't meet any other hikers; not many others had made the mistake of striking out when the sun was at its most brutal. Dust, stirred up by our footsteps, clung to our dampened skin. I dragged the back of my hand across my upper lip and tasted salt and dirt, the rich tang of minerals.

Pausing during a steep ascent, Tiffany exclaimed, "Look at that rock! It looks just like a howling wolf." She jabbed her finger toward an outcropping that resembled an animal on its haunches, snout lifted. "You four, get in front of it." She pulled her phone out of her back pocket and waved us into the frame.

"I can take it for you," I said, trudging up the sandy trail.

"*Hao de,*" she said delightedly, passing the phone to me and then hurrying to join the other women. They posed with their hips canted to one side, baring their teeth in big smiles.

From here, we had a vantage point of the stone coursing beneath us, every facet a different shade to form a prismatic terrain. The photo shoot continued, the women pairing up to take glamour shots of one another.

"Tuck your hair on one side," Tiffany was coaching Joyce, who sat on an arm of rock, ankles crossed underneath her and hands folded on her knees. She smoothed back a strand and turned her face wistfully toward one shoulder. "*Hao mei*," cooed Meredith. "This can be your new profile photo."

The pictures would go on WeChat, I knew, where my mother and her friends tracked the lives of those who hadn't immigrated. If she'd remained in Shanghai, my mother informed me, she would have also retired at fifty. She would be getting facials and massages between meals at fine restaurants that served quail with its shriveled, marinated head as a garnish. I wondered if it were another social media mirage, but I didn't argue: Didn't we all have alternate dimensions in which we were doing better? Anyway, she would say, it was impossible to go back; she had lost her Chinese citizenship. "And you're here," she used to add in an injured tone, as though it were a decision I'd made to spite her.

Their photo shoot continued along the trail. They took pictures mid-leap, hair splayed as if drawn by static electricity. They took romanticized pictures of one another's backs as they receded in the frame. At one juncture, I cowered in the shade of an overhang and sipped at my canister of dwindling water, trying to keep my impatience in check.

"Kathleen, don't sulk," said my mother when the others were up ahead. "Come be part of the group."

"I can already feel myself burning," I said. "I'll just wait here."

She slipped one arm from her backpack strap and swung the bag to her front, then unzipped the top to bring out a deflated tube of sunscreen. "Put some more on, then. Don't forget your face."

Too parched to argue, I uncapped the lotion and smeared dabs of it across my roasting shoulders, my flushed chest. It turned into a runny salve as it mixed with my sweat. Freshly slimed and coconut-scented, I returned the sunscreen to her backpack.

"*Ni kan*," she said, peering at something over my shoulder. "What are those drawings?"

I turned to look. Faintly etched into the rock face were a series of petroglyphs, their pale, evocative shapes just evading comprehension. Some ciphers were round and perched on limbs like animals and others snaked in geometric abstraction. I reached up to brush the impressions, imagining someone else making the same gesture thousands of years ago.

"Don't touch!" scolded my mother. She marveled at them for a moment before handing me her phone. Arranging herself under the petroglyphs, she swatted at me to step back. "Get as much of them as you can," she instructed.

I pointed the lens and thumbed the button, which produced a crisp shutter sound—which, I knew, most of the younger generation would never recognize. As she raised both her arms in a victorious V for one photo, then turned to the side and leaned against the rock face in another, reality seemed to skip, and I saw her in the flattened dimension of bathroom selfies, micro-influencers, targeted ads. I didn't want to make Luke's mistake of confusing image making with vapidity, so I joined in.

"Let's take one together," I said. I snaked my arm around her shoulder, and we grinned at our own likenesses.

I heard the shuffle of feet, the idle blabber of intersecting conversations, but it took a few moments for the source of the noise to reach us: a herd of tourists, most of whom looked to be in their sixties or seventies, their faces shadowed by the beaks of visors or the shade of lofted umbrellas. They spoke Cantonese and Mandarin and were dressed too warmly, the men in button-ups and the women in printed polyester blouses. A young woman wearing a khaki vest and waving a red pennant suddenly raised her bullhorn and chattered into it. Her fuzzy, blaring voice directed the group to notice the petroglyphs and to gather close behind her so that everyone had space to stand.

Either no one on the tour noticed that we were outsiders or no one cared. They pressed in close, giving us no choice but to inch toward the wall, shifting our weight like penguins. Slender curls of funk and acridity rose from our bodies.

"These drawings are around four thousand years old," said the tour guide, beads of sweat encrusting her temples. "They were made when the Native Americans living here scratched off the surface of the rock, which is dark because of a layer of minerals, to reveal the lighter rock underneath. Can anyone guess what these carvings show?" I couldn't understand all of the Mandarin words, but I fumbled toward meaning, filling in the blanks.

A man flapped his mouth a few times before venturing, "A snake."

"You are absolutely correct," said the tour guide, indicating the wall behind her without looking. It was unclear which glyph they meant. "Snakes were an important symbol for the indigenous people of the region, signifying cunning, longevity, and power. What else do you see?"

"That one looks like a tornado," said someone else.

"Excellent," said the tour guide. I scanned the wall for something resembling a tornado. "Tornadoes often tore through the area, destroying homes, and the native people believed that if they could illustrate these natural forces, they could better understand and control them. They drew scenes from everyday life, but they also used art for ceremonial purposes. It's likely that these etchings were part of a weather ritual."

"Do you think she's making this up?" I murmured to my mother. "Tornadoes aren't really a thing here, are they?"

"Who cares? It's more interesting this way. They paid to be entertained, not learn."

The guide recited a litany of increasingly questionable facts before guiding her audience to a yucca plant. We detached from the group to catch up with the rest of the bachelorette party, who had gone on ahead.

"Isn't that elder abuse, bringing those people on a hike in this heat?" huffed my mother, lifting her hat by the bill to fan herself with it.

We plodded uphill, skin clinging whenever our arms brushed together. I concentrated on keeping pace, impressed by her strength as she vaulted over boulders in our path.

"That man from yesterday," she ventured. "That was one of your clients. From that place."

I'd been expecting her to broach the subject. *"Dui."*

"Why is he here?"

None of the alternate stories I sketched out seemed plausible. The strange truth was the only thing to offer. Anyway, I was tired of pruned narratives and willful wording, tired of hiding. My mother had bared herself to me over the weekend, and if she entrusted me with her young mistakes, then I could do the same. I explained it all—how his lyrical, but rational, way of speaking about Diane had put me at ease, how his interest in my life had seemed reassuring and paternal, how I'd taken advantage of his softness to fashion a kind of partner for myself. I was mortified by my own honesty. It felt wrong to be speaking to Marissa this way. Usually, what we knew of each other's inner worlds were just projections of ourselves.

"And now?" she asked when I was done.

"And now it's over. All of it. I'm not going back to Midas Touch."

My mother stayed uncharacteristically silent. She was waiting for me to tell her what was next. A week ago, I wouldn't have had any idea, but a new thought had been circling: the possibility of going back to school and starting over with clinical psychology. I didn't want to spend the rest of my life in calibrated studies; I wanted to invest in long-term clients, excavating grief and celebration. I wanted to be able to look people like Phil in the eye with something mean-ingful to offer.

Before I could say anything, however, my mother wondered aloud, "How did they get so far ahead?"

I remembered that we'd been searching for the others. "They can't be that far. We stood back there for five minutes, *ʒui duo.*"

"We should've caught up to them by now."

"Do you think we made a wrong turn?"

My mother crunched ahead for a few more steps and then stood panting in the dirt, squinting back toward the way we'd come. "Maybe. Did you see a fork somewhere?"

"No, but I wasn't really paying attention. I was just following you."

She let her backpack slip down to the ground and crouched over it until she found her phone. "Do you have any service?" She frowned at her screen.

I checked. "No. Maybe we did miss a turn. Let's go back."

We turned around. The tourist group shuffled into view and filtered past us as though we were rocks in a river, shading us temporarily with their canopy of umbrellas.

"Excuse me, have you seen a group of women? Three women?" asked my mother.

A graying man with his hands clasped behind his back shook his head as he shuffled past. "Haven't seen anyone. Day like this, who would be out? We booked this tour months ago."

Eventually, we reached the petroglyphs again.

"I'm thirsty," I said.

"Let's rest," she said. "Maybe they'll come back for us."

We skirted the rock face, its surface like the skin of a huge, reptilian beast, until we found a patch of shade under an overhanging crag. In this small sanctuary, we tipped our water bottles into our mouths and each peeled a granola bar. My tongue probed the glob of oats and honey.

"I'm glad you're not going back to that place," said my mother. "You're lucky with Phil. It could've been worse. You could've met someone obsessive. Violent."

I loosened another inch of the silver wrapper. "I know."

"I think you know how stupid that was. I won't bring it up again."

"Yeah, right," I said, unable to stop myself from sarcasm.

"But when I saw you with him," she said, her tone softening, "even though it was someone I didn't know, a man, a man too old for you, I felt calm. You looked so peaceful. And he was lying there like a little boy. It was like a dream." She folded her empty wrapper in half and then in half again. "You're good at helping people. Growing up, you were always trying to help out. Maybe because you thought your mother was a total mess, and you were right. But it made you sensitive. You notice things. I want you to use it. You don't have to decide this moment, but you have to decide what to do with it. And it is not Mydol—Mydol—"

"Midas Touch."

My mother nodded. It had taken her effort to tell me this; I knew because it had taken effort for me to listen. With us, sparring came naturally, and silence was second best. Being earnest about our love and admiration—this was maudlin.

"Thank you," I said, and launched into a hug. Her small, firm arms wrapped around mine. Then, a bit embarrassed, I reached down and swished the dwindling water in my bottle. "What are we going to do if we run out?"

"We'll be back at the parking lot soon."

"Which way is that, exactly?"

She stepped out of the shade and surveyed the surrounding rock faces. Then she got close, placing an exploratory palm on the wall. She hooked one hand around a protrusion, the fingers of her other hand fidgeting for a hold.

"Mom. What are you doing?"

Grasping with both hands now, she leaned back to test her grip. "I'm going to get a better look at where we are," she said, and hoisted herself six inches off the ground, her left foot digging into a crevice for balance. She tilted her head back to survey the path upward. "It's only ten feet up; it won't be hard to get up there."

"It's still far enough to break an arm. Or worse."

Her free leg bent, straightened, and arced like an antenna, hunting for another ledge. Finding it, she stood up, a few inches closer to the top. With every movement, her muscles went taut and slack, taut and slack, revealing the architecture of her body. As stressful as it was to watch her ascent, I was amazed at this new mother of mine: scaler of canyons, tamer of rock. I had refused so many invitations to join her and Brian at the climbing gym, determined not to partici-pate in her farce, scared that I would be embarrassed by her earnest, girlish aim to please her partner. In all the scenarios I'd imagined, I'd overlooked the possibility that she would have a talent for it. Her

limbs moved with intelligence, patience, grace—she spidered across
the surface until, with a burst of power through her arms, she reached
the crest and clambered onto the highest point.

"*Wa!*" I exclaimed. "That was amazing!"

She shook her arms to relieve them, swung them across her body.
"You can see everything from here. *Tai mei le!*" She turned cau-
tiously, a dark figure against a blaring indigo sky. "There are mountains all around, like giant teeth."

"But do you see Tiffany and the others?"

She formed a brim with her hand. "No, I don't see anyone. Not
even the tourists." She paused. "I do see the parking lot, though. It's
way over there." She pointed to demonstrate.

"Really? Can you get us to it?"

My mother pulled out her phone and held it flat on her palm,
twisting her torso until she was facing the right direction. "We want
to do thirty degrees northeast," she said. "If we stick to that, we
should be there in about half an hour."

"Okay. But how are you going to get back down?"

Pocketing her phone, she approached the lip of the outcropping,
and for a wild moment I imagined her leaping off the edge, landing in
a superhero's stance with one hand bracing the ground and the other
raised like a wing. Instead, she started to descend the rock face as
deliberately as she had climbed up, her pointed toe tapping for an
indentation, her fingers glowing white with effort. I didn't realize I
had been holding my breath until she hopped down to the ground, a

puff of sand clouding her ankles. Her face was streaked with sweat. "You ready?" she panted.

I followed her down the path in an awed silence. Our staggered footsteps created an irregular beat. When the trail forked, my mother consulted the compass app on her phone and eventually we reached a flat stretch of scrub. In the near distance, I could see the parking lot. "Look!" I said.

"*Zongsuan zhaodao le*," said my mother, relieved.

Now that the end was in sight, my legs seemed to accrue mass with every step, dragging in the soil.

"Did I tell you? I thought of a song the other night. At karaoke. To play when I walk down the aisle," said my mother.

"Really? What is it?"

"That old song from the seventies, do you know it?" She began to hum, breathlessly at first, mincing the melody. Gradually, however, the notes swam together, and I recognized it as the song I'd once spied her dancing along to in the kitchen. *My feelings are real, and my love is real. The moon represents my heart.*

"*Yueliang Daibiao Wo De Xin*," I said.

"That's it!" she said, delighted that I'd named it. "Ingrid, maybe she can play a string version of it on the *guzheng*. It's so beautiful. I should have made you play an instrument. So many things I would do differently. Oh, there they are!"

We were close enough to the parking lot to make out our car and Meredith, Tiffany, and Joyce beside it, gesticulating to a park ranger who was speaking into a radio. He looked young, and got younger as we approached, no more than eighteen with his smooth, tapered face burdened by a frown. The women were too excited to notice us; they spoke over one another, Tiffany insisting, "We walked maybe two hours, then we lost them," while Joyce interjected, "I'm not sure, I think maybe was one hour? Let me see my photos, I check time." The boy raised the radio but didn't respond to the crackling voice on the other side.

"Shh, don't say anything," said my mother in a low voice, threading her arm through mine. This time, it felt like a natural gesture, welcome despite the broiling heat. We began to march in step. Her lips curled mischievously. "Let's see how close we can get before they realize."

Swallowing laughter, parched and electrified by the sun, we walked forward arm in arm. In a few weeks, we would do this again, though with more solemnity. She would be exquisite in her gown, a woman like a white river, adrift on her song. For now, though, we were just two girls in the thrall of a prank, rapidly closing the distance and waiting for the others to look up and recognize where we were.

Acknowledgments

So many incredible people and experiences converged to midwife this book, and I want to express my immense gratitude. Thank you to my agent, Sarah Bowlin, for believing in the manuscript when it was a narrative labyrinth—and for leading me out of the maze. Your sage edits, tireless championship, and bighearted guidance have been invaluable. Thank you to my editor, Alison Fairbrother, for loving these characters and urging me closer to the heart of the story with patience, intuition, and insight. I'm deeply indebted to Bianca Flores, Ashley Sutton, Viviann Do, and the entire team at Riverhead for embracing this book and humbled by the care and talent that have gone toward bringing it into existence.

I've had the luck and privilege of having many brilliant teachers over the years. Special thanks to Michelle Patterson, Rick Thompson, David Roderick, Vikram Chandra, Bharati Mukherjee, Daniel Alarcón, Jean McGarry, Eric Puchner, Alice McDermott, Stacey D'Erasmo, and Peter Ho Davies for your lessons on craft and carving out a writer's life. Thank you to the writing seminars at Johns Hopkins University and my wonderful cohort, especially Taylor Daynes, Jessica Hudgins, Molly

Acknowledgments

Lynch, Zehra Nabi, and Maddy Raskulinescz—you made Baltimore feel like home. Bread Loaf, MacDowell, Yaddo, Kundiman, Aspen Words, the Virginia Center for the Creative Arts, and Loghaven gave me the immeasurable gifts of community and time while I worked on this project.

Thank you to Alexandra Chang, Lydia Conklin, Jean Chen Ho, and Kyle Lucia Wu for your friendship and early support. To Denice, Sarah, Tonhu, Janine, and Su, my day ones. To Keena, Leti, and Jillian, who watched me struggle to microwave eggs and always make room on the twin bed. To Kim, anchor and slingshot, and my beloved co-op family, flung from coast to coast, too many to name: So much of you is in this book. I love and am continually astonished by our lives together.

And most important, thank you to my parents, Shen Wen and Xie Xiaohua, for holding me all these years. Your love, bravery, resilience, and support are everything.

DATE DUE

	AUG 9 2023		
	SEP 5 2023		
	SEP 27 2023		
JAN 2 2024			
	AUG 3 2024		
			PRINTED IN U.S.A.